JUNTA

JUNTA

JUNE DRUMMOND

LONDON
VICTOR GOLLANCZ LTD
1989

First published in Great Britain 1989
by Victor Gollancz Ltd,
14 Henrietta Street, London WC2E 8QJ

British Library Cataloguing in Publication Data
Drummond, June
  Junta.
  I. Title
  823 [F]

ISBN 0–575–04465–9

Typeset at The Spartan Press Ltd,
Lymington, Hants
and printed in Great Britain by
St Edmundsbury Press Ltd, Bury St Edmunds, Suffolk

This story is set some years
in the future

"A person precariously balanced on top of a pile of logs is aware of the hurt that will be done if it collapses. Not surprisingly he calls for stability, for change that is gentle.
"A person who is squeezed under the pile of logs is conscious of his present pain. He calls out to be freed, even if it brings down the whole pile."

The Archbishop of Canterbury
speaking in South Africa, 1986

1

On the evening of the first Wednesday in August, a German freelance photographer named Karl Stendal was murdered on the outskirts of Site Nine, a squatter-camp that had sprung up on the Cape Flats after the destruction of Crossroads.

Stendal's death was in some sense his own fault. Under the terms of the security regulations, no cameraman was permitted to enter any black settlement in South Africa. Furthermore, Stendal had been warned by the police that the township Vigilantes regarded all journalists as hostile to their cause, and would attack him on sight.

He had ignored both the law and the warning. It was not political conviction that drove him, for he had none. Thirty years of working in Africa . . . in Algeria, the Congo, Rhodesia and Mozambique . . . had made him indifferent to causes and policies, and indeed to human suffering.

One thing he knew. Bad news, well photographed, fetched money, and the latest clamp-down on the media by the South African government had upped the price. This time Stendal was after really big bucks, a story he could sell to the major networks around the world.

He had received the tip-off in the early hours of Tuesday morning. Minutes later, the violence erupted at Site Nine. By Tuesday night, over a thousand shacks had been torched, forty-one people were dead, scores injured, and thousands homeless.

The weather was bitterly cold, and with darkness, a heavy mist rolled in from the sea, thickening the pall of smoke over the Flats, and making the work of police and relief teams largely ineffective.

Most of the journalists covering the action were bunched at the barricades set up by the security forces, on the main access road to Site Nine. Stendal was not with them.

During Tuesday night, he had made his way to the boundary of the sector known as The Tanks. Evading the police and army detachments encircling the settlement, he established himself on a sandy knoll screened by heavy growths of Port Jackson willow and rooikrans.

At first light he studied the position through binoculars. The thicket that concealed him continued down to a shallow depression, along which ran a road, at present under repair. Piles of gravel had been dumped along it, and at a point a little to Stendal's right was a stack of drainage pipes, each a metre in diameter.

On the far side of the road, the ground rose again towards three rusting water-tanks. To left and right of these stretched a barrier of razor-wire, new, the silvery blades catching the light. Behind that lay the shacks; Vigilante territory, a jumble of rotting lumber, metal and cardboard, patched with black plastic refuse-bags.

A deep ditch had been cut into the far bank, between the road and the tanks. It stank of sewage.

Stendal calculated that it would be easy to reach the drainpipes unobserved. If need be, he could make it across the road, duck into the ditch, and move right up to the tanks.

It was a question of dodging the security patrols. Army vehicles passed along the road every ten minutes or so. They were using Casspirs, armoured transports manned for the most part by young conscripts. No doubt there were foot-patrols in the scrubland at his back. At intervals, an army chopper droned overhead.

The area destroyed by yesterday's arson lay on the far side of the camp. Stendal could see the blackened debris, and the ant-small figures crawling over it, salvaging what they could.

What struck him was the silence. Shanty-towns were usually noisy as hell, yet in this place no woman called to her neighbour, no child whimpered, no dog barked. It was as if sound had been crushed between the millstones of the leaden sky and the grey earth.

The camp was divided roughly in two by a corridor of empty ground, a sort of no man's land. South-west of this, the comrades ruled, young blacks born on the Flats and raised in its slums. Jobless, and without tribal ties, they ran in wolf-packs, maintaining their own discipline, admitting no law outside that of their People's Courts. They claimed allegiance to the ANC, but that organisation's control of them was at times tenuous.

The Vigilantes held the north-eastern sector. These were older men, for the most part, come to the Cape to support families starving in the so-called homelands. They too had their hierarchy, their pickets, their kangaroo courts. Their identifying mark was the white headband that gave them their name, the Witdoeke.

Most of the seventy thousand people at Site Nine sought neutrality, spending their energies on the effort to stay alive. The militants . . . comrades and Witdoeke . . . were locked in a battle to determine who, in the final analysis, would inherit the scorched terrain.

Stendal did not plan to waste film on either cadre. Shots of Casspirs, of stone-throwing children and rampaging men, were run-of-the-mill. He was after something more lucrative.

Over the past weeks he had picked up persistent rumours of a third force in the unrest; *agents provocateurs* who were said to be orchestrating the violence in the squatter-camps. Not local men, his informants had insisted, not Xhosa or Pondo or Zulu, but foreigners, white and black, who spoke tongues no one understood.

What Stendal was weighing in his cold little mind was, who owned and directed this third force, and for what purpose? The answers to those questions could reap handsome dividends for an enterprising newsman.

The sun rose higher, rolling back the mist. Stendal saw that trouble was building at the waste ground.

From north and south, people were massing on its fringes. The opposing ranks growled and swayed. From time to time a single figure leaped forward, gesticulating and stamping, taunting his adversaries. Through the telescopic lens of his camera, Stendal

9

could see the glint of cane-knives, assegais, axes. He guessed that the men at the back, out of sight of the police, would be carrying firearms.

He shifted his gaze to the water-tanks. No activity round there. He continued to wait.

The first charge came soon after eleven. Stendal could not have said who started it. As fighting dogs suddenly stop circling and spring, so the two lines rushed together. Dulled by distance came shouted orders, the screams of the injured; then shots, the crack of pistols and the heavier reports of rifles.

Up to this time the security forces had remained at the barricades on the edge of the settlement, but as the shooting escalated, four Casspirs lumbered in, lurching along the uneven track that led to the waste land. At their approach, the pattern of conflict changed.

The mauling factions broke apart and ran back to their former lines, turning to face the common enemy. Many of the comrades began a jigging dance, chanting freedom songs. Stones rattled against the metal of the Casspirs and tear-gas missiles arched back in response, the white-grey smoke streaming in the wind. The mob retreated, coughing and retching, to the warrens of the shackland.

After half an hour, the Casspirs withdrew.

So the day passed; periods of quiet while the opposing ranks built up, short bouts of hand-to-hand fighting, dispelled by the intervention of the Casspirs. Occasionally a police-truck raced forward to pick up a body, dead or injured, and carry it back to the ambulance-line at the barricade.

Stendal was irritated. Damp squib, he thought, nothing new. He dug a pack of cheese sandwiches from his kitbag, and ate them.

At four in the afternoon, as the light was beginning to fail, came the explosions, a series of coughing thumps in the area of the comrades' shacks. Stendal rolled to his knees and lifted his camera.

Away to the south, single flowers of flame unfurled and spread, people poured from the burning pondokkies, dragging children and livestock, precious blankets, pots and pans. Stendal's lens followed their surge across the open ground, focused on a woman with clothes burning, a child running blindly round her, mouth wide, arms upraised.

Sirens wailed on the perimeter roads, transports and armoured cars raced past, a chopper hovered overhead and then veered away south.

The Casspirs were advancing again, nosing into the mass of refugees. An officer in the leading vehicle yelled through a loud-hailer, urging them to move towards the safety of the barricade. Some obeyed, others huddled together, terrified.

A detachment of men in army drab trotted forward and tried to herd a group of women away from the burning zone, but at once a hail of stones whirled towards them. A soldier fell, blood pouring from his face. The man next to him swung round and fired a wild volley over the heads of the crowd, which spun back on itself, shrieking and trampling.

Stendal panned the camera across the site, searching for the springhead of this crazy three-cornered battle. Somewhere in that shambles there were men with motive and a plan. The explosions he'd heard weren't petrol-bombs, he was sure, but something more sophisticated; grenades, maybe incendiaries.

He was looking for the people who'd used them.

They wouldn't be on the waste ground. By now, they'd be headed out of the camp, and if his info was right, they'd leave by the water-tanks.

He crouched, waiting.

The sun was almost down when he saw one of the tanks move. It shifted in a smooth arc that left a gap between its side and the razor-wire. Directly below this gap was the drainage-cut.

Stendal started his camera. It picked up figures dodging along the path between the shanties. Bent low, keeping to the shadows, they slipped into the lee of the tanks. There were three of them, dressed in the shabby clothes of migrant-workers, each with a white rag twisted round his forehead.

Not Witdoeke, thought Stendal exultantly. Witdoeke didn't deploy like trained soldiers, didn't carry AK47s.

He glanced quickly at the sky. The light was lousy. He had to have identifiable faces, and voices for the sound-track. He had to get closer.

He squinted at the tanks. The men over there would be watching the road, timing the arrival of the next military patrol. Once it had passed, they would leave the camp by the gap in the fence, and make their escape northwards, away from the barricades. With luck, there would be a brief moment when their attention was fully engaged by the approaching patrol. That would be his chance to dodge down to the cover of the stack of drainpipes. From there he could get the shots he wanted.

He could hear a Casspir now, far along the road. Hurriedly, he checked his camera settings. The vehicle came in sight, travelling slowly, its lights piercing the semi-gloom.

Stendal crawled rapidly through the scrub, gained the shelter of the drain-pipes and lay still. There was no sound or movement at the tanks.

The Casspir passed. Stendal focused his camera on the gap in the fence. There was light enough if the men moved at once, and they did. First one, then another, slid past the wire and dropped down into the ditch. Both were blacks. A third man appeared in the gap and stood for a moment with head lifted, seeming to gaze straight into the camera lens. Stendal's heart lurched, sweat poured down his back. He knew that face, the swarthy skin seamed with deep wrinkles, the brutal turned-up snout and small flat mouth. It was a face hated and feared in half a dozen countries of east and central Africa. Seen in its present setting, at Site Nine, it was real pay-dirt.

If Stendal had lain still, he might have lived to collect his dues; but as the three men started to move down the ditch, he raised himself to get one last shot of them. The movement was seen by the man he'd forgotten, the man stationed inside the tanks.

A voice shouted in Portuguese: "Sousa! To your right, behind the pipes!"

At the cry, the swarthy man crouched and fired his AK in a smooth sweep. The concrete pipes next to Stendal shattered and the shards flew out like shrapnel, one of them slicing into his thigh just below the groin. He snatched at the wound, blood gouting between his fingers on to the sand. He tried to drag himself back into the scrub, but bullets pinned him down, and the two blacks in the ditch were already running down to the road. Seeing death approach, Stendal screamed in an agony of terror.

Then salvation appeared. An ambulance was making its way along the northern road. The swarthy man stopped firing and barked at the others.

"Wait! Keep down!"

The ambulance came on steadily until it was close to where Stendal lay, its bulk between him and the drainage-cut. Desperately he clawed himself into the roadway, screaming, lifting an arm in supplication. The ambulance slowed and stopped. As Stendal collapsed in the dust, the passenger door opened and a man jumped down, gazed at Stendal for a moment, then turned to stare at the opposite bank.

Stendal scrabbled at the man's ankle.

"Help me, for God's sake, hurry!"

Across the road, the swarthy man rose to his feet.

"Shoot him," he called, "and bring the camera."

Too shocked to utter a sound, Stendal made one last attempt to roll clear; but the man from the ambulance set a foot on his injured leg, and drawing a revolver, shot him through the back of the head.

2

On the evening of Stendal's death, the all-white House of Assembly of the Republic of South Africa was in emergency session, summoned to debate the collapse of the tricameral constitution, the rising civil unrest, and the strikes that threatened to paralyse the country.

"Tossie" Wendt, parliamentary reporter for the *Cape Mirror*, listened to a deputy-Minister stringing platitudes on the worn thread of government policy, and wondered why the hell he wasted his time here.

It was a situation of total sterility.

The liberal opposition, powerless in the face of massive security laws, had long ago resolved to break the system itself. The Conservative Party pursued its Neanderthal path, bent on seizing power and regressing to some Stone-Age Elysium. The governing National Party wallowed in the shallows of necessary reform, unwilling or unable to face the challenge of the open sea.

To compound the crisis, the resignation of the President became effective on Friday. His successor would have the right, as Premier and State President, to govern by decree, to overrule the decisions of any political structure in the land, and, in the final resort, to dissolve Parliament.

Lord, in fact, of Misrule.

There were three men in the race for the Presidency. The two front-runners had already spoken in today's debate. The third, the dark horse . . . whom Wendt privately considered the likely winner . . . sat silent in his place. His big head tilted towards the speaker, he looked the picture of earnest attention.

A messenger entered the House and approached the man Wendt was watching, handing him a folded note. The recipient

14

read it, rose at once, bowed to the Speaker and headed for the door.

Acting on a hunch, Wendt left the Press gallery and followed him.

"Well, Tossie, what can I do for you?"

The Minister had kept Wendt kicking his heels in the outer office for twenty minutes while he made acrimonious phone calls. Now the two men sat on opposite sides of the vast ministerial desk.

They had known each other for thirty years, and had perfected their own style of communication. By jibes, by denials, by reticences, they conveyed what could not be openly stated.

Wendt pulled two sheets of paper from his pocket and handed them across the desk. The Minister looked them over, then dropped them on his blotter.

"Kite-flying," he said.

Wendt shrugged delicately.

"Why now?" the Minister insisted.

"People want to know which way the wind will blow if you're elected. The question of Matlala's release is as good a kite as any."

"What do my opponents say about it?"

"Neither of them wants immediate release. Later, maybe."

"Umh! Now isn't the time to rush into print, you know."

"Granted. But off the record, what's your line?"

"I say, release him. In gaol he's a martyr, for the ANC to exploit. Out, he becomes their leadership problem. By releasing him, we silence overseas criticism and hamstring the sanctioneers."

These reasons were intoned with an expression that said, "This is old stuff, you know it already."

"If you release," Wendt said, "there'll be huge demos in the major industrial areas. The black unions will back them, so will the other radical elements."

"We can handle demos."

"By force of arms? Surely that would defeat the whole purpose?"

15

The Minister picked up a pen and rolled it over his fingers. He seemed to be weighing whether or not to speak. "We have to get black activists to the discussion table," he said at last. "To do that, we need an initiative. It has to be dramatic. One must break the old cycle, and start afresh."

"Is that what caucus believes?"

"It's what I believe!" The flash of arrogance in the eyes, the angry hunching of the shoulders, was typical. "I don't intend to be the prisoner of the Security Council. Look about you, man! The country's close to anarchy, white against black, white against white, black against black. We maintain order through the police and the army, not by the consent of the people. The war on our border is a wasting disease, we have to end it, we have to get the Russians and their surrogates out of Southern Africa, and to do that we need the support of the Western powers. You know all this. You say, 'Will caucus support you?' I say, 'If caucus elects me, caucus will support me.'"

"If they know your intentions . . ."

"They know me, they know my record, and they're looking for a lead. Tossie, don't you see, the time is long past when we can argue points, and form little committees? There has to be decisive action. One must break the patterns of the past, break society wide open, force a political regrouping."

"It'll cost you plenty, in voter-support."

"What we lose on the right, we'll recover from the centre and the left."

"Why Matlala? What makes you choose him?"

"Because of what he is. A young activist, with political magnetism, who can bring the trades unions to the conference table."

"Will they accept your . . . initiative?"

"Man, how can I tell? Will they accept, will black leaders accept, will the young comrades see Matlala as anything more than a useful figure-head, will Matlala himself be willing to play his part? I can't give you the answers. All I can tell you is, if we go on as we are, we're all going to drown in our own shit!"

The Minister dropped the pen he held and raised both hands,

palms together, almost in a gesture of prayer. "There are ways of doing things," he said. "It's not whether we release the detainees, but how." He lowered the hands, leaned back in his chair. "No kites yet, Tossie. I'll issue my statement at the proper time."

Wendt nodded, aware that the interview was over. He picked up his draft and moved to the door. There he turned.

"When will the caucus decide?"

"Tomorrow afternoon."

"Will you win?"

The man behind the desk hesitated. "Not on the first ballot," he said at last, "but on the second, yes, I'll win. Now get out of here, I'm busy."

Wendt left Parliament Buildings and strolled down Adderley Street. He had no qualms about what he was about to do. He was fifty-nine years old, a hack writer with nothing to show for thirty years of protecting his sources.

He turned into a shopping arcade, found a pay phone, and dialled a number. When he was answered, he paid in his money and identified himself by the agreed code-name. The message he delivered was short.

"I saw him. He says he'll win. He'll release Matlala."

After he'd hung up, he reflected that a thousand rand a word was the most he'd ever been paid for a story, even an exclusive like this one.

3

On Tuesday night, Ross McRae returned to South Africa to attend his father's funeral.

The journey from New York was roundabout, involving a stopover in Paris to allow him to put Jay on the special coach to Lourdes, then a day and a night in Zurich to settle the deal with Bernadotti, and finally the day flight to Johannesburg.

They landed in the early evening, descending smoothly to the camel pelt of the Witwatersrand. A minibus whisked them from the Boeing to the terminal, the luggage came through fast. Operation silk, Ross thought.

Three uniformed policemen stood near the customs desk. One of them, a chunky man with an opaque smile, greeted Ross by name. Ross wondered if he was Special Branch, but suppressed the idea. That kind of paranoia belonged to the past.

He called at the information desk to collect the keys of the office car, and instead was handed a key-case of ostrich-skin, embellished with a silver "J". Tucked inside the case was a note from Julie.

"I'm staying with Dad. No shortage of wheels here, so take the Lamb and drop her off when you get back."

The Lamborghini was in the lock-up garage.

Silk, too, thought Ryan, as he edged the elegant nose into the rush-hour traffic. He hoped he could handle the car to Julie's exacting standards. She was a great driver, better by far than her drip of a husband.

He took the link-roads, skirting the metropolis, aiming for the N3. Signs of the state of emergency were everywhere. He passed a number of troop-carriers, and at Alberton there was a road-block, the police searching all vehicles. Waiting in the queue,

Ross saw the sullen glow of fire in the western sky. He tried to remember which of the black townships lay that way. Thokoza, was it, or Katlehong?

The rents in the silk were becoming more obvious with each visit.

He drove through the night, a trip made dreamlike by jet lag; white stars in a black Free State sky, white mist on the pass at Van Reenan, rain and mist along the foothills of the Drakensberg, lifting as he reached Ixopo in the far south of Natal.

The farm Halladale lay south again, in the territory once called No Man's Land, soft country that rose from the coast through rounded hills and random forests to the seven-thousand-foot precipices of iNgeli, source of sixteen rivers.

Soon after eight on Wednesday morning he reached the village of Stannard's Post, and turned off the tar on to the unmade road that served Halladale and the Bengston's farm beyond. Ten minutes later, at the crest that marked the northern boundary of the McRae lands, he stopped the car and climbed out. There was a sharp wind blowing, and he stood with his arms wrapped across his chest, looking down at Halladale.

His gaze went first to the logan on the far side of the valley. The great rock balanced on a neck so slender that it seemed to float in mid-air. God's Judgement, his grandfather had named it.

Directly below the logan was the farmhouse, stone-walled, with a low-pitched roof of black corrugated-iron, and wide, cluttered verandahs. A half-moon of indigenous trees enclosed the house, its gardens, and a tractor-yard.

The years had brought few changes here. A new irrigation system was swinging columns of spray across the lucerne fields, the stand of bluegums behind the cowshed was gone, but everything else was as he remembered. The Jersey milk-herd in the home pasture, the beef cattle grazing on the floor of the plain, the cloud-shadow on the encircling hills and the smell of dung and saligna pine were all so immediately familiar that he half-expected to see Grandfather McRae's old bakkie come drumming towards him in a haze of red dust.

His aunt and uncle were on the front verandah to meet him. James McRae, his father's brother and the present manager of Halladale, came down the steps with his awkward, secretary-bird gait.

"Glad you could come, Ross, glad you could make it."

Ross put an arm round the older man's shoulders. It was certain that James felt this death more deeply than anyone. James had been described, once, as "a McRae left out in the rain". The uncompromising family features were in him softened and blurred, but his character was firm enough. There were tears, now, in his pale blue eyes, and he kept touching his fingers to his mouth, like a grieving child.

"I was with your dad only last week," he said. "He took Nola and me to lunch, in Durban. Fit as a fiddle, full of jokes. It was a terrible shock, losing him. I always felt I'd go first."

Nola McRae waited at the head of the steps, a tall woman, stout and stiff-backed; dressed, no doubt as a mark of respect, in a black suit and frilled pink blouse. She was James's second wife, city-bred, and had never tried to conceal her dislike of Ross. Bereavement wasn't going to make any difference. As she leaned forward to receive Ross's kiss, her black eyes raked the Lamborghini.

"That's no hired car."

"No."

"Where did you get it?"

"It belongs to Julie Aikman."

"Richard Wragge's daughter? I thought she lived in America."

"She's been here a few months."

"Why? Doing what?"

"Working at a clinic in Soweto, I believe. It's closed now, because of the unrest."

"I'd have thought she'd do better to sell the car and give the money to the clinic, if she's so charitable."

"She races the car, professionally."

"Where's her husband?"

"In Germany, with the Porsche team."

"So they're still married?"

"Far as I know."

20

Nola stopped staring at the car and turned back to Ross. "We expected you earlier," she said. "Did you have trouble at the airport?"

He smiled into her angry eyes. "None at all. I declared everything."

She made an impatient gesture. "I mean, trouble with the police?"

James said in a low voice, "Nola, please!" She shot him a contemptuous glance.

"I've a right to ask, in view of his record. My boys are in the army. I don't want them smeared with Ross's mud."

"No mud." Ross spoke mildly. "I'm a businessman on a routine visit. I come at least four times a year. They're used to me, by now."

"Well, I suppose money talks. I hear you've made a bundle, doing whatever it is." She turned on her heel and marched into the house. James shook his head.

"I'm sorry. She's touchy, these days. Simon and Brett are both on the border . . . and now Don's death, the uncertainty . . ." He gazed vaguely about him.

"James," Ross said, "understand one thing. There's no uncertainty about your position here. I don't want you and Nola to leave, I don't want to change one damn thing at Halladale."

"Everything's changing." James turned to face Ross. "You don't know what it's been like, this past year. The drought, sanctions, prices way down. We can't find enough work for our own people, and the squatters have been pouring over the border from Pondoland. Starving, poor buggers, but we can't keep them here, these lands are close to being over-grazed, as it is. Last week, the local blacks went for the Pondos, killed four of them. The Press called it faction fighting, but that's not so. It's hunger, hunger for food and for land, and God alone knows how we're going to cope with it." The gentle eyes were pleading. "I hoped you'd come home for a while? Help us sort things out?"

"I'm afraid that's not possible at the moment."

"Surely Wragge could release you for a few months? Ask him,

Ross! You've always loved Halladale. It would be good for Jay, too. Farm food and fresh air, she'd pick up at once."

Ross had a sudden vision of his wife, bird-thin, her thighs bruised by the daily injections of insulin. He didn't feel able to discuss her, yet. Instead, he said, "Tell me about Dad."

"Of course." James looked contrite. "It was very sudden. He never told me he had high blood pressure. Did you know?"

"No. I've only seen him twice in three years. We weren't exactly close. Where did he die?"

"Durban airport. He'd been in Joburg for a board meeting. Caught the late flight home, and as he stepped on to the tarmac, over he went. Massive brain haemorrhage." James sighed. "He left a request to be buried at Halladale, Lord knows why, he never could stand the place. You know, even as a kid, Don fought with our dad all the time. Cleared out when he was eighteen and only came back under protest. So why choose to be buried here? It's caused no end of problems. One good thing, though, it brought you home. This is where you belong, boy."

"Should an ex-gaolbird and profiteer inherit the earth?"

James shifted round to stand directly in front of his nephew. "Don't you pay any heed to Nola. She lets her tongue get the better of her, sometimes. You own the farm, and you'll decide its future." He patted Ross's arm. "We've put you in your old room. Why don't you have a wash and brush-up and come to breakfast?"

Donald McRae was buried that afternoon, in the burial-ground on the hill behind the house, alongside pioneer Malcolm McRae and eleven of his descendents.

A low stone wall enclosed the plot. At its northernmost corner, a kaffirboom was coming into bud, the still-green spurs raking the sky, and under this thin canopy the grave had been dug.

Down on the plain, the heat had driven the cattle to find what shade they could. Not so much as the chirp of a cricket disturbed the heavy stillness.

22

Mr Peattie, the clergyman from Stannard's Post, drove over to take the service. He had never known the dead man, disapproved of burials outside of church property, and recited the words of committal as if he were pressed for time.

Four black labourers, sweating in their best clothes, stepped forward to lower the coffin into the red earth, and James McRae, crumbling into tears, was led away by Nola and the priest.

The labourers peeled off their coats, fetched shovels from behind a tombstone, and prepared to fill the grave. When Ross attempted to join them, the foreman stopped him.

"No, 'nkosi, let us do this."

Ross studied the man's face.

"You're Mapumalo, aren't you?"

The man smiled, and nodded. "Yes, from the dairy."

"I remember. Your family is well?"

"Well, yes."

"Tell me, do the Matlalas still live in these parts?"

"Yes, yes, at their same place." The man raised his arm to point at the footpath that wound over the hill, past the logan, to the Reserve territory.

Ross thanked him, sure that his enquiry would be passed on. A few minutes later, he left the group at the burial-ground, and walked slowly back to the house.

"I don't know why he chose to be buried here," repeated James, after supper that night. "If he'd had a service in town, there'd have been a big crowd, all his pals, his staff, the Moths and Rotary. A proper show."

They were sitting on the dark verandah. Behind them in the lounge, Nola was watching television. She'd closed the french doors and the windows because the flying-ants were swarming. Hordes of amber bodies banged and bumbled against the glass, dropped their filmy wings and crawled blindly across the verandah tiles.

"When your grandpa died," said James, "all the neighbours came to the funeral. All the workers and their families. The singing was grand, it filled the valley."

Strange how much James wanted the pretence that someone had cared about Donald McRae. Ross closed his eyes, remembering how his mother had struggled to preserve the same fiction, anxiously trying to build a circle of friends around her husband's business ambitions. She'd drowned in that maelstrom, although the official record gave the place of her death as Hout Bay.

"Unsound mind," his father had said, standing with his back to ten-year-old Ross. "There's no stigma attached to suicide, you understand? It's a sickness of the mind. Nobody is to blame for it."

After her death the house became a place of icy silences, broken by violent quarrels, like the one about his decision to refuse army service. To Don McRae, veteran of Korea, conscientious objection was akin to treason.

"Good men died to make this country safe for you, and you propose to hand it over without a fight."

"Why do we have to fight? Why can't we reach a settlement?"

"The blacks don't want to settle, boy, they want the lot. You plan to stay in Africa, you'd better be ready to fight."

"Against my own people?"

"Against revolutionaries, man, against terrorists. They won't hesitate to cut your throat when the time comes."

"So you think I should go into the townships and shoot guys who are doing exactly what I'd do in their place?"

"And what's that?"

"Demanding their rights."

"Ach, don't gimmie that crap! I suppose it's your grandfather that's been filling you up with that crap!"

"I haven't discussed it with him."

"Your junkie pals at varsity, then?"

"I don't know any junkies."

"Political junkies, full of political crap."

"This isn't a political decision."

"Of course it damn well is! It sure as hell isn't religious. You never go near a church. I don't understand what the hell you're after."

24

"I won't go into the townships and shoot blacks, can you understand that much?"

"Sentimental, political crap!"

Later, rage turned to wheedling. "Think of us, Ross. Think what it will do to your grandfather, if you go to gaol. You will, you know. They're not going to make any exceptions."

Finally, bitter resignation. "Do as you please, then, wreck your whole bloody life. Just don't expect me to pick up the pieces."

Yet on the day he was released from prison, his father was at the gate, with Richard Wragge's offer of a job in his pocket.

James had fallen silent, thinking perhaps of the past. Ross said, "I'd like to talk to old man Matlala, while I'm here."

"Why?" James was immediately suspicious. "Has someone been twisting your arm, someone in the States?"

He was close to the mark. Five nights earlier Senator Cromlech, an important figure in US Defence circles, had cornered Ross at a party in New York.

"Ross McRae! I was sorry to hear about your dad. They told me you'd already left for Johannesburg."

"I leave tomorrow."

"How long will you be away?"

"About a month."

The Senator plucked a canapé from a passing tray and swallowed it. "Interesting times, over there. As in the Chinese curse: 'May you live in interesting times.' Who's going to be your next State President?"

"I'm sure you know more about that than I do, Senator."

Cromlech laughed. "Rumours, I hear rumours, nothing I'd like to bet on."

"Which candidate do you favour?"

"Oh no, no, one doesn't interfere in such matters." A sly wink denied the statement. "'Course, we'd like someone who'll give us deeds, not words. Release the detainees, for a start."

"You think it'll happen?"

"Have to, sooner or later. Myself, I don't think they'll do it all

25

in one go. They'll keep the Messiah under lock and key for a while yet, but it's on the cards they'll release John the Baptist."

"Who's he?"

"I'm guessing, but . . . I dunno . . . someone like Vusi Matlala? Young enough to draw the township militants, smart enough to harness the trades unions, tough enough to risk negotiating with you whiteys." Shrewd little eyes surveyed Ross. "If they do let Matlala out of the brig, you better take damn good care of him, because there'll be a pack of hyenas after his hide. Keep him alive, buy yourselves time to negotiate a real constitution. If you lose this chance, God knows when there'll be another."

There was urgency in Cromlech's voice. Ross said, "I don't live in South Africa, any more. I'm not active in politics."

"Maybe that's a pity."

"I've made a life here. I like my job."

"Yeah." The Senator talked for a time about Salectron's part in the new ground-to-air missile, and then drifted away.

Ross stared out at the dark fields of Halladale. His, now, though he felt no sense of ownership. This dark flesh of Africa could not belong to a man with an office and apartment in the best part of Manhattan, a ski-lodge in Aspen. Nor did he wish to come back. That would be to become a victim, again.

"Why Matlala?" James said. Ross looked at him.

"I owe the old man a visit. He was good to me when I was a kid."

"Because your grandfather was good to him. Don't go on any sentimental journeys, Ross. Things are a lot rougher, since last you were here. I think some of the local police are CP. People are being detained on suspicion, rumour, nothing at all. Nola's right about one thing, you do have a police record, and if you're seen to be tangling with militants . . ."

"I'm not tangling with anyone. I can't afford to."

"As long as you realise that."

Ross stood up and moved to the verandah rail. The half-moon was rising now, flooding the plain with light and turning the hills an eerie blue.

"The reason I have to stay out of trouble," he said flatly, "is Jay. She's going blind."

James stared at him, slowly shaking his head.

"It's the result of the diabetes," Ross said. "I've taken her to specialists, the best I can find. They say there's very little they can do. In a year or two, she'll be totally blind."

James found his voice. "Where is she now?"

"In France. Lourdes. She's shopping for a miracle."

"Then why aren't you with her, man?"

"She doesn't want me around. She says I lack faith. Seems that could set up the wrong vibes. God mightn't get the message."

"That's . . . very hard on you."

"It's no good arguing with Jay. We'll have to work it out as best we can. I'll be in South Africa for a month. See Dad's lawyers, help at the trade fair. I'll collect Jay on my way back to New York."

The bedroom he'd been given was at the north end of the house, unchanged since his childhood. Oregon floorboards, worn thin near the doorway, logs in a roughstone fireplace, three rush mats, a brass bedstead with a blue cotton quilt.

His running-trophies, meticulously burnished, stood on the chimney-piece, his photographs were under the glass of the bedside table; school and varsity groups, his father in airforce uniform, his mother at her writing-desk, some old sepia prints of past McRaes, remarkably alike, black-haired, light-eyed, stubborn-mouthed.

In pride of place was the snapshot he'd taken of Grandpa McRae with Simeon Matlala, at the door of the farm school.

That was where it began, Ross thought, the testing of one's deepest affections, the first step towards self-imposed exile.

Simeon Matlala was a Master of Arts, a graduate of the University of Fort Hare, ex-headmaster of one of the largest schools in the country. His translations of Zulu folk tales had been published by Oxford University Press in 1958, and articles by him appeared from time to time in the avant-garde journals of Britain and America. He had joined the African National

Congress in the days of the passive resistance campaigns, was a close friend of Nobel prizewinner Albert Luthuli.

In 1960, soon after Sharpville, he was banned.

The terms of his banning order forbade him to set foot in any place of instruction, to publish his writings, or to leave the district of his birth. It amounted to mutilation. Simeon came to live at the family small-holding on the reserve to the west of Halladale.

A week after he returned, Keir McRae rode over to visit him, taking Ross along. It had rained heavily during the night, and there was no sun, no breath of wind. The whole countryside was heavy with moisture; the grassland where thin cattle ranged, the stands of ripening maize, cabbage and sweet-potato, all pearled with tears. In the silence, the clop of the horses' hooves and the clunk of a hoe striking earth, somewhere far away, seemed like solemn portents.

The Matlalas' home was wattle and daub, whitewashed, with a narrow stoep that overlooked the river valley. Simeon was sitting there as the McRaes rode up the path, and he came forward to greet them.

While the two men conversed on the stoep, Ross sat on the steps, holding the horses' reins. His grandfather spoke about the school he hoped to build at Halladale.

"You'll have time on your hands now, Mr Matlala. We could use your experience."

"I'm not allowed to teach, Mr McRae."

"Help me draw up the plans for the schoolhouse."

"I know nothing about building."

"Makes two of us. Come over tomorrow, and we'll talk."

The project went ahead that spring. The two men picked the site, worked out specifications, laid foundations and set cement blocks. Their toil was viewed by most of the neighbours with amusement, by a few with profound mistrust.

"The man's a bloody Red, Keir, you shouldn't have anything to do with him."

But the school was built, and three years later the terms of Simeon's banning were relaxed enough to allow him to teach there.

28

In those years, his mother being dead and his father involved in making his million, Ross spent most of his vacations at Halladale.

He was never lonely. For company he had his step-cousins, other farm children, and Simeon's three boys. They ran as a pack through those sky-blue days, limping across the sunrise stubble to swim in the dam, helping to chase the cattle through the dipping-tanks in a clamour of noise and a stink of carbolic, gathering tinfuls of wild amatingula berries whose white milky juice curled the tongue, eating slabs of bread and syrup in the wattle-plantation, the air glazed with drifts of pollen.

Friday dawned cold, clouds banking up to the south. After breakfast, Ross ordered a horse saddled and made the journey to the Matlalas's house.

Two years of poor rains had seared the Reserve, and the foothills of iNgeli were scored with new dongas.

Simeon had become very frail. His skin was heavily wrinkled, his hands gnarled by arthritis. He welcomed Ross warmly and apologised for not having been at the funeral.

"I can't walk far, these days, and my brother has taken the car into town for repairs. He won't be back until tonight. I thought of you, though, Polela. I prayed for your father's soul, may he rest in God's light."

Polela was Ross's Zulu name. It meant, a place where there is quiet.

They went into the house and sat chatting while Simeon's sister-in-law made coffee. When she'd gone back to her kitchen, Ross said, "Baba, I came to tell you, Vusi may soon be released."

The old man watched him politely.

"Just before I left New York to come here," Ross said, "I spoke with a man who's on the National Security Council in the USA. He believes that certain of the detainees will be freed, soon."

"It's been said before. They're still in Pollsmoor."

"This man has always given me reliable information."

"Umh. And why does he do that?"

"He knows that I'll report what he says, to my boss. They scratch each other's backs."

"I see. Did he mention Vusi by name?"

"Yes."

"Did he give reasons?"

"In his view, there's a move to promote black leaders who can persuade the militants to negotiate."

"Doesn't he know that to the militants, negotiate is a dirty word?"

"In the present circumstances, sure. But if the activists are released, the ANC unbanned? Will they still refuse to talk?"

Simeon shook his head, staring at the floor. "I don't know. Polela, how long is it since you saw Vusi?"

"About fifteen years."

"He was then a boy, still green. He's changed a great deal."

"But not diminished. I know his reputation. He was gaoled because he has a massive following in the trades unions."

The old man said flatly, "If he rejoins the struggle, it will be on his own terms. I can't say what those will be. I do know that whatever he does will be dangerous for him. Did your American friend speak about danger?"

"He said the hyenas would be after Vusi."

"'Hyenas' is a very vague term."

"He's a devious man, he deals in hints and half-truths. All I can say is that you must be on your guard. Don't take anyone on trust."

"I trust you, Polela."

"You shouldn't. I can be used, and I'm expendable. I have the feeling that whatever game is being played out now, the stakes are very high."

"What do you want me to do?"

"Look after Vusi. When he comes out, he's going to need a safe place. People to guard him. Can you arrange that?"

"His brothers can. I'll speak to them."

"Where are they now?"

"Themba works at a chemical laboratory in Johannesburg. Zidon is at the new casino, the one they built at Bowers Bay. He knows how to send messages into the prisons. I'll go and see him."

"It's a long journey. Let me arrange for a car . . ."

"No, no thank you, that would attract attention. I shall go by bus, with my fare tied up in a handkerchief, the country kaffir visiting his rich son." Simeon rose with a smile. "Thank you for coming. How long will you remain at the farm?"

"I leave for Joburg on Sunday." Ross paused. "There's not much I can do for Vusi, but if I hear anything, I'll call you."

"Don't use this phone, it isn't safe. Leave a message with Vijay Ramdas at the supermarket in Stannard's Post. He'll see I get it." Simeon scribbled the number on a piece of paper.

Ross took it, and clasped the old man's hands between his own. "Stay well, Baba."

"Go well, Polela, my friend."

4

At nine-thirty on the morning after Stendal's murder, a man crossed the deserted beach of Walker Bay, and climbed the slope to an isolated cottage some two hundred yards above high-water mark.

Far to his right was Danger Point, where in 1852 the *Birkenhead* sunk, drowning four hundred and fifty-four British soldiers. As far to his left, and half-obscured by sea-wrack, lay the jet-set resort of Hermanus, filling now at the start of the Cape spring.

The man was tall and heavily built, naked except for a white cloth hat pulled down over his eyes. As he walked, he drove his feet deep into the white sand that slid under his weight. Particles of sand encrusted his legs and glittered on the teak brown of his body.

He reached the terrace in front of the cottage and bent to turn on a tap. The water ran, ice-cold, from the spring behind the building. The man let it fill the bucket under the tap, and then began to sluice himself down, sloshing water over his head, back and crotch. As he finished, a young coloured man in yellow shorts appeared on the verandah above.

"Fouché's here, Mr Mathias."

The big man nodded and climbed the steps to the verandah. A white beach robe hung over the rail, and he put it on, not troubling to tie the cord. Reaching out, he put his hand on the young man's shoulder, the ball of his thumb gently massaging the point where the jugular vein passed the collar bone. The youth stood stock still, half-smiling, his gaze fixed on the sea beyond the breakers.

Mathias released his grip. "Bring coffee later," he directed, and walked into the room that served him as an office.

The courier Fouché was waiting there. Khaki shorts, a faded shirt and cheap rubber sandals, did not succeed in making him look like a weekend fisherman. He was of medium height and spare-framed. His eyes were small and green behind his dark glasses, his hair and clipped moustache were streaked with grey. He had served fifteen years with the police department on the Rand, but had left nine years ago under suspicion of corruption.

Mathias dropped into an easy chair. "You have the film?"

"Yes, sir." Fouché was unlocking a despatch case. "The quality's only so-so. He was using a very light camera."

"Run it, we'll see."

Fouché crossed to the television console and slotted the cassette into the video machine. Light from the verandah patched the screen, and he moved to draw a couple of curtains before sitting down.

Mathias picked up the control box and started the tape. He ran it through without interruption, then backtracked to a point near the end. He froze the frame that showed the rusty water-tanks at Site Nine. After a moment he moved on to a close shot of a swarthy face twisted in a rictus of rage.

"Got the lot, didn't he?" said Fouché.

"Not quite."

"Must've been tipped off," Fouché said. "It's a pity Sousa was in such a hurry to waste him. Else we'd have got the informer's name."

"I doubt if Stendal knew it. An anonymous call from some township rat is all it took." Mathias switched off the tape. "Sousa used those tanks once too often. The shacks are full of eyes. Who else was with him?"

"Petros. He's not on the tape, he was inside the tank. The two blacks you saw were Gama and Nsanje. Finch and Reynecke were in the ambulance."

"Did Stendal have a back-up?"

"No. On his ace. Sousa checked the bushes where Stendal staked out. There was only the one set of tracks. He found Stendal's binoculars, some dried-up skoff, a water-bottle. He thought he'd better fake a robbery, so he took the binocs and

Stendal's watch and cash . . . and the camera, of course. Then he came back to Bellville."

"Where's he now?"

"We flew them all to South-West, last night. They'll disperse at Keetmanshoop and stay out of sight."

"Good. When was Stendal found?"

"Ha'past five last night. Two, three vehicles must've gone right past the bugger without seeing him. It was dark, and he was lying in a bit of a dip. Then a patrol-car spotted him, didn't stop, case it was an ambush, sent a Casspir back. They picked him up and shipped him to the morgue."

"Formal ID?"

"Done. Half his face went with the exit wound, but he was carrying his Press card. His prints matched."

"Who told you all this?"

"Colonel Volbrecht."

"He's in charge?"

"Ja, and mean as a meercat because the army didn't report the murder until four this morning. Going to take it up with the Minister, they say."

Fouché laughed, and Mathias stared at him in displeasure. "Don't underestimate Volbrecht. He can make waves, and we don't need that. What about Stendal's possessions?"

"Junked." Fouché was looking sullen. "Camera, binocs, watch, we sent the ambulance for respraying and tyre change. About that tip-off, why don't we take a look at Stendal's place? Might give us a lead."

"Don't be a fool. By now Volbrecht will have it under maximum surveillance. We must keep right away from the case. On the facts at his disposal, Volbrecht will probably decide the killing was unrest-linked. Stendal tried to get shots of the rioting, was spotted by Witdoeke and they killed him. End of story. Did you bring the report?"

Fouché scowled, annoyed at the sudden switch of interest. The big man turned to stare at him. Fouché found himself looking into the eyes of a shark, coal-black and without light. He rose quickly and fetched a bulky envelope from his briefcase.

"Thank you." Mathias signalled dismissal. "Burn the tape in the incinerator. Tell Abram I want coffee."

Fouché collected the tape and his case, and left the room. Abram was in the yard at the back of the cottage, hanging washing on the line. Fouché thrust the tape at him, saying sharply, "Destroy this, and take coffee to the Baas, fast."

The document handed over by Fouché was a pirated copy of a routine report issued by the Security Council to the Joint Management Committees. Attached to the top page was a scrawled note: *Check pages 37–49*.

There was no signature, but the writing was that of Raoul Creuse, director of the computer section of Mathias's undertaking in Bellville.

Mathias was the big man's surname in so much as it appeared on various of his passports. Nobody knew his given name, though he used the initial "A" for convenience's sake. His birth date, stated as July 1st, 1935, was an arbitrary one, based on the estimate of the doctor who had examined him in a Turkish refugee camp in 1939.

Nothing was known of the first four years of his life. He had been part of the flood of refugees rolled down Europe, through Bulgaria to Varna, and thence across the Bosporus to Usküdar. Since the child could not, or would not, utter a word of any language, it was impossible to determine his country of origin, or his parentage.

During the next six years, he was shuttled from place to place in the Middle East. He became a number on a list of displaced persons without known country of origin.

He had no home, he formed no friendships, no attachment to any living creature. His power of speech returned, however, and he learned French, German, English and Arabic with amazing ease. He was considered, by those who spared him a thought, to be of unusually high intelligence. He had a special aptitude for mathematics and finance. He was exceptionally observant, methodical and patient. His ability to memorise, collate and codify information amounted to genius.

By the age of twelve, Mathias perfectly understood the value of his talents. Information was a saleable asset. One took an amorphous mass of facts and figures, brought them into order, defined their significance, and exchanged the result for hard cash.

At thirteen, he stole a sum of money from the institution then sheltering him, and after some ups and downs arrived in Beirut. He found a place to live and established his first intelligence network.

At that stage, his data was the gossip of the market-place, and his agents eavesdropping guttersnipes. As time went on he began to bribe clerks, barmen, and people with access to official records. He found that secrets could be bought cheaply, especially when money was allied to other pressures.

His olders and betters were inclined to laugh at his efforts, but it must be said that the people Mathias spied on, assisted, bribed, blackmailed, or sold, did not regard him as a joke.

Very early on he grasped the simple truth of intelligence work . . . that eighty per cent of all information is gleaned from legitimate sources, from newspapers and journals, defence reports, stock-market indicators and shipping notices. He appointed agents to study and analyse this kind of material.

He was careful. He would have nothing to do with drugs or drug-traffickers. He steered clear of the political cadres with which the Middle East was riddled. He never directly involved himself in violence.

He sold advice based on accurate information.

By the time he was twenty, he had the reputation of giving value for money. He had stashed away a sizeable fortune in a numbered account in Zurich, and owned property in London and New York. But he was running into difficulties.

The tenuous peace of the 1950s was over. As regional disputes festered, and terrorist fought counter-terrorist in every country from Greece to Indo-China, Mathias attracted attentions he very much disliked. His lack of loyalty to any one cause had become a two-edged sword. He was nobody's friend.

Twice he was ambushed by jealous competitors and beaten

unconscious. Once he narrowly escaped death when Red September agents planted a bomb in his headquarters. More and more often, he was compelled to pay exorbitant bribes in order to stay alive.

It was time to move on. He intended to reach the heights of his profession, and to do that he needed to acquire the skills that are only to be learned within a professional intelligence service. It was time to decide where he would spend the next stage of his life.

Quietly, Mathias considered his options.

The best fact-finders in the world were, he believed, right next door to him, in Israel. The finest computer storehouse was at Wiesbaden in Germany. The richest profits undoubtedly lay in the United States of America. (He had already made up his mind to move west, rather than to an Iron Curtain country.)

Armed with information about the sources supplying high-tech weaponry to Egypt, Mathias approached the Israeli Secret Service. Agreement was reached, and for some five years Mathias co-operated closely with the Mossad, learning a great deal from them.

In 1963 he moved to the USA to study computer-science. He knew that these machines, still in the early stages of mass production, represented the *summum bonum* of information-storage. He saw how they would enable him to expand his natural skills to a degree that would give him colossal power. Computers became the first, and only, love of his life.

An ordinary man might have chosen, at that point, to remain in America . . . as, say, a consultant on corporate finance. Mathias was not ordinary.

The horror of his childhood had deprived him, once for all, of common humanity. He was unable to experience or even imagine the loves and hates that motivated those around him. His sexual appetite was small . . . on the whole he preferred boys to girls . . . and he never felt any kindness towards the objects of his desire.

He had no concept of abstract right or wrong, only of personal success or failure. He had read the great religious texts and found them ridiculous, no more convincing than fairytales.

He was shrewd enough to realise that his emotional sterility antagonised normal people. Unable to adapt to their world, he looked about for a place he could shape to his own peculiar needs.

What he envisaged was a country small in the international sense, but large in opportunity. It must have multiple problems which he could exploit, and a government that was both rich and security-conscious.

For a while the South American states tempted him, but checks confirmed that their regimes were politically and financially bankrupt. The Far East presented difficulties of language and creed, and much of it was disrupted by war.

Mathias focused his attention on Southern Africa.

In 1967, two years after the Rhodesian UDI, he arrived in Pretoria. He brought with him much information relating to the Rhodesian economy, its negotiations with sanctions-busters, and the strength of its rival factions.

Having so to speak caught the eye of certain powerful individuals, Mathias made known his requirements. He would, at his own expense, establish an organisation to gather information that would "serve the financial interests of the Southern African region". He would strengthen the links he had already forged with agencies in North America, Europe and Israel. While he would not be directly attached to any government, he would co-operate with those governments which were prepared to encourage and reward his enterprise.

It was a piece of gross impertinence, but the powerful personages were attracted by the potential of such an unofficial agency, and certain that if Mathias should allow his ambition to overstep the mark, his services could easily be terminated.

Over the next decade he built his empire. He was the Mr Know-all who could supply the details of an arms or oil market, the name of a shipper who was prepared to dodge sanctions, the whereabouts of a financier who could launder dirty money.

In the process of enriching others, Mathias greatly enriched himself.

He set up headquarters in Bellville, his "front" being a kosher import-export agency. He travelled a good deal . . . he owned apartments in New York, Washington, London, Paris, Berlin and Tel Aviv . . . but his life style was so laid-back, so seclusive, that few people knew of his existence.

His greatest self-indulgence was his beach cottage on this isolated stretch of the Cape coast. Here he had his own computer-room, insulated against the threat of the salt sea air. The acres around the cottage were secured by electronic and human guards against uninvited visitors. A helicopter-pad lay in a convenient fold of land, out of sight of passing boats.

Mathias was well aware of the animosity his business aroused in certain quarters, and he took out the right kind of insurance. He secreted, in various places around the world, not only vast funds, but a mass of sensitive information about people and institutions.

Those who tried to push him around were quickly dissuaded. When the Information Scandal broke in 1977, destroying many reputations, Mathias's name was never so much as breathed. As one disgraced official remarked bitterly, the man was untouchable.

Yet 1977 marked a turning-point in his career. The see-saw that had lifted white baaskap to its zenith, was starting to tip the other way. In the townships the cry of Amandhla Awetu, Power to the People, grew daily louder.

Mathias watched, assessed, and pondered. The conclusions he reached had diverse results, one very minor one being the death of Karl Stendal.

"Your coffee."

Abram was standing in the doorway with a tray in his hands. He was nineteen years old, a descendent of the Koi folk who had once roamed this territory. He was delicately built, with smooth coppery skin, broad cheekbones, and a chin small and pointed as a cat's. His eyes, sloe-shaped and merry, betrayed the habitual liar.

"Daardie moffie," Fouché called him, "that little poof."

Abram was not in fact homosexual, nor had Mathias ever tried to seduce him. The bond between them was not lust, but empathy, a shared joke.

They had met when Abram attempted to defraud one of Mathias's technicians. The method he used was simple but ingenious, and instead of turning the boy over to the police, Mathias took him into his own employ. Time showed that Abram lacked the logic and patience that make a good computer-man, but he was an expert in the art of disinformation.

The spreading of calculated lies to conceal one's true aims had become an important part of Mathias's work. Abram could spread a rumour faster than fire in a hayloft. He spoke good Xhosa, as well as English and Afrikaans, and because of his colour he was able to move freely in the townships. He seemed actually to relish the dangers this entailed.

Master and servant were two of a kind. Mathias had created a warped world to suit himself. It suited Abram, too. They got along fine.

"Put it on the desk," Mathias said. He was studying the report Fouché had brought.

Abram set down the tray, poured coffee into a mug, added cream and two spoonfuls of sugar.

"Is it true what Fouché says? You wanted Stendal to be chopped?"

The big man glanced up. His eyes had a squinting concentration, as if he hadn't heard the question, but after a moment he shook his head.

"It's nothing to me."

"The bugger could've got away and sold that fillum."

"Luckily, he didn't."

"People in the townships, they suspicious now. They don't believe me when I say it's the police pays Sousa."

"They can believe what they like, so long as they stay at one another's throats. Did Fouché burn that tape?"

"He give it to me to do."

"So do it. And tell Fouché I'll be leaving here directly after lunch. If he wants a swim, he must go down now."

Abram went out grinning. He knew, as did Mathias, how much it annoyed Fouché to be given instructions through a coloured man.

Mathias returned to studying the report. It was a summary of unrest over the past week, and listed all known incidents, from major rioting, arson, and murder, to a stay-away of forty-one schoolchildren in the Northern Transvaal.

It confirmed what he already knew, that the situation in the country had become anarchic.

Which posed the question, what would the new President do about it?

Tossie predicted that the outsider would come in, and Mathias was inclined to agree with him. From that certain results would inevitably flow, demanding certain counter-measures. It was time to set things in motion.

Mathias strolled to the north end of the office. He placed his palm against an electronic screener in the wall. His palm-print identified, the door of the computer-section slid open. Mathias stepped through and closed the door after him.

The computer itself was housed in a glass cubicle at the far side of the room. Immediately to Mathias's right was a long bench equipped with sending and receiving radio, and telephones fitted with scrambler aparatus.

Mathias chose a chair and pulled a phone towards him. He pressed buttons, the code 0955 for Brazil, then the code 21 for Rio de Janeiro, followed by other digits.

After a short pause a voice answered, repeating the number in Spanish.

Mathias said, "Moondog."

This time the answer came in softly-spoken English. The accent was hard to place. It contained elements of America's deep south, overtones of waterfront New York, a sing-song cadence that was not American at all.

"Yes, my friend. How may I help you?"

"The matter we discussed. It will almost certainly be coming down within the next two weeks."

"'Almost' is not good enough. I have other clients to consider."

"I'll confirm within the week, but I must have your agreement to the terms."

"How long for the whole job?"

"Five or six days, including travel time. That is, if you fulfil your part."

There was a brief silence. "You said one hundred thousand US dollars?"

"Yes. Fifty thousand at once, the balance on completion. We'll use the O & A Bank, that should save you thirty thousand in tax."

The other laughed, enjoying the joke. "What if you have to abort?"

"We can come to an arrangement about that. I suggest we meet on Thursday next. Lusaka, as before."

"Very well."

"You accept the terms?"

"In principle, yes."

"Lusaka, then. Thursday next."

Mathias hung up without saying goodbye. He returned to his office, securing the door to the computer-room.

He strolled to the front windows and gazed down at the beach. It was empty. Fouché had not gone for his swim. Too cold for him, no doubt.

Mathias turned from the window and headed for the kitchen. He had ordered crawfish for lunch and wanted to be sure Abram remembered the Roquefort dressing for the salad.

5

At three-thirty on Thursday afternoon, the executive jet carrying Mathias as its only passenger landed at a small airstrip north of the dorp New Hebron. North again, the Snowberg lived up to its name, glittering under a cloak of white. The air at four thousand feet was bitterly cold, and as Mathias left the aircraft he jerked up the zip of his anorak.

Some hundred yards away a farm-house lay tranquil in thin sunlight. Four cars were parked on the scrub grass to the left of the porch.

Mathias ordered the pilot to stay with the plane, and headed for the house. A black servant admitted him and led him to the living-room. This was in the Cape Dutch style. It contained some fine antique furniture, three Baines paintings and several Rorke Drift rugs. A huge stone fireplace took up most of the far wall, and four men were seated in armchairs, facing the fire.

The man who was host . . . he liked to be called "General" although he had no right to the title . . . rose as Mathias entered, and came to meet him.

"Afternoon, mister. What will you drink?"

"Nothing, thanks." Mathias glanced quickly round the room. "Where's Rosendal?"

"Sent his apologies. There's trouble at his Benoni works. He has to be on tap."

Mathias nodded and moved to take his place. He opened his briefcase and took out five folders, retaining one and handing out the others. The host, still standing, said, "So you were right, Mathias. The tweegatjakkals won."

"On the second ballot. A comfortable victory."

43

Mathias settled himself comfortably, watching the four read his report.

He had from the beginning accustomed himself to thinking of them by their code-names, which he had himself chosen at random, from a school atlas.

His host, and the leader of the group, was Senekal; a big old man, bleak-eyed, sharper than his slow speech suggested. The names of his forebears were a drum-roll of Afrikaner history. Missionaries, trekkers, heroes of the Kaffir and Boer Wars, they had helped to forge a nation.

This one's soldiering had been cut short by the outbreak of World War II. When South Africa opted to fight alongside Britain against Hitler, Senekal resigned his commission. By doing so he remained, in his own view, true to his blood, ready to uphold the glorious past; an unrelenting Calvinism, an Afrikaner exclusivity that rejected blacks, communists, Jews, all those who spoke with other tongues and claimed other allegiances than his own.

His immense wealth, founded on land-ownership, was fostered by this exclusivity, for the brothers of his sect scratched one another's backs. His life style was simple, which allowed him to sink huge sums into certain covert operations in Africa south of the equator.

He regarded Mathias as a foreigner, and disliked him, but was prepared to accept his expertise.

Next to Senekal sat Kestell. Small, exquisite in his London-tailored suit, his French shirt, his Gucci shoes, he made no attempt to fit into the rural simplicity of this room.

He had a pinkish, oval face, the skin stretched by a recent face-lift which had been done, Mathias knew, by the best man in New York. His mouth was small and full, giving him a pouting look. He wore half-moon spectacles with gold frames, and read with great speed, flicking over the pages with neat, precise movements.

Kestell had made his millions in the manufacture of arms. Few people knew exactly how many factories he controlled in Africa, Germany and France. Mauritian-born, he spoke fluent

French, English and Italian, passable German, and some Russian.

He had many friends in high places. He had been married three times. His present wife was thirty years his junior and they had two young sons, to whom Kestell was devoted. His weakness, in Mathias's view, was his too-close links with that other family, the Italian Mafia. The Mob was apt to call in its loans without considering the consequences to others.

The man on Senekal's left was Breyten. He alone of the present company possessed neither wealth nor social standing. Breyten had been invited to join the group because of his knowledge of the security networks of the sub-continent.

Locked away in his foxy head was a matchless dossier covering every aspect of the police, the armed forces, the Joint Management Committees, the township informers, the secret swat-teams, the mercenary bands. Breyten knew how the Cape nuclear station was protected, what routes the ANC used to send in their operators, how oil and other sanctioned materials reached South African ports.

He would certainly have reached top rank in the security field, but for one fatal flaw in his character. He was a hater. Time and again, when he should have been concentrating on work of national importance, Breyten had allowed himself to be side-tracked into some personal vendetta. More than once he had abused his powers in order to persecute those who displeased him. He'd made potent enemies. When the Information Scandal broke, the long knives flashed for Breyten. He had been disgraced and deprived of office; but he kept up some of his old connections, and these the group found invaluable.

Next to Breyten sat the elderly Cradock; legs elegantly crossed, one long bony hand holding the report, the other resting on the arm of his chair. Mathias wondered if Cradock practised these poses before a mirror. He was certainly vain about his good looks, the finely-angled bones of cheek and jaw, the smooth olive skin, the snow-white hair and deep-set eyes. An aristocratic face. Cradock liked to be termed aristocratic, liked to refer to his

French-Huguenot ancestry, his ties with some of the great houses of Europe.

He was the only Cape member of the group, having been born and raised on the beautiful wine estate which he now owned. His wealth was sunk in numerous blue-chip investments, but he referred to himself, charmingly tongue-in-cheek, as a farmer.

A graduate of Stellenbosch, Oxford and Harvard Universities, he had enjoyed a distinguished academic career, and had for some years advised the government on communist strategy in Africa; but his excessive dread of Marxism had eventually become too much for even officialdom to stomach.

He was now, reflected Mathias, a senile old *flâneur*, given to sentimental gestures that embarrassed his friends and were a danger to the Junta; but Senekal thought highly of him, and refused to dump him.

Rosendal, the absent member of the group, surprisingly sided with Senekel in this. "Cradock can move in diplomatic circles without attracting attention. He gets us useful information. He stays."

The men finished reading. Their eyes turned towards Senekal, but he remained motionless, head bowed and hands clasped, as if in prayer.

It was Cradock who broke the silence, saying in his fluting voice, "An excellent report, Mr Mathias. As always, your facts are admirably presented. I'm not sure that I go along with your extrapolations. Do you really believe our new President will commit such follies?"

Mathias hunched a shoulder. "I remind you of his record, sir. He's been a maverick for years. He condemned the Seychelles exercise, the raids on Botswana and Lesotho. He hobnobbed with the Commonwealth Support Group. He is presently in touch with radical thinkers in America and Britain. He's pressing for free elections in South-West Africa. So yes, I believe my predictions are correct.

"He will release the detainees, end the state of emergency, and unban the ANC. He will repeal the Group Areas Act, the

46

Population Registration Act, the Land Act. He will push through laws to bring blacks into Parliament."

"And," said Kestell deliberately, "as he has repeatedly stated that he dislikes military solutions to political problems, he will slash the defence budget, first chance he gets."

Cradock smiled. "Talk is one thing, action another."

"He'll act," Kestell answered, "and he'll bleed us white in the process."

Senekal raised his head. "I cannot understand him. What drives him to betray his people in this way?"

"Vanity, General." Mathias was brisk. "The manikin has a mission. He sees himself as the saviour of the country."

"Can he be bought off?" Kestell asked. "Frightened off?"

"No, I don't believe so."

"What do you suggest we do?"

Mathias shifted a little, so that the firelight glinted on his face, giving it the exaggerated planes of a gargoyle.

"If we accept that the President has the support of the National Party caucus, then we will have to look for a solution outside of Parliament."

"The electorate?" Senekal shook his head. "It won't serve. He'll lose votes, but not enough to cost him a general election. He may even gain seats from the left, or achieve a coalition."

"I agree, sir, and in any case, the election is too far off to help us." Mathias turned to Breyten. "If we take executive action, can we count on support from enough people in the security forces?"

Breyten's expression was guarded. "Enough? I can't say. Enough for what?"

"To protect our operations."

"That, perhaps. Not more."

Cradock leaned forward in agitation. "What are you talking about? What do you mean by executive action?"

"We mean," said Breyten flatly, "that we have to stop the bastard in his tracks."

"Assassination?" Cradock peered from one face to another, seeing an acceptance that appalled him. "No, that's impossible. I

47

won't countenance the thought. He's one of us, a brother, an Afrikaner. Kestell, surely you agree with me?"

"I am neither a brother nor an Afrikaner," Kestell said coldly. "I'm a Mauritian Jew. Not that that is relevant. We are here to protect our interests. We're attempting to assess the cost to each one of us if this lunatic is allowed to carry out his threats."

"Precisely," said Senekal. "He's a traitor who's ready to sell us out to a pack of black revolutionaries. The survival of our white nation is at stake. If survival demands extreme action, then we cannot flinch from our duty."

Mathias let them argue. He took a sardonic pleasure in their hair-splitting. These men sniffed round death like witches at a smelling-out; greedy for sacrifice, yet needing to go through their little ritual dance.

After a while he said softly, "Gentlemen, it never occurred to me to murder the President."

Four heads snapped towards him.

"As Breyten says, we have to stop him in his tracks. That doesn't mean we must make a martyr of him. All we have to do is ensure that his initiative is rejected by the blacks he hopes to draw into his net."

"No time," said Breyten decisively. "It would take a huge campaign, months of work."

"There's an alternative. The President's first step, so I am reliably informed, will be to release a number of key blacks. Activists. One of them must be our target."

"Man, you're crazy," Breyten said. "It'll start a blood-bath."

"Which will force the government to revert to tough security action, bring back the emergency, arrest thousands of blacks, and shelve all controversial legislation. Isn't that what we want?"

"It's still murder," Cradock protested, "and I want no part of it."

"You have a better suggestion?" Mathias watched Cradock as one watches an insect that may do something interesting. He was not disturbed by the professor's resistance, had in fact expected it.

48

"As it happens, I do." Cradock glanced at Senekal. "If I may have the indulgence of the meeting. . . ?"

The old man grunted assent.

Cradock addressed Mathias. "I take it that in your capable way, you have already decided which of the detainees should be our . . . target I think was the word you used?"

"Yes." Mathias was matter-of-fact. "His name is Vusi Matlala. He's thirty years old, detained last year, a man with a big following, not only in the trades unions but also among the young people in the townships. He's a good negotiator, a charismatic speaker, fire in his belly as the saying goes. From our point of view, he's very dangerous. We'll have to get rid of him, sooner or later. Sooner has many advantages for us."

"When is he to be released?"

"Within the next few days . . . if my information is correct."

"I have seldom found it otherwise," said Cradock graciously. He steepled his fingers. "To come to the nub of the matter . . . our purpose is to discredit and defeat the President's initiative. Right?"

"Right."

"I submit that that may be achieved without recourse to violence."

"How?"

"By showing that this Vusi Matlala is a government puppet, in the pay of the President. I'm sure, Mathias, that it's not beyond your ingenuity to arrange some sort of cash exchange . . . some deal we can expose, and publicise?"

"I can bait a hook, sure, but I'll tell you now, Matlala won't bite."

"Why not?"

"Too smart."

"If the money was big enough?" suggested Senekal.

"The amount won't make any difference. Matlala won't take funds from an unproven source."

"So dress it up, make it look kosher. Is that impossible?"

"No. Merely a waste of time, and time is what we don't have."

Senekal sighed. "That is true. Well then, gentlemen, we have a proposal, let us vote on it. Breyten?"

The red-headed man looked up. He seemed to be in the grip of some private excitement. His eyes had a flat shine, like those of an animal caught in a beam of light. "I agree with Mathias," he said. "Bribery's a waste of time and money. Kill him."

"Kestell?"

Kestell's hesitation was brief. "I support Mathias."

"If Rosendal were here," Cradock began, but Senekal shook his head.

"You know the rules, there is no proxy vote. Like you, I hate violence, but I agree with Mathias that we have to act at once. So this time, old friend, my vote goes against you." He glanced round the circle. "Is it agreed that we adopt Mathias's proposal in principle?"

Breyten and Kestell nodded agreement. Cradock spread his hands in resignation.

The old man looked at Mathias. "Goed, meneer. We are ready to discuss the practical details."

It was after seven when the meeting ended. The night had closed in, snuffing out the sun with no spark of stars. A high wind keened in the cold beds of the mountain streams, and tore pale wisps of snow from the crests.

Senekal said, "That is settled, then. A brandy, my friends, before you leave?"

Cradock handed his copy of the report to Mathias. "Nothing for me, thanks General. I have a long journey ahead of me. Kestell, are you coming?"

"Yes, yes, one moment. General, what about Rosendal? We must have his support, he'll have to look after the finance."

Senekal nodded. "I'll speak to him tonight."

Kestell and Cradock said their farewells and made for the door. As Kestell passed Mathias, he gave him the shadow of a nod.

Senekal went to a table and poured brandy into three balloon glasses, handed one to each of his companions. Outside, two cars started up and drove away.

Breyten said, "I don't trust Cradock. He could do something stupid."

Senekal eyed the foxy man with distaste. "He's a man of honour. He won't go back on his word."

"He never gave it. He just went along with the decision."

"It comes to the same thing, among gentlemen." Senekal turned to Mathias.

"When will you make the move?"

"Immediately. Once Matlala is freed, his legend will build extremely fast. We mustn't give him time to consolidate his support. He'll go first to the Eastern Cape unions. We'll take him there, at East London."

Breyten said, "You'll use Sousa's team?"

"Only as back-up. The hit itself requires a special operator."

"And of course, you've already approached someone?"

"I have someone in mind." Mathias's smile matched Breyten's in malice. "A Swedish national based in Rio de Janeiro. He used to do contract work for the Mob. Now, he's freelance."

"How much is he asking?"

"A hundred thousand dollars. Half at once, half on completion."

"That's a lot of money."

"A fair price, for what we want. There's a high risk-factor."

"Who makes the arrangements? You?"

"Initially, yes. I'll need the committee's backing, shared responsibility for costs. Aside from the actual hit, there'll be a lot of follow-up work. Our key people must be advised what they will have to do. We must be especially careful in regard to the security forces. The top echelons are solidly for the President, but we have our friends. We must see they're fully utilised."

"The black townships?" Breyten said.

"There we can employ the Cheetah squads, for disinformation, incitement, whatever is required. And we mustn't overlook the far-right whites. They'll be hysterically opposed to the new regime. We must exploit that hysteria."

Senekal looked troubled. "I'm not sure we're ready for such large-scale action."

Mathias put a hand on the old man's shoulder. "General, we aren't trying to seize power. We merely want to advance our cause. Gain a little high ground. Matlala's death will delay black-white discussions for months, if not years. We'll use that time to replace this Cape rubbish with someone more to our taste."

"You're right, I know. I'll speak to Rosendal tonight. Do you have any message for him?"

"Warn him we'll need a lot of money, and fast."

6

Ross McRae returned to Johannesburg late on Sunday afternoon. He went straight to the apartment block owned by Richard Wragge's company, Salectron, in the suburb of Killarney.

Security had been tightened since his last visit. There was a uniformed guard in the foyer, and the lower windows of the building had been fitted with shatter-proof glass.

The company apartment on the fifteenth floor had the impersonal comfort of all such places. No one really lived there. Anonymous ghosts had placed a pot of white crysanthemums in the living-room, switched on the air-conditioning, stocked up the bar with bottles and ice.

On the table in the bedroom Ross found a small pile of letters addressed to him, expressing sympathy on the death of his father. There was also a request from the executors of the estate for an early meeting.

He showered and shaved, dressed in slacks and a light sweater. Back in the living-room he sat at the bar and drank two whiskies, slowly. At exactly seven o'clock he put through a call to his wife, at her hotel in Lourdes.

There was a short delay before her voice came on the line, quick and cool.

"Hallo, Ross. Where are you speaking from?"

"The flat in Joburg. How are you?"

"Tired. It's been miserable weather, but the sun came out today. There's a nice garden where one can sit." A pause. "How did the funeral go?"

"All right." He smothered an impulse to invent an incident, something bizarre to shatter her composure. "James and Nola send you their love."

"Thank you."

"You'll need a car and driver, Jay. If you like, I'll arrange . . ."

"It's all done." She sounded impatient.

"How are you feeling?"

"I told you, tired, I'll be better tomorrow."

"I could come over, you know. I could leave right now."

"No!" Into that syllable at least she put emotion. After a moment she said, more quietly, "It's better for me to be alone. I need to . . . to concentrate. To understand."

"Well, if you need me, whistle."

"I'm all right."

"I'll phone tomorrow night."

"No, I'll call you in a day or two. Please."

"Very well."

"Thank you." She sounded humble, but relieved. He said goodnight and replaced the receiver, sat for some time without moving.

He didn't know how to talk to Jay any more. Try as he might, he couldn't understand her attitude. Her anger was normal, the specialists said. It was a stage, it would pass in time. At present, she couldn't be reached. The faith that should have comforted her was like a hair shirt. She mortified her own flesh, and Ross's. How long since they'd slept together? Seven, eight months? He could have accepted the physical denial, if she'd allowed him to share her anguish of mind, but she would not. Ross must keep his distance, must not use any endearment, must not speak of Jay's deteriorating vision, must not encroach in any way on the holy ground of her suffering.

He remembered a carving of the Medusa's head in the Louvre; a face of dreadful agony, the eyes starting, the snakelocks writhing. It was that pain that turned the viewer to stone.

The telephone rang sharply, and for a moment he hoped it might be Jay, but the voice was Julie Aikman's.

"Ross?" She sounded breathless, as if she'd been arguing. "It's Julie. Pa just phoned from the Cape. He's been at Ster Hoogte for a few days, with Renier van der Sandt. He'll be back tomorrow afternoon, and he'd like you to come to dinner here."

"Thank you."

"He said, if you're tied up with family matters . . ."

"No. I'd be delighted to have dinner with him."

"Good. Ross? Are you OK?"

"Sure."

"Your voice sounds funny."

"I'm fine, Julie."

"Have you had supper?"

"Not yet. I expect the good fairies have left stuff in the fridge."

"What a fate! Come and eat with us. Hal's here, doing sums, you can help him. Steak, Greek salad, wine, come at once."

She rang off without giving him a chance to refuse.

The suburban streets were almost empty now. He pushed the Lamborghini along, fighting irritation.

It annoyed him that he'd allowed Julie to spot his depression. Women, too clever by half. Like Nola, lynx-eyed at the mere mention of Julie's name, scenting the truth.

He thought about Washington, five months ago. Salectron had thrown a party there, to grease the egos of a bunch of politicos. Jay had stayed home in New York, but Julie and her husband Dave were among the guests.

Dave had arrived drunk, picked up a showy blonde within ten minutes, and towed her off to the bar. Ross danced with Julie, had supper with her at a window table above the terrace still streaked with snow, the river glinting beyond.

Around midnight, when Dave left the hotel with his blonde, Ross and Julie, no word spoken and none needed, went up to her suite and made love.

It was an encounter born of mutual despair. Neither of them had expected more than a few hours' solace, neither had been armed against lasting tenderness, a constant longing to meet again, to share a common life.

Impossible, in their circumstances. They'd agreed on that. No letters, no phone calls, no private meetings. So why had

Julie lent him her car, why had she asked him over tonight, and why in God's name had he been fool enough to fall for it?

Richard Wragge lived at Malbrook, a five-acre property opposite the Melton Country Club. The three-winged mansion was guarded by an electrified fence, security gates, and patrols with mastiffs. Protection for Wragge's collection of modern art was the given reason. The truth was that Richard had a morbid fear of being kidnapped.

He was a lonely man. His French wife had divorced him when Julie was three years old, and he'd never remarried. There'd been a string of pretty ladies ready to play chatelaine of the fortress.

Wragge entertained lavishly; visitors from the neighbouring states and from overseas, businessmen, journalists, diplomats and artists. Once a year, he imported an entire polo team from South America, complete with wives, managers, and hangers-on. Their horses were provided locally.

The stable yard was at the back of the house, and at right angles to the stables were garages for six cars. Ross parked the Lamborghini in the space nearest the house. A uniformed guard approached him, recognised him and accompanied him to the back door.

Julie and Hal Ensor were in the kitchen. Julie was busy with feta cheese and olives, Hal sat at the breakfast table, poring over sheets of figures.

Julie smiled at Ross but kept her distance.

"So, how was Halladale?"

"Looking good."

"What are you going to do with it?"

"James and Nola will stay on, I hope." He picked up a bottle of red wine that stood on the draining-board. "Shall I open this?"

"Please." She dismissed him with another smile, and went back to tossing the salad. Ross dealt with the bottle of wine and set it on the table. Hal Ensor looked up at last.

"Oh, Ross. Hi!"

"Hi!"

"Sorry about your Dad." Hal was frowning, evidently debating whether commiseration was necessary. He was a man who found it hard to give his mind to anything not directly connected with his job.

An actuary and computer-analyst, he held one of the top positions in Wragge's business empire, but he still lacked social confidence. He liked to blame this on the fact that he was half-Jewish: "Neither flesh, fowl, nor good pickled herring."

He was forty-two years old, slender, and smooth-featured. His eyes were smoky blue, magnified by thick lenses. He had a small birthmark shaped like a rose on the right side of his face.

"Best way to go," he said. "Quick."

"Yes." Ross pulled out a chair and sat down. Julie had put the steaks on the griller, and the room filled with delectable smells.

"Did you see Weingarten in Washington?" Hal asked. Weingarten was Salectron's White House watcher. "Will the Yanks dump gold?"

"Only if it suits Uncle Sam's pocket. In any case, they'll wait to assess their new President . . . and ours."

"Ours." Hal tugged at his lower lip. "Bull in a china shop, if you ask me."

Julie brought the steaks to the table, served the salad. She was not really beautiful, Ross thought; light years away from the current plastic mould. Her chestnut hair, cut short, curled on to a broad forehead. Her eyes were hazel and slanting, her thin nose took a faint twist to the right. Her mouth was her only regular feature, something out of a seventeenth-century painting, delicately curved, eloquent, sensuous. Her skin was normally pale, but when she was excited or angry, colour burned on the cheekbones. She had a tall, stylish figure, the sort that could make slacks and a patchwork sweater look great.

"Did you hear anything about the detainees?" she asked.

Ross took the bottle of wine and moved round the table, pouring. "Only rumours. Why?"

"There've been rumours here, too. About release?"

He resumed his seat. "Cromlech thinks some of them will be freed by President's decree."

Julie nodded. "I'm scared."

"Of what?"

She took her time answering. "You know I've been helping out at Theo Kaplan's clinic in Soweto? We had to close, last week."

"I heard."

"It's a bad sign, Ross. Theo's always been able to go into the townships. He has a huge black practice. When the police told him he should close the clinic, I thought he'd buck like hell, but he agreed at once."

"Did he tell you why?"

"He said, 'For the moment, the people don't want us. They're waiting for something. They don't want us.' It's true. You can feel it, the waiting, the tension. The last day we were there . . . a week ago . . . there was a fire in the shopping centre, not far from us. The emergency teams came in to fight it. By the time they arrived, there was a big crowd blocking all the approach roads.

"The fire engines and troop-carriers came towards the crowd, kicking up a dust, you know, bells ringing? I thought, now it will be the old story, stones and tear-gas and shooting. I thought, maybe this is the day I get killed. But at the last minute, the people moved aside and let the engines through. There was no shouting, no singing. They didn't make a sound, just waited, and watched. When the fire was out, the troops left and the crowd melted away, in absolute, total silence."

Julie lifted her glass, and Ross saw that her hands were trembling. "That's what scared me, the silence. As if the people were . . . of one mind . . . just waiting for a signal."

"A signal for what?"

"Nobody knows, not the police, not the informers, not the people themselves."

"It's the strikes," Hal said. "Too many men hanging about with nothing to do but make trouble."

Julie ignored him. She looked at Ross. "Have you ever been in an earthquake?"

"No, thank God."

"I have, in Japan. Ten minutes before it hit, the birds stopped singing. That same silence. Something you feel in your blood, long before it happens."

"Never mind that," Hal said impatiently. "What else did Cromlech say? Did he talk about our products?"

"We discussed the ground-to-air missile components, for a short while."

"I thought so. The old bastard's been sniffing around. Lesurier says he's had US agents at his French factories, asking questions about shipments to North Africa."

"Cromlech's a friend."

"Friend?" Hal looked waspish. "I'll look on the Yanks as friends when they lift sanctions and buy our goods."

He left soon after, gathering up his papers with an angry movement, stalking out with the barest of thank yous to Julie.

"I should go, too," Ross said.

"No, stay. I want to talk about Dad, that's why I asked you."

"What about him?"

"Well . . . I told you he's been at Ster Hoogte. He came back in a crazy kind of mood. Euphoric, you know how he gets? Convinced that the new President is going to work miracles, and that we must back him to the hilt, because that's the way to end the strikes. That's all he can think of."

"He's responsible for thousands of jobs, Julie, he does care about that. You can't blame him for seeing things from the business angle."

She gave him a strange, almost pitying look. "Oh yes. He's a jealous god."

"What exactly are you afraid of?"

"That he'll rush in . . . try to manipulate the situation . . . and it's a very dangerous one, Ross. I want you to talk to him, warn him not to go overboard."

"I'll try."

The percolator at her elbow bubbled, and she poured coffee for them both. He asked the question that had been in his mind all evening. "And you, why are you in Africa?"

59

She traced lines on the table. "Couldn't take it any longer, waiting for Dave to kill himself."

"If he's good enough for the Porsche team . . ."

"He's not. They didn't renew his contract."

"Oh."

"The truth is, Dave's too old for any kind of racing. His reactions are too slow, he's a danger to himself and everyone else on the track." Her face was desolate. "He blames me, says I make him nervous. So I came away for a while."

"Will you go back?"

"Don't know. We've been through a lot together. We're married. That still matters."

Like Jay and me, he thought.

"Matters to me." Julie spoke in the careful voice of one avoiding tears. "Not to Dave. I think he'll ask for a divorce, soon. I expect I'll give it to him. I didn't mean to mention it, it's not your problem, nothing to do with you."

"Julie . . ."

"No, don't." She pushed a hand through her hair. "I think perhaps you should leave, now."

It was good advice and he took it. She saw him to the door, insisted he take the Lamborghini. He wanted to say, "I'll call you in the morning," but didn't. He drove back to the apartment feeling sad, for Julie and for himself.

7

"Vusi Matlala? One heard rumours, in the Cape, that he might be released."

Ross looked sharply at his host and met Wragge's disarming smile. "Trades Union kingpin, am I right?" Wragge said. "New Brighton unrest? Went to gaol about six months ago?"

"A year," Hal Ensor corrected.

"Long ago as that, was it?" Wragge's tone was elaborately casual. "Is Matlala ANC?"

"UDF." Hal closed his eyes, reciting as if from a mental checklist. "Union leader, also edited an illegal news-sheet. Detained without trial for seven months in '88. Charged last year with receiving American funds for an affected organisation." He opened his eyes. "Maybe other offences, I don't remember. I think he got two years."

Wragge looked at Ross. "You know when he'll be out?"

"No." Ross had the uneasy feeling that Richard did know, that he was taking a quixotic pleasure in the knowledge. "As you say, there've been rumours, nothing specific."

The three men were standing at the bar that filled one end of the glassed-in terrace that overlooked Wragge's demesne; pool, tennis and squash courts, sauna and jacuzzi. Beyond his boundary could be seen the lights of a dozen satellite towns.

Wragge wore jeans and a cashmere sweater, Hal Ensor a suit formal enough for the Salectron board room. Julie, in a shapeless garment belted low on the hips, stood some way off, gazing at nothing, one finger continually tracing the rim of her glass. She looked lonely and vulnerable.

The resemblance between her and her father was superficial. They had the same fine, curling hair . . . turning grey in

Richard's case . . . same hazel eyes, but with very different expressions.

Richard's gaze queried everyone and everything. On the surface he was urbane and full of *bonhomie*, generous to friends, staff and charities. In politics, he was tolerant, or perhaps uncaring. There was something Florentine about Richard, glimpses of dark motives, of the benevolent despot.

The story ran that his great-grandfather had founded the family fortune selling quack medicines to the Matabele tribe. Three generations later, behold Richard, civilised man, but with his granpappy's acquisitive genes.

He was genuinely devoted to Julie, had raised her to inherit the earth, and was puzzled when she seemed disposed to give it all away. She had none of his lust to possess, none of his aggression.

"Ross?"

Ross turned to find Richard watching him with a quizzical tilt of the head. "You with us?"

"Sorry."

"I asked if you know Vusi Matlala well."

"I did years ago, when we were kids at Halladale."

"Not since?"

"Our paths diverged." Ross had no intention of telling Richard about his visit to Simeon Matlala. That was a private matter, between friends.

"So what sort of man is he? Reasonable? Approachable?"

Ross thought about that. "He's a leader," he said at last. "People follow him. Love him."

Richard stared with narrowed eyes. Before he could pose any more questions, there was the sound of the front door slamming, and a few moments later, Theo Kaplan erupted on to the terrace.

When he saw the group at the bar he hesitated, as if he contemplated flight. Then he came slowly towards them.

"Sorry I'm late, Richard. I was . . . delayed."

"Plenty of time, boy, fix yourself a drink."

Theo went to the bar counter. He was a small man, thin, with hair that frizzed up in a cockatoo-crest. They saw that he was

62

shivering, his skin putty-coloured. Julie, who had joined them, put a hand on his arm.

"Theo? What's wrong?"

He turned to face her. "Aggie Dhlamini was necklaced this afternoon."

"Necklaced?" Julie shook her head slowly. "That doesn't happen, Theo. It doesn't happen any more."

"It happened this afternoon." Theo pushed her hand away. "I'm going to get drunk," he said. "I shouldn't be here. I'll leave."

"Wait a moment." Wragge reached for the whisky, sloshed a double measure on to ice, handed it to Theo. "Who's this Aggie?"

"She's the cleaner at my clinic." Theo's teeth chattered on the rim of the glass. "Was. They killed her right outside the front door."

"You saw it?"

"No, no. Her son saw it. They hacked her arms first, so she couldn't defend herself, then they put four tyres round her body and set them alight. They danced round her till she was dead, and then they went and torched her house. Jabu . . . the boy . . . got away and came to me. I had to get him to my place . . . see . . . see him settled, make arrangements with the police about Aggie's body."

"Who did it?" Julie demanded.

"Jabu didn't know them. Young boys, he said, people he'd never seen before."

Hal Ensor muttered. "What do you expect? They're savages, these Comrades."

Theo wheeled on him. "It was not the Comrades. Jabu would have recognised them."

As Hal looked ready to argue, Julie intervened.

"Why Aggie? A harmless old charwoman?"

"They were shouting that she was a police informer."

"Total rubbish!"

"Of course, but that didn't save her."

"What does Jabu think?"

63

"He's past thinking, poor child. I had to sedate him. Maybe tomorrow I'll get more out of him." Theo held out his empty glass for Richard to refill. "I know why they killed Aggie. They want me out of the townships. This was their final warning."

Wragge said, "Theo, you're taking this too personally."

"Am I? I'm afraid I don't have your godlike detachment! When a woman I love and value is butchered . . ."

"Please, don't misunderstand me. What I mean is . . . why would a bunch of illiterate kids campaign to get you out of Soweto?"

"Because they were paid to do so. The children are merely instruments. They're paid to do these things."

Wragge said quietly, "Do you have proof of that?"

Theo looked at him. "I've been told by a senior member of the Security Police that there are gangs at work, right across the country. Their job is to spread lies, incite violence, destroy the last few bridgeheads of goodwill." The disbelief in Wragge's face seemed to infuriate Theo, who began to shout.

"You think I'm making this up? Tell me, did you read about Karl Stendal? The journalist who was murdered last week?"

"Yes, but I don't see what . . ."

"According to my informant . . . who I assure you is no romancer . . . Stendal was killed by a gang known as The Cheetahs . . . paid thugs who've murdered scores of people here and in Natal, as well as in the Cape. Every one of their killings has had a political spin-off. Unrest, disaffection, more killing."

Wragge was silent for a moment, frowning at Theo. Then he said, "Who runs this gang?"

"No one knows . . . or no one's saying. Perhaps Stendal came close to finding out, and died for it. Perhaps he got something on film. The killers stole his camera."

"They would do, wouldn't they? A valuable item like that?" Wragge set down his empty glass. "I know you've been under great pressure, recently . . ."

"I am not paranoid, Richard, if that's what you're suggesting. Nor am I sucking this out of my thumb. The trouble with people like you and Hal is, you never see what you don't want to see."

"The black power-struggle produces a great deal of mindless violence . . .

"Dammit, will you listen to me? These gangs are not part of the black power-struggle. They're not part of any known political group, black or white. These people . . . whoever they are . . . are highly organised. They have money, big money. They have access to the latest automatic weapons, to tear-gas, and explosives. They can launch an attack and then vanish into thin air . . . which is another way of saying they have sophisticated means of transport, including helicopters, and safe houses to run to.

"Some of them are black and can move in the townships. Others are white . . . English, Portuguese, German, Spanish . . . and could pass unnoticed in your workshops or offices. All of them are highly trained mercenaries. If that doesn't scare you, it sure as hell scares me!"

Wragge seemed taken aback by Theo's vehemence. He greeted the dinner gong, which sounded at that moment, with evident relief.

"We'd better go in. We can talk at the table." He turned to Hal. "There are a few details about the trade fair I'd like to clear up."

He drew Hal indoors. Julie followed, but Ross hung back, catching at Theo's arm.

"I spoke to Cromlech a few days ago. He said Vusi Matlala is going to be released."

"When?"

"Soon, I think."

Theo's tired face twisted in a grimace. "Then all I can say is, they'd better keep him under wraps. If they let him run loose in this climate, I won't give ten cents for his chances of survival."

At dinner, Richard placed Theo at his right hand, and Hal Ensor at his left. He kept the conversation general, kept the wine flowing, apparently anxious to restore ease, if not enjoyment, to the evening.

It proved an impossible task. Theo stuck to his declared

intention of getting drunk, swallowing glass after glass of wine. Next to him, Julie sat with her wrists on the edge of the table, drinking nothing and eating very little. She seemed to have withdrawn into a silence as broad and deep as the sea; to float there, within sight, but out of reach.

After a while Richard gave up the pretence of playing host, and talked business to Hal, occasionally tossing a question at Ross.

Ross watched Julie.

That sod of a husband, he thought. He has no right to abandon her like this.

He remembered, not so much in his mind as in his flesh, the smoothness and softness of her body against him, under him, and he found himself sweating with the effort not to reach across the narrow gap and grasp her hand.

8

Mathias phoned Senekal late on Monday night.

"Matlala is to be released tomorrow."

"Is the source of your information reliable?"

"The same as before."

"Then our arrangements must go forward at once."

"There's a complication. I heard from Breyten. He says a fund has been launched for Matlala. The Stormont Merchant Bank is holding the money."

"Foreign money?"

"No. Local."

"Who's putting it up?"

"Breyten isn't sure, yet. There appear to be several backers . . . the usual set of do-gooders. As soon as he has the details, he'll inform us."

"Is Cradock involved?"

"Cradock, and possibly Rosendal."

"I cannot believe Rosendal would do anything so foolish. I spoke to him on Saturday. He accepted our decision without reserve."

"He's still capable of breaking loose. He thinks money can achieve anything, provided there's enough of it."

"How much is there, in point of fact?"

"The launch target is ten million rand. There could be more coming through other banks."

"It alters things."

"Only to a degree. It's a question of keeping tabs on Matlala. If he decides to consider this offer, he'll have to meet with their agents. We may have to act accordingly. If he rejects the offer and goes straight to East London . . . then our plans remain unchanged. We must be prepared to be flexible."

"How flexible is your friend from Rio?"

"Perhaps we'll have to increase his fee."

"By how much?"

"An extra twenty thousand should do it, but I'd like room to bargain, if I have to."

"Very well. I leave it to you to bring him to terms. What are we to do about Cradock?"

"I'll find out how far he's involved. My guess is, he's done some talking, and will leave the action to others."

"It's a very grave offence, to break a joint decision."

"We can worry about that later, General. At the moment we have work to do."

"That is true. Well, I leave matters in your capable hands."

That night the old man sat for long hours in front of the fire. He thought about the treachery of Cradock, and perhaps others. There was no faith left in the world, he decided. The old days of loyalty and brotherhood were dead and buried.

One felt a darkness closing in.

9

The President announced the release of Vusi Matlala in his first address to the nation, at eight o'clock on Tuesday night. Ross caught the televised speech at the Electronics Trade Fair.

There had been an official opening at six, with speeches by the Minister for Posts and Telecommunications and assorted boffins. The hall was packed with members of the trade; the importers, manufacturers and corporate buyers for whom the silicon chip was the centre of the universe.

Tomorrow, the laymen would flood in to gape at gimmicks and robotech, the twentieth-century computer freak-show. The classified material, the electronic input to military equipment and the space research programme, was not on show. Those were the contracts that counted, that local manufacturers would kill for.

Ross did a circuit of the stalls, chatting to old friends. The talk was of their work, sanctions, their families. Nobody mentioned politics.

Just before eight, he made his way back to the Salectron stand. This was occupied by Richard Wragge and a bunch of his cronies. Financier Adrian Kalmeyer was among them, building a punch-line for an attentive audience. Philipe Lesurier, whose factories produced components for SADF aircraft, was arguing heatedly with two officials from ARMSCOR. He saw Ross, and quickly turned his back.

Ross detested Lesurier. The man looked like a leech, his beaky mouth the perfect sucking device, his pale brown body grown plump on other men's blood. He appeared to be losing the battle with ARMSCOR, and presently moved off, looking murderous.

At eight o'clock, the music blaring from the overhead amplifiers was doused, and the mammoth television screen at the end of the building filled with the President's face. As his first words boomed and rolled among the iron roof-trusses, the crowd in the hall fell silent.

Richard Wragge beckoned, but Ross stayed where he was. He had no wish to join Wragge's coterie. Their slick opinions irritated him. When he was with them, he felt alone.

The man on the giant screen was alone.

Ross stared at the huge face puckered in concentration, the ridges of the eyebrows beaded with sweat, the eyes urgent with a passionate need to be understood.

"At this last minute of the last hour, we must pull back from the brink of destruction. We must end the wars in Southern Africa, we must break the political deadlock in our own country. We must halt the unrest, the polarisation, the economic stagnation. We must abandon the dead past, abolish apartheid in law and in practice . . ."

The words were hackneyed, mouthed a million times, here and in the outside world. What was new was the man, this man, saying these things at this time, and with such a desperate intensity.

He was pledging himself to immediate and dramatic action. He spoke about shared power and a constitution built on the consent of all the people. He stated, almost casually, that he intended to consult with the true leaders of the black majority; "to which end I have ordered the unconditional release of certain detainees, among them Vusi Matlala. I emphasise the word 'unconditional'. In the past, leaders have been freed under conditions that made it impossible for them to function as leaders. That will not happen this time."

Jason Hopner, the American Press Attaché, appeared at Ross's elbow. "The man's mad, to make promises he can't hope to meet."

Ross shook his head. He was thinking, a prophet doesn't speak by reasoned argument. His utterances have nothing to do with possible success or failure. They come through the prophet, not from him. His god, or his madness, speaks through him, and those who hear, accept or reject by faith, not reason.

"You think he'll do all this stuff?" Jason asked.

"I think he'll have a damn good try."

Jason regarded him, chin on chest. "Come to dinner, some night, and we'll talk about it."

He wandered away, and his place was taken by Wragge, his face jubilant. "Great speech, wasn't that? A real breakthrough, something we can sock to those bloody sanctioneers."

"If he succeeds, yes."

"He'll succeed. It'll happen. It's already begun. Kalmeyer tells me that Matlala was released, early this afternoon."

Ross said quickly, "Do you know where he is?"

"No." Wragge was gazing round the hall, his eyes blazing with excitement. "Look at the buggers! The new boy's knocked 'em sideways! That's what the country's been crying out for, a leader with the guts to make a bold strike."

His glee was so intense that he laughed and reeled like a drunk man. Catching hold of Ross's shoulder, he said, "You're right, though. We have to find out where Matlala is. I must talk to him. He'll need plenty of backing, if he's to achieve anything worthwhile."

"Richard," Ross said, "for the love of God, don't pull any stunts."

"What do you mean, stunts?"

"Don't try to buy Matlala. It won't work."

"You think he's some kind of saint?" Wragge sounded like a sulky child. "That he can work miracles, with no money?"

"He won't take money from you."

Wragge's scowl deepened. "Let me tell you something, Ross. Matlala will come to me for money, sooner or later. They all will, the new boy included." He waved a hand towards the now darkened screen. "This initiative of his is going to cost billions. When he runs short of cash, he'll come to big business, to people like me. The Presidents and the Matlalas of this world . . . they know how to wave a begging-bowl!"

71

"Then wait till you're asked, don't volunteer. Things could go bloody wrong, Richard."

They were interrupted by Lesurier and Hal Ensor. Lesurier caught hold of Wragge's arm.

"Richard, we have to phone Paris, right away."

"Later, later."

"Now!" Lesurier's unnaturally smooth face glistened like a plum about to burst its skin. "We have to protect the Sabre contract. There'll be defence cuts, a complete repositioning . . ."

"Paris can't renege on our contracts."

"They can do anything, in these circumstances." Lesurier's voice was cold with rage. "Come along."

Wragge frowned, then shrugged, and went off with the fat man towards the central office that housed the telephones.

Hal Ensor said, "Philipe's right. No matter what Richard likes to believe, that speech will affect us. The SADF is our biggest customer."

"Cheer up. We may find peace even more profitable than war."

"One has to face the financial realities."

Ross let that one slide. "Hal," he said, "don't let Richard offer money to Vusi Matlala."

Hal's gaze clouded. "Why should he want to do that?"

"When Richard sees a big act, he wants to be in on it. Politically, he's twenty years behind the times. He still thinks there's a role for Big Daddy . . . that he can hand out cash and counsel, as and when he pleases. Try and get it into his skull that Matlala will see anything of that sort as another form of exploitation." As Hal stared at him blankly, Ross insisted, "Whatever is done now, must come from within the struggle."

"Is the President 'within the struggle'?"

"Yes. Yes he is. He put himself right in it, tonight. Richard doesn't want to do that. He doesn't want to put his company, his career and his life on the line. He wants to make gestures, from a safe distance. That isn't feasible, any more. Tell him to stay clear. Tell him that for once, he'll have to mind his own bloody business."

Hal frowned. "You always exaggerate so." His gaze strayed to the Salectron stall. "I have to talk to people," he said, and ambled away to join the group gathered round Kalmeyer.

Ross headed for the bar at the south end of the hall. People stopped him on the way, shouting above the music which was now at maximum pitch.

"What about the Yanks, Ross? Will they take a softer line now? Have to give us a break, won't they? What about the EEC, what about UNO?"

Everyone saw Matlala's release in terms of his own little cabbage-patch. It was hardly surprising, after all. At this moment in London, the ANC and the British Foreign Office would be putting their respective slants on the new boy's words. In Moscow and Washington, Delhi and the Vatican, experts would pronounce and pressmen speculate, each according to his own peculiar bias.

Let them. He wanted no part of it. Whatever was about to happen here, he wanted no part of it.

Queuing for a beer, he was cornered by a Hollander in search of political insights. How genuine was the President? Could he be trusted? Was his move pragmatic, cosmetic? Was Matlala truly a freedom-fighter, might he not have been brainwashed in prison? Could this all be some kind of massive confidence trick?

To escape, Ross carried his can of beer out to the car-park. The night had turned bitterly cold, the grass verges were grey with frost, the car hoods misted over. The sky above the city seemed solid, like clouded amber.

He thought about Vusi, free now, drinking a beer with friends, or perhaps looking at the stars above Halladale.

A man fresh out of prison looked at the sky. In the final analysis, freedom meant being able to see the whole sky, any time of the day or night.

I will not go back to prison, he thought, I will not go back to politics, I will not feel guilty about not going back.

He'd bought his absolution, paid for it in lost friends, ostracism, a smashed nose and three broken ribs, four hundred and seventy-one days in a cell, sixty-nine of those in solitary confinement.

Odd to remember that prison was the one place he'd felt completely free of guilt.

Maybe it was true, as Jay maintained, that in distancing himself from his family, his country, and his political past, he had merely exchanged one prison for another.

At least it was a prison of his own choosing.

Tonight a man had stepped forward, barehanded as it seemed, to deliver a challenge. Whether or not Vusi Matlala decided to take it up, was Vusi Matlala's business.

Ross raised the beercan and drank, eyes closed. He said aloud, "Hey, Vusi! You're on your own, man!"

Footsteps crunched on the road behind him, and Hal Ensor appeared, shivering and out of temper.

"Ross, what the hell are you doing out here? I've been looking for you all over. Richard wants you to meet someone."

"Who?"

"I dunno. Some geek from a casino. You better hurry."

Ross swallowed the dregs of his beer and followed Hal into the hall.

When Ross reached the Salectron stall, the Kalmeyer clique had left. Wragge was talking to a man who looked like Henry VIII, lardy cheeks, small shrewd eyes, a fringe of red-gold beard. Wragge introduced him as Charles Sickert, security chief at the Bowers Bay casino.

"Charlie has problems," Wragge said. "He wants advice on electronic security systems."

"Teething troubles, Mr McRae. We're very new, you know." Sickert's voice was at once high and husky. "See, it's the slot-machines. We've installed over seven hundred at a cost of R14,000 each. You'll admit that's a big investment."

"What make of machine?"

"ALDO, from Japan. I'm not complaining about the machines, they work fine."

"Then what's your worry?"

"Cheats," said Sickert. He blinked rapidly. "The old-time sluggers used a ticky on a string . . . dropped it in, pulled it out again. Today, we're in a different league. The boys we have to deal with now, know how to blow a computer's circuits. Did you know they run special schools in the States, schools for cheats? The casino could be taken for a million rand, in one night."

"Mr Sickert, I'm not an expert on fruit-machines. Why don't you talk to the ALDO suppliers?"

"No time." Sickert shook his head mournfully. "We've had a tip-off, see? There's this gang of pro gamblers moving in on us. They really cleaned up, in Mauritius. Tricks like mini-computers in the soles of their shoes, so they could keep track of the cards in play. Magnetic devices to blow the slot-machines. Maybe other things, too, things we don't even know what to look for."

"Do you have electronic surveillance at the casino?"

"Sure, the best. We monitor the gambling-rooms, the machine-halls and the counting-house. Mauritius could do all that, too. It didn't help them. The gang got past all the checks. Mr McRae, if you can spare us a couple of days, just the time this lot will be at the casino, help us work out how they operate . . . you'll be doing us the helluva big favour."

Ross glanced at Wragge, who was listening with a half-smile. Wragge's shoulders moved in the faintest of shrugs.

"By what you say," Ross said to Sickert, "you can identify these people."

"No, that's the trouble. We're fairly sure that the leader is a Greek-American called Stavros Pampallas, also known as Nicky Niarchos, or Stacy Palmer. He's one of the best blackjack players in the world, uses the Thorp system. But we can't identify the rest of his team."

"Do you have a photograph of Pampallas?"

"Mauritius sent us some they took. It doesn't help us too much. Pampallas isn't in the Griffin book."

"What's that?"

"A publication put out by a private agency in Vegas. Lists all the convicted gambling sharps. Pampallas has no criminal record, yet."

"Why did you accept his booking?"

"He booked weeks ago, under the name of Palmer. We had nothing against him at that stage, and now we don't know where to reach him."

"Warn him off as soon as he arrives at the hotel."

Sickert spread plump hands. "Mr McRae, it's not that simple. We've no proof that Pampallas cheats. Even if we catch him in the act and move him along, he could still leave his pals behind. Then there's the publicity to think of. We can't have our patrons saying that soon as we see a big winner coming, we warn him off."

"Even if the man's a cardsharp?"

"Ah, but we can't say so! That'd be libel, wouldn't it?" Sickert wiped a hand across his wet forehead. "I'll be honest with you, there's a special reason we don't want trouble next week. We've got the Pro-Am golf at Bowers Bay. We're booked to the roof, people coming from all over the world. They come to gamble, as much as to watch the golf. We don't want any scams, Mr McRae. We can't allow anything to destroy public confidence in our gambling systems. Once that happens, we're dead."

Ross shook his head. "It's outside my competence."

Wragge said gently, "Mr Sickert's offering you the hospitality of the hotel, Ross, in return for a little advice."

"Best suite in the place," said Sickert eagerly, "and if you fancy watching some golf, the best seat in the stand."

"I'm sorry," Ross said. "I came home to settle my father's estate. I have appointments with his executors, all next week."

Sickert sighed. "I see. Well, if anything happens to change your mind . . . please, we need your help. I'll be at the Carlton until Sunday morning. Call me any time."

He gave Wragge a nod, and moved away, his red head with its bald spot marking his passage through the crowd.

Ross turned to Wragge.

"Are you by any chance sponsoring the golf?"

"Good heavens, no!"

"Any of your pals involved?"

"No. Why?"

"You seem damn keen on obliging Sickert."

"I thought it might make a pleasant break." Richard's smile was disarming. "And Ross, we do have a stake in computer security. Any big computer fraud . . . even if it only involves the humble fruit-machine . . . hits the trade as a whole."

"There are a couple of hundred technicians in this hall who are experts on computer security. Sickert can ask one of them."

"Of course. It's entirely up to you."

Wragge drifted away, leaving Ross to feel a heel. It was part of the well-known Wragge technique for getting his own way.

10

On Tuesday evening, Vusi Matlala sat on the stoep of his father's house, and watched the sun go down. That piece of sky above the farthest hills, the groups of huts there, and there, and the dam that always held the red colour a little longer than the river . . . he'd thought of them often, in prison.

In prison, people tried to make you forget who you were.

They tried to scour out your mind, the way the flood water had scoured out that hillside. They told that this friend, or that good union man, had turned State evidence. Sometimes you came close to believing all the shit they shovelled at you. You began to fall apart.

Then you thought about this house, the valley and the people living in it, and you told yourself, "That is Vusi Matlala's place. The man who will live there one day is Vusi Matlala, and I am that man." You found the spirit of your ancestors. You found yourself, again.

He heard steps behind him. His father and his brother Themba came out of the house, each carrying a wooden chair. They set the chairs against the wall, and sat down, with a certain solemnity.

Simeon was still very emotional about having Vusi home. Whenever he looked at his son, the tears came to his eyes and he wiped them away carefully with his handkerchief, smiling at the same time, and shaking his head.

Voices carried from the kitchen; Simeon's brother arguing with his wife Nomsa. Presently the woman emerged, carrying a tray with glasses and a jug of home-brewed beer. She set it down next to Simeon and marched away without a word.

"She doesn't like having us here," Themba said. "She's scared the cops will come and arrest us." He laughed.

78

He was very like his brother, and not only in looks. They both had the same immense physical energy, but in Vusi it was packed down and controlled, while in Themba it was volatile, ready to explode at a touch.

Vusi said calmly, "The police won't worry us."

"They're watching this place," Simeon said. "Mchunu, down at the store, told me they've got men on all the roads, too."

"For once," Vusi said with a smile, "I don't mind having a few dogs at my heels. They won't bite me."

"How can you be sure?"

"I'm exhibit A in the world show," Vusi said. He poured beer for his father and brother, then helped himself. "Say what you like about Nomsa, she makes the best brew in the country."

"What are you going to do about the letter?" Themba demanded, and immediately answered his own question. "You have to refuse, man! It's a trap, anyone can see that. We haven't been able to raise a cent for months, now suddenly there's a million with your name on it? They're just trying to put a hook in your mouth."

Vusi shrugged.

"Listen," Themba insisted, "Zidon's been asking around. New York, London, Paris, everyone says the same thing. It's dirty money, don't touch it. They want to tie you in to the reactionaries. Then you'll be finished, for sure."

"We have to check it out, Themba. We need cash."

"We need you more!" Themba was suddenly enraged. He was committed to the struggle, he had risked his life for it more than once, and would do so again. He knew his own value. He could plan and he could administer, but he could never lead, as Vusi could lead. He was jealous of Vusi, even while he loved and admired him. The combination of jealousy and love made him angry. He shouted, banging down his fist.

"You're a bloody fool, man! They'll kill you if you go to that place! Leave it alone."

"I have to check it out," Vusi repeated. "I won't swallow any hooks."

79

"They'll kill you." As Vusi made no reply, Themba said in exasperation, "All right, then. But if you go, I go with you."

"Good," Vusi said.

At his cottage on the coast, Mathias considered the effects of Vusi Matlala's release.

The news had made headlines, around the world.

The governments in London, Washington, Paris, Bonn and Rome had already indicated approval and optimism.

In London, *The Times* wrote that the new developments in South Africa would no doubt form an important part of next week's meeting of the Commonwealth Heads of State.

The *Independent* printed an in-depth interview with the ANC's man at UNO.

The *Daily Telegraph* called for an immediate easing of sanctions against South Africa.

The *Washington Post* said: "This initiative is being taken seriously by the White House. It is felt that the way is now open for that National Convention of South African leaders which liberal thinkers have been urging for decades.

"Matlala is a significant figure, an opinion-former who has the charisma and the political know-how to create a power-bloc of the younger black politicians, and to attract young white activists as well.

"How he will use that power remains to be seen, but his freeing, together with the measures the President of the RSA announced last night, present Southern Africa and indeed the world with a unique opportunity to sweep away the rubble of apartheid, and to replace it with an equitable system of government."

Within South Africa, the English-language Press acclaimed a watershed decision. The Afrikaans Press, more cautious in style, also tossed bouquets.

Black reaction was harder to assess.

Many black leaders were in gaol or in exile, and those at hand were suspicious both of the government and the media. They welcomed Matlala's release "in human terms", but insisted that they must meet and talk to him, before passing further comment.

They pointed out that reforms had been promised before, with little result. Let the President convert promises to action; then, perhaps, there could be talks about talks.

On the extreme right, there was a considerable white backlash. The Conservative Party had launched a virulent attack, that morning, in the House of Assembly, labelling the President a sell-out and demanding his immediate resignation.

The Weerstandsbeweging had announced that on Saturday evening it would be holding a mass rally in Pretoria to condemn the initiative.

The heads of various right-wing cultural organisations, along with conservative academics and churchmen, were getting up a petition to protest against the "wilful destruction of the rights of the white man".

The release of Matlala, these people averred, would be the signal for bloodshed and racial hatred on an unprecedented scale. "What began as a lunatic notion in the head of one man," thundered one editorial, "will end in the overthrow of the forces of law and order. It will mark the end of civilised, Christian rule for our nation. Africa will become, once again, the Dark Continent."

With all this, Mathias was reasonably well satisfied.

Financially speaking, there were no surprises.

Matlala's release had, as he predicted, produced optimism on the major stock-markets. Mathias, having taken his profits, had quietly dumped all but a few blue-chip stocks.

Not that these moves were of any great importance. One did not make money by playing the markets, but by advising others how to play them.

He was retained by some of the wealthiest and most influential people in the world. His advice to them at present was to stay out of the Southern African arena. When, in a few days' time, the death of Matlala caused the markets, the President, and possibly the South African government to tumble, Mathias could rely on his clients to show their gratitude in the usual handsome terms.

An amateur attempted to foresee events. A professional structured events to his own advantage.

He considered the Matlala affair. It must not be bungled. This was a matter not of professional pride, but of economic necessity. His ascendancy over his rivals in the field depended on his record of success. Let that sag, and the big backers would go elsewhere.

He leaned back in his chair, and closed his eyes, reviewing various facts.

Since learning of Cradock's idiocy, he had extracted from an official of the Stormont Bank (in settlement of past favours) the names of two of the men behind the attempt to buy Matlala.

He knew which firm of Johannesburg lawyers had been instructed to make the initial approach.

He was keeping a close watch on Matlala, and knew that his first meetings were to be held in East London.

He was not yet sure if Rosendal was involved in the deal.

The question was, whether to challenge Rosendal, and scuttle the scheme at once, or to let it continue.

After some thought, he decided that the latter course would be less risky.

That settled in his mind, he picked up the telephone and directed his office in Bellville to book him on the Thursday morning flight to Lusaka.

At his home, on Wednesday night, the President talked to two of his trusted friends.

The first of them, an ageing politician, was close to panic.

"Ou maat," he said, "I have to warn you, my constituency won't accept what you're doing. The resignations are pouring in, my desk is swamped with telegrams, the phones haven't stopped ringing . . ."

"Then we'll just have to find you a safer seat, Paul. We can't afford to lose you."

"Man, it's not just my seat! It's seats right across the platteland! You've moved too fast, the people won't take it. There's going to be big trouble."

"We'll contain it." The President's voice was dry. "Aren't you always telling me, we have the best law-enforcement machine in Africa?"

"If you turn the police loose on our own voters, they'll go over to the CP, once for all."

"The police have orders to keep a low profile."

"And will they do as they're told?"

"A few won't. Most will."

The politician shook his dewlaps. "I hope you know what you're doing. Where's Matlala now?"

"At his father's house, on the Reserve near Stannard's Post."

"How long do you think he'll stay down on the farm?"

"He'll move soon. The informers say, to East London."

"Ja, to drum up a mob of supporters!"

"I hope so, Paul. That's why we let him out of the tronk, you know. If he can't attract a following, then he's no use to us, no use at all."

The old man muttered, "I suppose we can always put him inside again."

The President leaned forward. "I want it understood," he said, "that Matlala is free in the fullest sense of the word. I won't tolerate anything . . . from anyone . . . that makes his freedom look phoney. If that happens, our credibility flies out of the window. The whole initiative collapses. It takes me with it, and perhaps the government."

"So you admit, you are gambling with the future of the entire country."

The President shook his head. "No, Paul. A gambler has options. I don't. I have no choice but to do what I'm doing."

When the old man had departed, the President touched a buzzer under his desk. The door behind him opened, and a man in a blue track suit stepped through. He was above average height, wiry, lantern-jawed. He needed a shave and his deepset eyes looked tired.

"Sit down, Dion," the President directed.

Dion Volbrecht held a top security post in the Western Cape.

He was an unusual sort of policeman; introspective, imaginative, and impatient of protocol. He was here tonight because the president had faith in both his ability, and his loyalty.

"You heard what my old friend said?"

Volbrecht nodded. "Where he comes from, they still think the earth is flat." He settled into his chair, folding his legs back like a schoolboy. His dark eyes were fixed on the President's face.

"You must watch what you say, sir, even to old friends."

"What do you mean?"

"There've been leaks, sir, over the past few weeks."

"I assure you, I don't gab. I talk only to people I know to be trustworthy."

"Like your old friend Tossie Wendt."

The President looked up sharply. "What about Tossie?"

"Did you tell him you were going to release Matlala?"

"I . . . yes, I did. But I won't believe . . ."

"Wendt's on the skids. He's been taking backhanders for months. This Monday he paid ten thousand in cash into his Claremont account."

"That doesn't mean he sold me out."

"No, but you're vulnerable. I thought I should warn you."

The president opened his mouth to argue, met Volbrecht's eyes, and sighed. "Will you question him?"

"No. We'll keep him under observation. We need to know who paid him so much money." Volbrecht took a pack of cigarettes from his breast pocket, looked at it and put it away again.

"Smoke if you want to, Dion."

"No, I gave it up yesterday. About Matlala, sir. If you would just let us offer him protection."

"You know that's impossible."

"What you're asking of us is impossible, Mr President. We have to keep Matlala alive, but we can't go near him, we can't talk to him? You realise that if he crosses into one of the homelands . . . Ciskei, Transkei . . . we have no authority to act in those places? None at all."

"I've done my best to explain . . ."

84

"Ja, sir, and I understand. I'm just telling you, there are a lot of people who want Matlala dead. So don't be surprised if we get unlucky."

"Tell me what you've arranged so far."

Volbrecht outlined his plans for Matlala's safety, and the man behind the desk listened without interrupting. At the end, he nodded approval. "That sounds comprehensive. When do you leave for East London?"

"Tonight, sir. From here."

At the door, as they shook hands, the President said, "Understand, if you need anything, tell me. Money, men, I'll see you get whatever you ask for. Whatever it takes to keep Matlala alive. That's your job, Dion, from now on. Keeping Matlala alive."

11

Mathias disliked Lusaka.

Like most Third World capitals, it displayed some of the trappings of a modern city; a fine university, some tall new buildings along the old Cairo Road; shops that sold an odd assortment of luxury goods and ticky-tack; a market for fruit, lake-fish, vegetable and spices; two golf courses, a vast brewery, various factories. These marks of development quickly gave way to the general poverty of Africa, to squalid shanty-towns and squatter-farms patched with scrawny maize.

The vigorous copper-boom was over, the splendid mines at Rokana and Chingola now producing more than the world wanted. The rich supplies of cobalt and uranium, lead and emeralds, gold and amethysts that lay under the Zambian earth were not yet being exploited to the full. Each year the economy sagged a little lower, leaning more heavily on foreign aid and injections of private capital from South Africa, America and Europe.

It was not Mathias's cup of tea.

Yet Lusaka had its uses. Like Cairo and Casablanca in the forties, it was an ant-heap of intrigue. Here diplomats, trade missions and financial wheeler-dealers toiled at operations that covered every facet of life on the African sub-continent.

It was from Lusaka that Russia and the Western Five controlled their interests in Angola, Zimbabwe and Mozambique. It was rumoured that on one or two occasions, representatives of the South African government had conferred here with members of the ANC. Certainly a good intelligence agent could pick up much useful information from Lusaka's Arab dealers, French mercenaries, men of God and men of The Devil.

Care was taken to preserve the ant-heap, for if it were to be trampled, it would have to be repaired, at serious inconvenience to every ant in the business.

In Lusaka Mathias passed as the representative of one of his front firms, Belpearl Metal Industries. He had a small office in the city centre, and rented a colonial-style bungalow in the suburb favoured by wealthy Zambians. This house was very private, screened by banks of overgrown bougainvillea and bamboo. The front gate was served by a tarred road, the back by a dirt track that led to Chawama, a council housing estate.

On this Thursday night, the moon not yet being up, Mathias left a light burning in the kitchen. Its soft bloom spread only a few yards. He heard the truck approaching long before he saw it.

It was a rusty bakkie of the make much used by local farmers. It coasted to a halt, the lights were doused, and a tall man slid from the driver's seat and advanced without haste to the kitchen door.

Mathias admitted him, closed and locked the door, and led the way to the living-room. The curtains were close-drawn. Drinks stood ready on a tray, and he glanced enquiringly at his guest, who shook his head and dropped down on to the sofa.

Still without speaking, Mathias moved to switch off the central light, leaving only one lamp burning in a corner. There was a projector on the central table, and he set it running before he took his place on the straight-backed chair beside it.

On the screen at the far end of the room appeared the blown-up photograph of a black man. It was an arresting face, narrow and high of forehead, the nose thin with flared nostrils, the mouth wide and full-lipped. The hostility in the eyes, as much as the number stamped across one corner of the frame, confirmed that this was a police mug-shot.

"Vusi Matlala," Mathias said.

There followed profile shots of the same face, then snapshots taken over a number of years, a family group, a school picnic, a soccer team. In every picture, Matlala's face was instantly identifiable.

The stills gave way to action footage of a funeral procession. Thousands of mourners trudged across a dusty hillside. Matlala was one of the six pall-bearers carrying the coffin. In the background, banners waved; Viva Mandela, Viva UDF, Amandhla Awethu, Workers Join the Struggle. Further back still, a cloth crudely daubed with a hammer and sickle billowed for a short space in the wind, then disappeared.

The scene changed to a mine compound, neat offices within a tall security fence, pithead machinery, and a mass of men in overalls and miners' helmets, shouting, waving clenched fists at the camera.

"Strikes of '87," Mathias said.

The camera panned across the shouting men. It picked up a figure pushing through the throng, scrambling to the top of a stack of oil-drums. The man turned and began to address the miners, right hand stabbing the air. The camera zoomed in close, isolating him from the crowd.

"Hold it there," said the man on the sofa, and Mathias froze the frame. Matlala's gaze blazed at them, through them. Energy seemed to pour from his body like an aura.

The man on the sofa grunted, and Mathias let the film run again. It showed shots of an open-air rally. Blacks and a few whites packed the stands of a sports stadium. Matlala stood at the rail of the speaker's podium. He leaned forward, smiling down at a mass of schoolchildren who swayed and stamped, their hands raised in salute.

The final footage showed township rioting. Matlala stood with a group of men while behind him, on a road hazed with dust, youths skirmished, hurling stones at a line of police vehicles. Matlala ran towards the youths, shouting at someone off-camera. His face in this sequence was blurred by movement.

"The bugger never stands still," Mathias complained.

The film clattered to an end and he switched off the projector, moved across the room to an easy chair.

The tall man stretched his arms along the back of the sofa. His eyes, thick-lidded and goatish, squinted at Mathias as if along the barrel of a rifle.

88

"Not good enough, man."

"Best we could get, in the time."

"Listen. You want me to shoot the right guy, you better gimme good identification. All blacks look alike to me, you know how it is." His smile was a grimace.

"We've arranged for you to get a close look at the mark, before you make the hit."

"Where?"

Mathias ignored the question. "I've had problems," he said. "Top brass has been buggering me about."

The tall man grinned. Mathias never worked for anyone but himself. Whatever the operation, he was in charge. Things came out the way he wanted them to.

"I had to make a few changes," Mathias said.

The tall man's grin vanished. He held up both hands, palm forward.

"No changes, man. We have a contract, we stick to it."

"I've arranged an increase in your advance," Mathias said smoothly. "You get seventy thou up front, fifty on completion."

He paused, letting the bait dangle.

The two men eyed each other. They were much alike, in their psychopathic coldness, their admiration for the technically expert, their contempt for ordinary humanity.

"So what's the switch?" the tall man said at last.

Mathias lowered his gaze. "At the moment, Matlala is at his father's house, in Natal. My information is he'll leave there tomorrow. He won't go directly to East London. He'll go first to see his brother, to discuss money."

"What sort of money?"

"That needn't concern you."

"Where is this brother?" The tall man sounded offended. "That does concern me, right?"

"He works at the casino at Bowers Bay."

The tall man shot to his feet and advanced on Mathias. "A casino? Are you crazy? Security crappers all over the place, video surveillance, a hot line to the cops? Forget it! No ways, no ways!"

He seemed ready to storm out of the house. Mathias said soothingly, "It's safer for you there than in East London. There's surveillance, sure, but it's designed to catch gamblers, and you won't be gambling. You'll have time to look around, choose your time and place. If you make the hit there, getaway will be easy. There's an airstrip, good roads. We can even take you off by boat if we have to."

"You conned me. You set this up without telling me."

"No. Matlala changed his plans today."

"Yeah? How come you know about that?"

"We have an agent at the casino. It's a good place to launder money. The agent told me that Zidon Matlala . . . the brother . . . asked permission to have his brother to stay in his quarters, for a couple of nights."

"So there'll be cops everywhere!"

"The local police. Homeland boys, amateurs, not like the SAP. No chance they'll identify you."

The tall man stopped his pacing and jerked a thumb at the projector. "Talking about police, there's a lot of police footage on that film. How come?"

"We have useful friends."

"Pigs? Look, I don't like to work with people who pal up with pigs, I don't like to work anywhere near pigs, they got dirty habits. You do a job, and when it's done, the pigs see you get blasted to hell. I seen it happen too often. So don't think you can pull that kinda shit on me. I took out some insurance, you understand what I mean?"

It was bluster, Mathias knew. The creep was desperate for cash, couldn't pay the protection money he needed to operate in Rio, couldn't look for contracts in the USA because if the Feds didn't get him, the Mob would. He was a man with important enemies. That vulnerability was one of the reasons Mathias had picked him. Another was his undoubted skill as a marksman. There was a third reason which Mathias had mentioned to no one, not even to old man Senekal.

Now he said resonably, "Another thing, it'll be easier to get you in that way. The border restrictions aren't so tight."

The tall man said pettishly, "You're asking me to ad lib, risk my neck for a lousy twenty thousand."

"I might stretch to twenty-five."

"What if there's a screw-up? What if I have to abort?"

"Then we revert to the original plan, no sweat, and you're still twenty-five thousand to the good."

Calmly Mathias rose and crossed to the tray of drinks. He piled ice into two glasses, added vodka and lime juice. Out of the corner of his eye he saw that the tall man had gone back to his seat on the sofa.

Carrying the drinks, Mathias moved to join him.

12

At eight o'clock on Saturday night, Ross called his wife in Lourdes, person to person. Her voice, when she answered, was so full of antagonism that he found himself making apologies.

"I've been expecting you to call . . . you said, in a day or two . . . I was worried."

"I've been seeing doctors."

"Oh. Good. What did they say?"

"Exactly what your doctors said, that I'm going blind."

"Jay, they weren't my doctors, they were . . ."

"What does it matter? It doesn't matter a damn."

"When do you go to . . ." he couldn't think of the right word ". . . the Grotto?"

"Tomorrow." Jay spoke briskly. "And after this is over, I shall stay in Europe."

"Well . . . sure . . . if that'll help. I can come back to fetch you, say in six weeks' time?"

"I mean, stay for good. Live here."

"I don't understand. Jay, we can't just move . . ."

"Alone," Jay said. "I want a divorce."

Ross could see, as clearly as if she were here in the room with him, her small pale face, the chin thrust out, the eyes defiant. Thoughts flooded into his mind, protests and angry questions. All he could find to say was, "You don't mean that. You've said often enough you don't believe in divorce."

"I have to be alone." Her voice had the sharpness of pain. "I have to be rid of your damned pity. If God intends me to go blind, I'll do it without you."

"Darling, we can't talk about this on the telephone. I'll come over, I'll make arrangements right away . . ."

"I don't want you!" She almost screamed the words, then repeated them with cold emphasis, "I don't want you, Ross."

"You're ill, Jay. I can't allow you to make this kind of decision without seeing you." As she was silent, he said angrily, "At least tell me what brought this on."

He heard her give a long sigh.

"You don't feel for me. You do everything you can to help me, you're a tower of strength, but you don't feel a damn thing."

"For God's sake, of course I do!"

"You love your work. You love causes, and ideas." She sounded almost dreamy. "You don't love me. I don't know if you love anyone at all."

"I love you. Believe me, I love you very much."

"Then perhaps I'm at fault. Perhaps I can't be loved, any more. I only know I want to live alone, away from you."

"Jay, just listen to me. When we meet, when we talk . . . we'll work something out." He waited. "Jay? Are you there?"

"Leave me alone, Ross." Her voice was thin now, like the wind in the reeds. "I'll write to you, but don't try and come here. Just leave me alone."

The line clicked dead.

He tried to call her back. The hotel in Lourdes said Mrs McRae was taking no more calls tonight.

He went to the desk in the living-room and wrote her a letter. It came out hurt and angry. He tore it up and wrote another, which he also destroyed. The trouble was, he knew what she meant. Good times, or bad, he'd always been able to understand Jay.

Thinking about their years together, he realised that she'd always been one jump ahead of him. Ahead in wanting marriage, in pressing for a bigger house, in seeking out people who could help his career. Jay's people were from Vermont, wealthy and well up the social ladder. She'd been, when first they met, a leader of her clique, a fine skier and horsewoman, good at conversation and at forming friendships. All that had fallen away as her health deteriorated.

93

Maybe they'd never had love, but they'd been good companions, he thought, had some great times together, a marriage at least as good as those around them.

All that couldn't be ended by a telephone call.

Yet if she wanted time to herself, there ought to be enough respect left between them, for him to honour the request.

He went and took a shower, then dressed in slacks and sweater, drank a couple of whiskies. He switched on the television and watched, for a few minutes, some old movie he'd seen years ago.

There was a stillness in him. He felt detached, floating. It was a trick he'd learned in prison, a bad trick as he now knew, because it was akin to the immobility of madness.

He decided to go out to a steak house, and was on his way to the door when the telephone rang.

It was Hal Ensor.

"Ross? Hal. I'm at Richard's place. Do you know where he is, tonight?"

"Dining at the Kalmeyers', I think."

"He never told me!" Hal sounded agitated. "I should have been told. Something important's come up, and I can't . . ."

"Phone him at the Kalmeyers', if it's so important."

"You know he doesn't like that."

"Leave a message with Julie, then."

"She's not here either. She's gone to Bowers Bay."

"The Casino?" Ross was startled.

"Richard sent her," Hal said. "Something about getting her away from politics."

A number of facts meshed in Ross's mind. He said harshly, "When did she leave?"

"Yesterday, I think."

"Why did she go?"

"How should I know? She'll see the golf." Hal sounded wistful.

"Is that the only reason she went? To take a break? Richard didn't have any wild scheme. . . ?"

"Scheme? Not that I know of."

94

"You did warn him to stay away from Matlala?"

"Well, yes, I mentioned it, but you know Richard. He does what he wants."

"OK. Thanks, Hal. Listen . . . I'll be tied up for a few days . . . some private business. Tell Richard, will you?"

"Where will you be?"

"I'll be in touch," Ross said, and rang off.

He went to the steak house round the corner from the apartment, ate a steak, drank half a bottle of Cabernet, followed it with black coffee.

He thought about Julie at Bowers Bay. He thought about Richard's reasons for sending her there. He remembered his conversation with Simeon Matlala. Simeon had mentioned that his son Zidon worked at the Bowers Bay Casino.

It all fitted too neatly.

In growing anger he reminded himself that he was on leave, that he didn't have to concern himself with Richard's lunatic impulses, that it would be good sense to stay away from Julie.

He was back at his apartment at five-past eleven. At ten-past he put through a call to Charlie Sickert at the Carlton Hotel, and arranged to travel with him to Bowers Bay next morning, in the private jet owned by the casino.

13

"Bowers Bay," Sickert said, at the same time jabbing a thumb at the starboard windows of the plane.

They had been flying along the coast for twenty minutes, wild country whose rocky cliffs were thickly wooded and pierced at intervals by rivers turgid with floodwater.

Now the Beechcraft banked steeply over a stretch of sea protected by a low bluff. Bright-sailed surf-boats skimmed along the fringe of breaking waves. Inland, the coastal forest gave way abruptly to the fever-green of an eighteen-hole golf course, and the sprawl of the hotel complex.

Ross glimpsed an Olympic-size swimming-pool, sundecks, squash and tennis courts, bowling rinks, stables. On the parking-lot to the north, rows of cars glinted in the sun.

The landing-strip lay inland again. Their pilot brought them down smoothly and taxied to a hanger. From there, a minibus whisked them to the main entrance of the hotel.

Sickert signalled to a uniformed attendant to take in his and Ross's luggage, and led the way across an enormous foyer, to a reception counter manned by six clerks at computer terminals, and a troop of porters.

"We've put you in the Tanga Suite, Mr McRae," Sickert said. "That's on the third floor, overlooking the pool deck. If you don't like it, say so, and we'll move you. Would you like to go up now, or look round first?"

"I'll go up," Ross said. "Meet you back here in a quarter of an hour."

The Tanga Suite consisted of a double bedroom, bathroom with jacuzzi, and sitting-room with bar. The furnishings were luxurious. Lavish bowls of indigenous flowers stood on low white tables. The windows faced the sea.

He crossed to the telephone and called the lobby.

"I want to speak to Mrs Julie Aikman. She's a guest in the hotel. I don't know her room number."

There was a brief pause, then the clerk said, "The room number's 607, sir, but Mrs Aikman is not in the hotel at present. She's booked for a wind-surfing lesson. Do you wish to leave a message?"

"No thanks. I'll call her later."

Back in the main foyer, Sickert was at the reception desk. He handed Ross a sheaf of travel brochures.

"These'll give you the layout of the place. What do you want to see first?"

"The slot-machines," Ross answered.

Sickert conducted him across the foyer, past a double bank of elevators, and through an archway the size of a theatre proscenium.

"We're in the casino complex now," he said. "The entrance to the roulette, blackjack, et cetera, is over there, to your left. The main slots hall is straight ahead."

They entered a circular arena, windowless and lit by brilliant electric chandeliers. The carpet was crimson, the curving bowl of the walls a dull metallic ochre, pierced at intervals by pink-tinged mirrors. The effect of the decor was deliberately feverish. It shut out the real world and focused eye and mind on the banks of one-armed bandits ranged round the circle.

At many of the machines, gamblers were clotted like flies, absorbed in the business of feeding in coins. Music throbbed from hidden speakers. The air was over-warm, over-scented.

"Dante's Inferno," Ross muttered.

"Something for nothing," Sickert said, with surprising bitterness. "Isn't that what we're all after?" He caught Ross's look of surprise, and at once reverted to unctuousness.

"Over seven hundred machines, we operate, Mr McRae. Four hundred here, the rest in the hall over on the north side. That's near the fast-food outlets. We get a lot of day trippers, they don't want to waste time eating in a posh restaurant."

"How about machines under repair?"

97

"Twenty or so, any day of the week. We make regular spot checks."

"Security measures?"

"Total electronic surveillance. TV scanners at key points, right through the public rooms, and particularly in the gaming areas. We can see what goes on, at all times. In the counting-house we have a voice monitor. For obvious reasons, we can't let too many people see what goes on in there. I'll show you the surveillance centre later. It's down in the basement."

At that moment there was a flurry of movement round one of the machines. A fat woman in a blue sun-dress set up a wild screeching and broke into a jig, the flesh of her upper arms swinging, her big breasts bouncing to the beat of the piped music. Other gamblers clustered about her, laughing and gesticulating.

Sickert chuckled. "Now look at her! All she's won is five or six hundred. It's all relative, eh?"

"What's your maximum possible jackpot?"

Sickert sobered at once. "Half a million. If Pampallas could get his paws on that lot . . ."

"What about human guards?"

"We have plenty of those. Here on the arena, they pose as members of the public. Trouble is, your pro gambler can pick out a security man, no matter how you dress him. They send in decoys to distract our boys . . . pumped up blondes in bikinis, little old ladies with phony heart attacks, anything to create a diversion. Meanwhile, the sluggers are working over the slots.

"How?"

"Well, it doesn't take much to blow an electrical circuit. We caught one bright boy using a little drill. Neat, you could've held it in the palm of your hand. He was boring a hole right through the side of the machine . . . setting it up so's a pal could come along later, and jam the works to make the right bars come up. They use magnets, aerosol spray, you'd be amazed what they dream up."

"Do you trust your guards?"

"Honest as the day is long. I hand-pick my staff, and I see they get top pay." Sickert winked. "Mind, we also run checks on them. They know that's part of the deal."

"Who watches the watchers? You?"

Sickert shot him a quick glance, as if he didn't like the question. "Yeah, sure, I'm in charge of security. The buck stops with me."

Ross didn't press the point. He said, "Pampallas specialises in blackjack?"

"That's right. He's smart enough to win without cheating. Memory like an elephant."

"Would an expert like that descend to playing a fruit-machine."

"Not him. His team. That's what's giving me the shits, pardon the expression. Say we kick him out, and they stay behind? It could take us days to identify them."

Ross nodded. "Why don't we take a look at the casino?"

They left the slots hall and made their way to the suite of rooms behind the reception desk. From there, a staff elevator took them up one floor, to an office whose decor was in marked contrast to that of the rest of the hotel.

Three large windows overlooked the golf course and the sea. Three white desks matched the windows. At the first, a svelte brunette cooed into a telephone, at the second a grey-haired woman checked accounts, and at the third a youngish man in a grey lounge suit and Gucci shoes pored over a sheaf of computer print-outs. Sickert introduced him as Derek Marciano, casino manager.

"Mr McRae is from Salectron, Derek. I've invited him down to advise us on computer security. He'll be staying a couple of days, free run of the hotel. Anything he wants to know about the gambling side, I can count on you to arrange it, OK?"

Marciano nodded, staring at Ross with dislike. He touched manicured nails to an ear and murmured, "Of course. Naturally."

Ross came straight to the point. "Do the slot-machines come under your control, Mr Marciano?"

"The admin side, yes." Marciano sounded bored. "Not security. That's Charlie's worry."

"It's everyone's worry," said Sickert, in the tone of one who's been through the argument before. Marciano shrugged.

"Who programmes the slots?" Ross enquired.

That was an attention-getter. Marciano's head turned sharply and Sickert's smile became even more unctuous.

"The original programming," Sickert said, "is done by Aldo in Japan. We can reprogramme if we need to . . . alter the percentage take, and so on."

"Who's 'we'?"

"Myself, Derek, and of course the Aldo rep, Garth Gummer."

"You're all computer trained?"

"We know the basics. We're not experts, like you."

"Who does the routine maintenance?"

"We have engineers on our permanent staff. They're responsible to our surveillance controller."

"Can they programme?"

"No, no. They're just mechanics." Sickert frowned at Marciano, who seemed about to interrupt. "I know what's in your mind, Mr McRae. You're thinking that Pampallas is no small-time slugger, he won't frig about with drills and hairspray, he'll find a way to fox the computer programmes . . . which means, buy one of the programmers. Am I right?"

"The thought crossed my mind."

"Quite. And that's my reason for asking you to help us. If Pampallas hits the jackpot, it's me the hotel owners are going to skin . . . me, or Derek, or Gummer. We're the fall guys."

"There must be checks built into the computer systems, to prevent fraud?"

"Sure there are, but you and I know there's ways around them. So that still leaves me in the hot seat, and I tell you straight, I don't want to spend the next ten years in chookie for something I didn't do."

"What exactly do you want of me?"

Relief shone in Sickert's small eyes. "Well now . . . if you could have a chat with the chief maintenance engineer . . . give the machines the once-over . . . check out our security systems and tell us if you see any way Pampallas could break them.

People will take your word where they won't take mine, or Derek's."

At this, Marciano's expression became openly hostile, and Sickert said hastily, "No offence, Derek. It's the way things are." He turned to Ross. "I'd like to show you the view gallery. This way."

He shepherded Ross through a rear door that gave on to a broad balcony running round the four sides of the main casino area, which was divided into half a dozen rooms. The floor and rear walls of the balcony were carpeted. The front walls were glazed, the heavy panels extending from the balcony rail to the ceiling. Sickert tapped the glass with a fingernail.

"One way view," he said. "From down there it looks like mirror, up here it's transparent."

They were standing above the main roulette room, in the centre of which the table seemed to float, like an island in a sea of dark blue Wilton. A dozen people stood or sat round it. The voice of the croupier quietly called for bets. He spoke English, Ross noted, no French mystique on this stretch of coast; but the gamblers' tension, their rapt absorption, that never seemed to change, anywhere in the world.

Ross said, "Marciano didn't seem pleased to see me."

"Derek's a fool," Sickert answered. "He thinks he just has to say, 'My nose is clean', and the world will believe him."

"Is it clean?"

"Sure it is." Sickert's usually pallid cheeks were pink. "So am I clean, Mr McRae. The Board believes it, the bank believes it, so do our insurers."

"But someone doesn't."

"Eh?"

"Someone made you invite me here."

"No, no, no! It's not like that." Sickert looked quite panicky. "I'm in charge. No one tells me how to do my job. I wanted your advice. I made the decision."

Ross met the small blue eyes. He said deliberately, "I believe you have a man named Zidon Matlala working here?"

Sickert was not thrown. His smile was confident.

"We do. He's our surveillance controller. If you'd like to meet him, I'll take you down there at once."

They returned to the office. Marciano had vanished. Neither of his assistants glanced up as Ross and Sickert passed them.

The staff elevator carried them smoothly down to the basement. They stepped out into a small lobby. Opposite them was a massive steel door fitted with a combination lock, which Sickert opened. They passed through into a corridor pierced by three more steel doors. There were television monitors set into the side and end walls of the passage. Ross guessed that the casino takings were stashed down here, before being banked.

The first door bore a plastic plate. SURVEILLANCE. Sickert pushed a button and spoke into a voice monitor. Someone replied from inside the room, and the door swung open. Sickert signed to Ross to go through, and followed.

The surveillance centre was divided in two by a metal partition. To their right, an open door afforded a glimpse of recording and copying equipment, shelves of tapes, filing cabinets.

The area in which they stood had the green gloom of a fish tank. Rows of television screens were set into the east and north walls. The pictures showed people moving about the reception foyer, the gambling halls, the restaurants.

Two men sat in chairs facing the screens. One of them was a stocky youth wearing denims and a white T-shirt. He took no notice of the new arrivals.

The second man rose and faced them. He was tall and thin, dressed in brown slacks and a cream shirt with a button-down collar, a darker cream tie. His face was narrow, the light-brown skin shining over high cheekbones and bony forehead, the eyes masked by spectacles with gold rims. His smile displayed good teeth.

Sickert said, "This is Zidon Matlala, our surveillance controller."

The dark man raised a hand, palm forwards. "We've met. Hi, Ross."

"Hi, Zidon." Ross moved to take the outstretched hand.

Smiling bright-eyed, Sickert said, "I'll leave you two old friends to talk."

"Well, Ross?" Zidon Matlala's smile addressed the years that had elapsed, as much as Ross's presence here and now.

"It's good to see you, Zidon."

"I heard you were at Halladale. Then Sickert told me you were coming to give us a hand."

"You think you need one?"

Zidon's expression became guarded. "Pampallas could make a killing, but he'll have to get past these babies to do it." He jerked his chin towards the television banks. "I've been tracking you, you know, ever since you got off the plane. Like God." He laughed.

"Or the Devil," Ross said. The picture on the screen nearest him showed the roulette room. A man in a white track suit was leaning forward to place a bet. Ross reached over and adjusted the set's tuner. The camera shifted at once to close-up, the detail of the gambler's face and hands showing clearly.

"What else can you do," Ross asked, "apart from this sneaky stuff?"

"We can make still photos, or a complete video. We'll have Pampallas on tape from the moment he arrives until the moment he leaves. Let's hope that won't be too long."

"Sickert seems to be more scared of the rest of the gang."

"Ach, we'll pick them up . . . if they stay. Most likely the whole team will move out when we tell them to."

"Sickert said you had a photo of Pampallas."

"Snapshots." Zidon crossed to a desk in the corner, unlocked a drawer and pulled out a cardboard file. He brought it to Ross, and flipped the pages until he reached a fuzzy picture of a man who resembled a small-town banker. Plump-shouldered and pale, black hair thinning over a polished skull, drooping black moustache and drooping eyelids, the soft beginnings of a double chin.

"Doesn't look too dangerous," Ross said.

"Just don't bet against him, man!"

A typewritten report faced the photograph:

STAVROS NICHOLLAS PAMPALLAS.
Alias Nicky Niarchos, alias Stacy Palmer.

Parents: Apollo and Caliope Pampallas, born Piraeus, Greece, emigrated 1929 to Iowa City, USA, became US citizens 1935. Prosperous family catering business.

1935   Stavros born. Home life stable, education good.

1952   Enrolled University of Wisconsin.

1957   Graduated summa cum laude in mathematics.

1958   Appointed maths teacher at Parabola High, Des Moines.

1959   Quit teaching and moved to Chicago. During the next five years, held various posts, while training as a computer technician. Also became addicted to gambling.

1964   Employed by the Federal Bureau of Investigation in section dealing with large-scale evasion of Federal Tax.

1965   Shifted to specialist division of FBI, to head a committee investigating nation-wide gambling frauds. Responsible for training agents to identify members of gambling rings and expose corrupt practices.

1967   Left US Government employ and became a professional gambler. Said to own a school for gamblers in Dallas, Texas, and to instruct "students" in illicit gambling methods.

Persona non grata at Las Vegas, Monaco, and the larger Far East casinos. Now frequents lesser casino circuits in South America and Africa.

Rich. Owns property in New Orleans, Buenos Aires, Rio and Cannes.

Has never been prosecuted for a gambling offence.

Ross handed the file back to Zidon.

"If he's known to be a crook, how come he's never been prosecuted?"

Zidon shook his head. "It's hard to nail these boys. There's no law against winning at blackjack or roulette. You have to catch the man crooking, and even when you do, it's hard to prove how much he took you for. A court won't convict on 'ifs' and 'maybes'."

"So what will Sickert do?"

"Warn him off before he has time to start anything."

"You think he'll leave, simply on a warning."

"Probably."

"Mr Marciano, upstairs, seems to think Sickert's making a fuss over nothing."

Again, Zidon was blank-faced. "Not for me to judge. Pampallas skinned them in Mauritius. We don't want that to happen here."

"When's he due to arrive?"

"Five o'clock this afternoon. We had a message yesterday."

"How's he coming?"

"Private car. I'm told he has a chauffeur, doubles as body-guard and valet but doesn't play the tables."

"Can we watch from here?"

"Certainly. Front-row seats." Zidon's eyes flickered towards the youth in denims. "I'm on lunch in ten minutes' time. Why don't we leave Sean here to watch the shop, and go and grab a burger from Fast Foods? Then I can show you the slots halls, repair shop, the works. We can talk as we go."

They collected hamburgers from the cafeteria and carried them out to the golf course, settling to eat on a bench near the first tee. Groundsmen were working on the fairway, some way off.

"No beady-eye, out here," Zidon said.

Ross remembered Sickert's remark about keeping checks on the staff.

"How often are you on candid camera?"

"Sickert doesn't tell us," Zidon said drily.

"You don't mind being spied on?"

"It's routine at a place like this. And after all, I'm Vusi Matlala's brother. Could be a terrorist in disguise."

"So why did they employ you?"

"I'm useful to them. I can do the job all right, and I'm a token black to show the overseas visitors. We have to show them this is an independent black state, right?" Zidon chewed and swallowed. "You want to see a citizen of this independent state, look over there."

Ross turned his head. Some ten yards from their bench, an urchin squatted in the shade of a thornbush. He appeared to be eight or nine years old. He wore a filthy and tattered shirt, from which his scaly arms and legs protruded like lichened twigs. Grey snot caked his nose and upper lip. His eyes were fixed on the food in Zidon's hand.

Zidon beckoned. "Weh, umfaan!"

The child got up and trotted towards them, stopping a short way off. Zidon said in Xhosa, "What are you selling today?"

The child tilted the tin he was carrying, displaying a few prickly pear fruits, squashed and dusty-looking. Zidon drew a coin from his pocket and held it out. The child set the tin down carefully and ran forward, hands cupped. Zidon placed the coin and the remains of the burger in the hands, which closed over like claws.

"Go home to Mama, son," Zidon said. The child started to scuttle away, remembered the fruit and ran back to empty the tin on to the grass at Zidon's feet. He flashed a wide grin, and fled.

Zidon screwed up his eyes, tilting back his head. "Maybe we should put these on the hotel buffet tonight. Crayfish, salmon, caviar, and prickly pears."

Ross looked at him. "You have a degree in engineering. What made you pick this god-awful job?"

Zidon stared straight up at the sky. "You mean it's a long way from the freedom-fighters? But not so far as you are, Polela, in little old New York."

Polela. The use of the nickname softened the rebuke. Ross said quickly, "I'm sorry. I meant no offence. It was a stupid question."

"True. So here's another. Who sent you here?"

106

Ross knew that his answer would determine whether or not the conversation continued. He said, "I'm not sure. My boss, Richard Wragge, hinted I'd be doing him a favour if I accepted Sickert's invitation. I don't know why that should be. I really don't know what the hell's going on."

Zidon turned to face him. "My father came to see me. He told me you visited our house, while you were at Halladale. He told me what you said about Vusi . . . that he'd be released . . . that he would be in danger. Is that all you know?"

"Yes, I swear it."

"Who told you?"

"An American, Senator Cromlech."

"He didn't say what kind of danger?"

"Zidon, what I know, you know."

"This Richard Wragge," Zidon persisted, "what are his politics?"

Ross half-smiled. "He doesn't fit into any political category. He just imagines he's God."

Zidon did not return the smile. "What do you mean?"

"He spoke about financing Vusi. I told him to forget it."

"What bank does he use?"

Ross straightened. "Look, Zidon, it wasn't serious. I mean, the notion floated into the man's head, he spoke it. He's like that."

"I said, what's his bank?"

"First National."

"Is he close to the Government?"

"He's on the President's Economic Advisory Council, but he's no supporter of the National Party."

Zidon looked away, across the clipped turf, to the line of blue sea. "They'll try and buy Vusi," he said, "and if he won't be bought, they'll kill him."

"Who will? Who are you talking about?"

Zidon slowly shook his head. He seemed on the brink of a confidence, but the moment passed. He got to his feet.

"We better move, Ross. Get our inspection done and be back downstairs in good time to see Mr Pampallas make an entrance."

*

107

The tour of inspection took them until four-fifteen, and convinced Ross that his trip to Bowers Bay was a waste of time. It was plain that the casino was doing everything possible, electronically speaking, to prevent computer fraud. The men in the repair shop were no more than mechanics, capable of doing simple maintenance work on the slot-machines, but not of bugging them.

He agreed with Zidon. Once Pampallas had been sent packing, the danger to the casino would be over.

Which made him wonder why Sickert had been so anxious to lure him down here?

As they left the repair shop, they saw a luxury bus under the portico of the hotel, surrounded by passengers and baggage.

"Golf," said Zidon succinctly. "They've come to watch the Pro-Am. You coming downstairs with me?"

"I must make a phone call, first."

"Tell the desk when you're ready, and someone will bring you down."

Ross returned to his suite and called room 607. This time Julie answered.

"Hi, Julie."

"Ross?" She sounded surprised and pleased. "What are you doing here?"

"The question on everyone's lips. I was about to ask you the same thing."

"Holiday, golf, gambling, the sea. How about you?"

"I think your father arranged my trip."

"I don't understand."

"Makes two of us. I need to talk to you, Julie. Have dinner with me later? I've an appointment at five, but it shouldn't take long."

"How about seven o'clock in the Crow's Nest?"

"Fine. See you then."

Ross returned to the lobby, and a security guard conducted him to the surveillance centre where Zidon and an assistant were waiting. The latter settled himself in the chair facing the east bank of screens, leaving Ross and Zidon to watch those on the north wall, which covered the reception area of the hotel.

As they took their places, Zidon said, "The guard on the main gates will let us know when Pampallas comes through. We'll pick him up a few minutes later." He indicated the screen at the upper left-hand side of the range.

"Screen One covers the portico and the entrance to the hotel. Screen Two covers the lobby . . . you can see the reception desk at the back of the picture. Screen Three operates from behind the desk, facing out, so we'll get Pampallas whichever way he goes.

"From Three we shift to Four. That covers the elevators and the entrance to the gambling areas. Five to Twenty is the gaming rooms. Whether he heads for the tables, or for the slots, we'll be able to track him all the way. Most likely he'll just take the lift straight up to his suite."

"Which is. . . ?"

"302."

"Next to mine?"

"Yeah."

"Is it bugged?"

"What goes on in the bedrooms is none of my business."

Ross sat back, at that, letting his eyes grow accustomed to the multi-faceted action on the screens.

In the event, they almost missed seeing Pampallas.

No signal came from the guard on the road. At five-thirty Zidon called him, to be told that Pampallas's car had not yet come through.

There was now a steady stream of guests flowing through the hotel doors. None of them resembled the photographs of Pampallas.

At a quarter to six, the stream became a flash-flood.

A television van dumped a crew weighed down with equipment, and two luxury buses from Cape Town disgorged a horde of golf fans, young and old, black, white and brown, local and foreign. They packed together in a noisy throng, showing no disposition to budge from the centre of the lobby.

Their reason for loitering became plain when a private coach halted under the portico and set down three world-famous golfers, their entourages, and a mound of expensive gear.

The fans surged forward to mob their heroes. Sickert and two uniformed helpers emerged from the casino and bored in like collie dogs, cutting the golf-stars from the herd and sweeping them over to the reception desk. A TV cameraman, missing no chances, climbed on to a chair and began filming the scene.

Ross said, "Who's the big fair man in the blue shirt?"

For answer, Zidon jabbed an urgent finger at Screen One.

"Pampallas," he said. "The bugger came on the bus."

The second Cape Town bus was still standing at the hotel entrance. One last passenger was alighting from it. He was small and plump, dressed in dark slacks, a white shirt, a blue blazer. His face was obscured by the brim of a panama hat.

As they watched, he advanced through the main doorway, passing directly under the TV scanner. Now they could see only his back as he walked across the lobby. He was followed by a hotel porter carrying two small suitcases.

Muttering, Zidon leaned forward to adjust the picture on Screen Two. The plump man was cut from the crowd and enlarged.

"I didn't see his face," Ross said.

"I did. It's him. We'll get him in close-up, on Three."

Pampallas kept going, skirting quietly round the crowd that milled and jostled in the centre of the foyer. Screen Three picked him up as he reached the reception desk. Ross saw neat features, a skin pallid and unlined, eyes veiled by downcast fleshy lids.

Pampallas reached for the register and signed. The reception clerk, murmuring some pleasantry, handed over a key. Pampallas took it with a nod of thanks and signalled to the porter to take his baggage upstairs.

110

It was then that the incident occurred, if something so trivial could be termed an incident. The porter bent to pick up the suitcases. Pampallas straightened and began to move away from the desk. As he did so, he appeared to see someone, or something, that transfixed him. His air of lazy detachment vanished, his head jerked back so that it was possible to see his eyes. They were large, luminous, and highly intelligent. The expression in them was, quite unmistakeably, one of profound shock.

An instant later he was on the move, heading for the elevators so fast that the porter had to trot to keep up with him.

"Give us the whole lobby, wide-angle," Ross said. "I want to see what he saw!"

Zidon widened the picture on Three. It showed, dead centre, the big fair golfer. He was smiling as he chatted to the TV interviewer. To their left, a black man in a caddy's track suit hefted a bag of clubs to his shoulder, three porters piled luggage on to a trolley, and a vortex of faces blurred and spun as the fans dispersed to their own pursuits.

"Something phased him," Ross said.

"Sickert, most likely." Zidon was scowling at the screen. They watched Sickert swim out from the thinning crowd, making angry thrusts with his arms. He reached the desk and plunged into heated conversation with the reception clerk.

"Who runs Sickert?" Ross asked.

Zidon looked at him. For the second time that afternoon, Ross felt himself under scrutiny, as if Zidon hung on the edge of a confidence. It never came. Zidon said flatly, "The Board, I suppose."

Ross said in a low voice, "All this could be important, from Vusi's point of view."

"We can look after Vusi." Zidon's expression was telling Ross to back off, but he persisted.

"Will you give me copies of Tapes Two and Three? I'd like to run them again."

"I can't do that. It's against the rules."

"Break them."

For a moment their stares locked. Then Zidon shook his head. "Just leave me to handle things, Ross."

He got up and walked into the adjoining room.

Ross asked the assistant to give him safe conduct back to the world above-stairs.

14

From his suite on the fifth floor of the hotel, Derek Marciano made a long-distance call. His tone was belligerent.

"What's Sickert up to? Bringing some computernik down here to check our systems? Our systems are OK. You should have warned me you were sending someone."

"I have not sent anyone."

"Then who is this man?"

"You tell me. His name, first."

"McRae. Ross McRae. He asked a lot of questions."

"From where?"

"Johannesburg. An apartment in Killarney."

"Police?"

"I don't think so. There's enough of them, already. Listen, what's going on? I haven't been told. I don't like that. How can I do my job here if I don't know what's going on?"

"Your job," came the gentle answer, "is to run the casino efficiently, and answer any questions I care to ask. Asking questions is my job, not yours. Understand?"

Marciano hesitated, then said in a very different voice, "Yes, sure, I understand. I thought you should know about McRae, that's all."

"Good. Now I know, and you can get back to your work."

The phone went dead. Marciano sat for a moment or two staring at the receiver in his hand. His eyes were frightened.

By a quarter to seven, Ross had showered, shaved and dressed. With fifteen minutes to fill before he met Julie, he stepped on to the porch outside his bedroom.

It was a cold night, the moon laying baleful fire across a

viridescent sea. The golf course was ready for tomorrow's tournament. Television towers had been erected at strategic points and there were stands for spectators at the third, ninth and eighteenth holes.

Not a soul moved in the grounds. The deserted swimming-pool looked gelid under its arclamps.

Lights glowed in most of the windows of the two residential wings of the hotel. At this time, the attention of the occupants, whether guests or staff, was focused inwards. The five restaurants, the many bars, the theatre and cabaret stages, the slots halls and casino tables, were about to fulfill their purpose of entertaining the customers and stripping them of their money.

Ross thought about Julie, whom he wanted; about Sickert, whom he mistrusted; about Zidon, whom he no longer seemed to know.

Far away, on the other side of the building, he could hear the continuous drumming of vehicles on the car-park.

He could leave now. He could walk out and catch a bus. He could throw all these people on the ash-heap, and forget them.

He could get away, before the big seas caught him and carried him far out, to the drowning-waters.

He stood for a few minutes longer, staring at the breakers. Then he took the lift upstairs to the Crow's Nest Restaurant.

Julie arrived ten minutes late and apologetic.

"A phone call just as I was on my way. I had to take it."

He suppressed an urge to ask who the caller was.

She looked gorgeous. The hair curling on to her forehead was slightly damp and shining. Her skin, her eyes, her delicately tinted mouth shone, not just with the burnish of health, but of some emotion within her, light through alabaster.

She was wearing a yellow silk blouse and a white silk skirt. Her long brown legs were bare, and her white kid sandals had thin gold heels.

She ordered a Daquiri. "Right for the occasion, don't you think? Scott Fitzgerald, end of an era, society about to fall apart?"

"How was the wind-surfing?" Ross said.

"Fun. I'd like to learn to do it properly. You should have joined me. Where were you, all day?"

"Snooping." He watched her face as he said it, but saw no more than a mild curiosity.

"I was invited here," he said, "by the security chief, a Mr Charles Sickert, on the pretext that I could help prevent a gambler named Stavros Pampallas from beating the casino at its own games."

She frowned. "What makes you think Dad arranged it?"

"He introduced me to Sickert. They seemed like old friends."

"Could be. Dad comes here, from time to time. I don't see why he'd want to get you here, though."

"I think it has to do with Vusi Matlala. The night of the trade fair . . . the night Matlala was released . . . Richard was on one of his highs. He talked about financing Vusi."

She stared. "He must be mad."

"So I told him. So Hal told him. I don't think we convinced him, because the next thing, he introduced me to Sickert."

"I still don't see the connection between Vusi Matlala and this place."

"Vusi's brother Zidon works here, as a security officer."

"But would Dad know that?"

"When Richard wants something, he ferrets around. Maybe he found out about Zidon. Maybe he decided this would be a good place to do a deal with Vusi, maybe he thought I'd be a suitable go-between. I used to know the Matlalas when I was a kid. They lived near Halladale."

Julie regarded him steadily. "And when you declined the offer, maybe Dad decided I'd do instead. Is that what you mean?"

"It crossed my mind."

"Well, he didn't ask me."

"Did he give you a letter, or anything, to bring here?"

"No."

Ross sighed. "I suppose I'm being paranoid. I just have this feeling I'm being set up."

She thought for a moment. "If you are, then it would have to involve Vusi's brother what's-his-name."

"Zidon."

"Yes. Have you spoken to him?"

"I warned him Richard might offer Vusi money."

Julie coloured. "There's nothing criminal in that, is there?"

"That depends. Legal or not, it would be suicidal for the Matlalas to accept what might be seen as a bribe. Richard doesn't always see the implications of his actions."

"He's generous," Julie said defensively. "He tries to do good. The reason I'm here is, he wanted to get me away from the troubles in Soweto. He was thinking of me."

Ross saw that there were tears in her eyes. He reached over and took her hand. "I'm sorry. I didn't mean to upset you."

Her fingers laced with his. "It's not you, it's bloody Dave. That call tonight was from one of his mechanics, to say they're moving to Italy. That's the way it is between us. I have to wait for a mechanic to tell me where my husband is. I haven't spoken to Dave in five weeks, I don't know what he's doing, what's in his mind, I just . . ." She broke off, making a small gesture of despair.

"Join the Lonely Hearts Club," Ross said. As Julie looked up enquiringly, he said, "Jay wants a divorce."

"When did this happen?"

"Last night. I called her, and she told me."

"She's ill, Ross. People say things when they're in pain."

"I know."

"Will you go over to her?"

"She doesn't want that. I'll have to wait. See how things turn out."

Ross found he was still clasping Julie's hand, and he gave it a shake. "I tell you what we'll do. We'll have another drink, some seafood, some wine, and then we'll go and bust the casino. If this is going to be the twilight of the gods, we may as well send up a few last rockets."

After dinner they spent an hour in each of the slots halls. Ross won, Julie lost, neither of them enough to write home about.

If there was thievery going on, Ross couldn't spot it. The

116

crowds seemed to be amateurs hoping for miracles. No big winners to disturb the peace.

At eleven o'clock they moved to the main roulette room. Sickert was there, talking to a group of golfers who'd latched on to the tall fair man Ross had noticed at the reception desk. Sickert caught Ross's eye and came over.

"Evening, Mr McRae . . . Mrs Aikman. Going to try the spin of the wheel, are you?"

"In a moment," Ross said. "First, I want to know if you spoke to Pampallas?"

"I did, sir, I did." Sickert was sleek with satisfaction. "I'm glad to tell you, he's left."

"No argument?"

"None. I went up to the gentleman's suite and we had a nice little chat. I told him the management wasn't about to let him and his pals rip us off. Told him we'd like to see the back of him. He muttered something about he had as much right to bet here as the next man, but I could see his heart wasn't in it. Pretty soon he was saying he wouldn't stay where he wasn't wanted, and twenty minutes later, he left. Never even unpacked his bags."

"Strange that he folded so fast."

"Not really. I can be tough when I have to. He could see I wouldn't stand any nonsense from him."

"It didn't strike you that Pampallas was scared of someone else?"

"Now what makes you say that?"

"I was in the surveillance centre when he arrived. Zidon and I watched him on the scanners. While he was standing at the reception desk, we had him in close-up. I got the impression he saw somebody in the lobby . . . somebody who scared the hell out of him."

"Is that so? Well, now, that's very interesting, Mr McRae. Could be he spotted someone he fleeced in the past, eh? Skipped on a debt, crossed up a pal? So long as it helped to get him out of my hair, I'm happy."

Ross nodded. "Quite. With Pampallas out of the way, you won't need me any longer. I'll be getting back to Joburg."

Sickert's smile vanished. "No, no, please. There's still his associates, remember? He tried to tell me he was on his ace, but I don't believe that. There's others, and we'll have to keep our eyes peeled for the next day or so. We need your help."

The group of golfers had moved to the roulette table. Ross indicated the fair man, who was already seated and engaged in arranging a stack of chips before him.

"Who's he?"

"That's Per Frolich. Up and coming on the international circuits. Swedish born, but lives mostly in America. Travels like a bloody film star, I can tell you, brings his business manager, his masseur, his caddy, even."

"I think he's the one who scared Pampallas."

"Eh?"

"Pampallas was looking towards where Frolich was standing."

Sickert seemed taken aback. He stared at the Swede for a moment. "Well . . . I suppose it's possible. They tell me that Frolich's a heavy gambler. They could've met. I'll find out, if I get the chance." He smiled brilliantly. "But I'm wasting your time, aren't I? See you around Mr McRae. Mrs Aikman."

He rolled away towards the door. Ross took Julie's arm. "Let's try our luck."

They took up a position behind Per Frolich, and when the seat next to his fell vacant, Julie slid into it. Frolich shot her a glance that took her in from head to toe. He had the almost albino fairness of some Scandinavians, his eyes ice blue and rimmed with white lashes, his skin blotched with large pale freckles.

He was evidently a practised gambler. He placed his counters with quick precision, and more often than not, he won. Winning seemed to amuse rather than excite him. He laughed a good deal, showing large even teeth.

Julie began to follow his bets, placing her chips where he did. He turned to smile at her. His pale eyes lifted to check if she was accompanied, saw Ross, and switched back to the turning wheel.

By midnight, Julie had won over a thousand rand. Frolich grinned at her.

"I bring you luck, huh?"

"You did. Thank you."

He stood up, gathered his chips and dropped them into his pocket. His freckled hand brushed Julie's shoulder.

"Tomorrow I have an early match. I must get my sleep. You are staying for the golf?"

"Yes."

"Good. Perhaps we try our luck some more . . . you, me, your husband." The smile he directed at Ross was a challenge. Ross decided that if winning golf-titles was the Swede's top priority, women probably came a close second.

"You watch out for that one," he told Julie, as Frolich headed for the door.

She laughed. "Don't worry. I have enough trouble."

"Shall we stay here, or go and watch the cabaret?"

"The cabaret."

They cashed her chips and were on their way across the lobby when a page blocked their path.

"Mr McRae? Call for you, sir, at reception."

Ross went to the desk. The caller was Zidon Matlala. He sounded anxious.

"Ross, man, can I see you right away? It's important."

Ross glanced at Julie, who was standing some way off. She walked across to him.

"Something's come up," he said. "Can we take in the show tomorrow night?"

"Of course." She smiled at him, then leaned forward and kissed him on the mouth. "See you tomorrow." She walked quickly away towards the elevators.

Ross turned back to the phone. "OK. Where do we meet?"

"Stay at the desk," Zidon said. "I'll come and fetch you."

15

"What's the problem?" Ross said.

They were outside the hotel, walking along a paved path that skirted the tennis courts and branched right, to a row of bungalows that housed the senior staff members.

The grounds looked deserted. Straining his ears, Ross could hear nothing but the distant surge of the surf. Yet he felt that he was observed, every step of the way.

Zidon said, "Vusi's at my place. He wants to talk to you."

Ross glanced back at the hotel. "Do they know?"

"Sure. He's a free man, he can go where he likes, now."

His manner had altered since their meeting that afternoon. He seemed to have resolved some indecision within himself, and in doing so to have put more distance between them.

They passed through a gate and up a short path to a white door. Zidon unlocked that and gestured Ross through. They stepped into a living-room dimly lit by two standard lamps, the curtains close-drawn. There was a sofa and two easy chairs, a side cupboard with books and a music-system.

The man standing in the centre of the room came forward to meet them.

"Polela! How are you, man?"

Twelve years had changed Vusi Matlala a great deal. There were the unmistakeable Matlala features, high-domed forehead, high cheekbones, narrow nose. A neat beard outlined the jaw and mouth. The build was spare, well muscled.

At fifteen, Vusi had possessed an ebullient energy that expressed itself not only in physical action, but in a kind of ribald amusement, a twos-up directed at the world's pomposity.

That energy was still present, but the laughter was gone. This man was like a fighter watching for an opening. There was no friendliness in the eyes, no hint of memory of other times and places.

Ross shook the outstretched hand. "Good to see you, Vusi."

"Right." Vusi gave a short jerk of the head, like a horse impatient of delay. "Zidon? You got any beer?"

Zidon lifted cans of beer from the cupboard and doled them out. Vusi snapped the tab from the can and drank, watching Ross all the while.

"Zidon says Charlie Sickert invited you down here."

"That's right."

"And you don't know why?"

"I don't know the real reason. I guess it has to do with your release . . . the fact that we know each other."

Vusi sat down in one of the easy chairs. The fingers of his left hand traced the pattern of the upholstery.

"I guess you're right." He smiled. "Or it could be money. You know something, Polela? Someone offered me a million rand. You are looking at a maybe millionaire. How do you like that?"

"I'd like to hear about it."

"And I'll tell you." Vusi finished his beer and dropped the can to the floor. "When they let me out of the tronk, I was flown to Durban, and from there I went straight to my father's house. I was tired. Needed time to think. You know how it is."

"Yes."

"I expected . . . moves . . . you know? But not so fast. There was this letter waiting for me. I thought it must be from the Prime Minister, because who else would know where to send it?"

"What was in the letter?"

"It was very interesting. It said, certain people in the business community want to set up a fund for me. The Vusi Matlala Fund. The aim of this fund is to help the said Vusi Matlala in his wonderful task of bringing peaceful change to our troubled land. A nice phrase, don't you think? Nice ring to it? A bit old-fashioned, but nice."

121

Vusi was using his voice like a flick-knife, making small feints, letting the light catch the blade. Ross said quietly, "May I see the letter?"

"Sure." Vusi reached into the pocket of his jacket, brought out a bundle of papers and selected one. Ross took it.

The letterhead was that of a well-known firm of Johannesburg lawyers, the signature that of a senior partner, the text as Vusi had described.

"You know these people?" Vusi enquired.

"Yes. They look after my family's business affairs."

"They are also retained by your firm, Salectron?"

"Yes." Ross handed the letter back. "What did you do?"

"I phoned this gentleman," Vusi tapped the signature, "to tell him the offer was not acceptable, unless I had the names and addresses of these generous benefactors. The man said, 'I'm sorry, that information is confidential.' 'In that case,' I said, 'It's no deal.' And I rang off.

"I thought that would be the end of it; but the next day, Thursday, I received a message from the gentleman. He suggested that I should come to Zidon here, at the casino. He said, if I did that, I would receive evidence of the good faith of these people. Like a miracle, you know, a voice coming down from Heaven? He said there could be discussions. I could decide whether or not to accept the money.

"Well, I talked it over with my father and my brothers. I decided to come, and here I am, Polela." Vusi spread his hands. "And here, to my amazement, are you."

Ross was suddenly out of patience with the verbal fencing. "I'm as amazed as you are," he said. "Suppose we take it from there? Do you know the names of the donors?"

For answer Vusi held up two pieces of paper, one in each hand. "I arrived here on Friday," he said. "I heard nothing. But at midday today, I received these. A letter from the same lawyers, and a cheque for one million, signed by Richard C. Wragge. Did you bring it, Ross?"

"No." Ross paused. "For what it's worth, Richard hinted he might try something like this, and I told him not to be a fool."

Vusi nodded. His gaze never left Ross's face. "These things didn't come by post. There must have been a courier."

"It wasn't me."

"Who, then?"

"At a guess, Charlie Sickert."

Vusi handed the cheque to Ross. "Is that Wragge's signature?"

"It appears to be."

"Can he afford to sign a cheque for a million?"

"Yes. He's a multi-millionaire. I would expect him to have spread the burden . . . as the letter suggests he has done."

"How did he make so much money?"

"Salectron is a leader in the computer world. He built it up."

"Computers. And munitions?"

"Modern armaments include a lot of electronic equipment."

"Which Salectron makes?"

"Yes."

"Salectron has buyers all over the world, right?"

Vusi's gaze was piercing, intent. Ross said slowly, "We sell to certain countries."

"No questions asked?"

"On the contrary. There are strict international laws about arms-dealing. A lot of states embargo our goods."

"You can get round sanctions, if you know how."

"Our trade is legitimate."

"Yeah? So tell me, Ross, do you think I should take Mr Wragge's money?"

"No."

"Why not? Why should I turn down a million of these legitimately earned bucks?"

"Because if you take it, it will look as if you're taking a bribe." As Vusi remained silent, Ross added. "And because you don't know who's behind it."

"Behind Mr Wragge, you mean?"

"Somebody could be using Richard. He's naive about politics."

Vusi laughed. "But I'm not." He took the cheque from Ross's outstretched fingers, tore it in half and then in half again. He slipped the pieces into the envelope and handed it to Ross.

"You go back and tell Daddy-O, I mean no offence, I appreciate his generosity, but I don't want to kiss any capitalist bums, right now."

In the background, Zidon said quietly, "Cool it, Vusi, man."

Ross slid the envelope into his pocket. "Understand one thing. I came here in good faith. I wouldn't do anything against your interests."

"I believe you," Vusi said, but lightly, as if it didn't much matter.

"Where will you go now?" Ross asked.

"I leave tomorrow for East London. I have meetings there. Next Thursday, I move to Durban to talk with AWASU."

Ross stared. AWASU was the Zulu-sponsored Trades Union, set up to rival the UDF's COSATU, now emasculated. The two groups were virtually at war. Anyone who could secure a truce would command enormous power.

"You really think they'll listen to you?"

"I know they will." There was no vainglory in the words, merely a calm conviction.

"And after Durban?"

"The Rand, Free State, Western Cape. There's so much to do." Vusi seemed to be speaking half to himself. "All that stuff in the papers . . . demos, marches . . . that's just fart. We have to consolidate, plan, bring the leaders together to form a new strategy. The Freedom Charter's not enough. Not any more."

"You'll never unite all the factions."

"I will unite them, and I will form a lawful political party based on the labour movement."

"Vusi, the authorities will never let such a thing get off the ground!"

Vusi stood up. He said quietly, "You haven't grasped it, yet, have you Ross? I was released to do what no one else can do . . . create a black bargaining force. The man back there in Cape Town understands it, I understand it. It has to be done, and we have to do it. There's no room left for anyone in between. The love-play is over, man. It's fucking time."

He spoke flatly, as if he had keyed himself up to this interview, and now wished it to end.

"Give my regards to your boss," he said, and nodded dismissal.

Ross remained seated, staring up at the dark face, trying to read the expression in the eyes. He remembered how, a few days ago, Richard Wragge had asked, "What sort of man is Vusi Matlala?" and he had answered, "People love him."

The man he faced now was not lovable. That quality was gone, left behind, perhaps, in Pollsmore prison, or burned out by the fire of an ever-present danger.

"Believe me," Ross said, "I do understand."

Vusi laughed again. "And you think that to understand is enough?" He placed both hands on his chest, bending forward so that the light shone on his eyes.

"Some men went into exile," he said. "I stay here. When I raise my fist, I salute the brothers and sisters who live and die here. When I say 'Amandhla Awethu', I mean power to the people who are here, and now. The struggle is here, and now, and it is ours. Go back to New York, Ross. You have made your choice, and believe me, I also understand."

He turned on his heel and quickly left the room. Zidon came forward. He looked distressed.

"Vusi is under so much strain."

"What he said is true."

"Don't think we are not grateful. We had to be sure whether the cheque was . . . honest."

Ross stood up. "Zidon, I don't know what's going on, but I do know one thing, Vusi's in great danger."

"He's always in danger."

"But especially now, because he's uniquely important to this country."

"He knows that."

Ross nodded. "About the cheque," he said. "I'll talk to Wragge, find out what's behind it. I'll let you know."

"I won't be here, for a week or two. I'm going with Vusi. You can send a message to the store at Stannard's Post. They'll see I get it."

"About those tapes, the copies you said I couldn't have . . ."

Zidon hesitated, then said, "I made them. I'll leave them at the desk for you, tomorrow." He held out his hand. "I won't see you. We'll be out of here by seven."

"Thanks, Zidon."

"So long, Polela."

As Ross walked back to the hotel, he saw two black policemen, armed with rifles, move across the lawns behind the tennis courts. They gained the shadow of a shrubbery, and were lost to sight.

The arclights over the swimming-pool had been doused. A warm off-shore wind was blowing. It carried the bitter smell of veld-fires.

The man in room 413 watched Ross return to the building, as he had watched him leave it.

Since his arrival at the hotel, he'd seen all the people he'd been told to look out for.

The fat guy, Sickert.

The young guy, McRae.

The casino manager, Marciano.

The goodlooking woman with the legs.

Vusi Matlala. He'd got a good view of that one through the lens, as he went into his brother's pad. Could have taken him then, but the circumstances weren't right.

They never would be at this place. Too many pigs around, and then, the mess-up with Pampallas.

He'd felt like quitting when he spotted that slob, but it would have been stupid to run. Call attention to himself. Better to leave quietly, in the morning.

He'd go to East London, do the job there, as planned.

He glanced round the room. He'd unpacked nothing, been careful to leave no prints, here or in the bathroom.

His hold-all and the bag of golf-clubs stood at the foot of the bed. He went over and opened the zipper top of the golf-bag, reached down past the clubs, and drew out a long, flat box.

It contained his rifle, the detachable stock separate from the

126

barrel, the special ammunition with explosive heads cradled in a special container. It was a sniper's weapon, made in South Africa. That had been stipulated in the contract.

He had a permit for the gun. The papers he carried described him as a hunter. Wouldn't fool anyone who knew guns, but it was a nice touch. He had a letter that explained that Howard C. Latimer was entitled to shoot one lion, in some way-out place in the Transvaal.

It was all kosher. Only thing was, he'd be getting his lion a little closer to the coast.

Smiling to himself, he replaced the box in the golf-bag.

He lay down fully clothed on the bed, switched off the bedside lamp, and in a short while was sound asleep.

16

Ross took the elevator to the sixth floor and knocked on Julie's door. She opened it, keeping the chain on, saw Ross and let him in.

"I'm sorry to wake you," he said.

"I wasn't asleep." She was tying the belt of a white satin wrap. "What's wrong, what happened?"

"Richard offered Vusi Matlala a million rand."

Julie sat down on the edge of the bed.

"Are you sure?"

"I've just been talking to Vusi, in Zidon's house. He showed me Richard's cheque."

"I didn't bring it, Ross, I swear."

"I know. It was probably Sickert."

Julie muttered, "What can have got into Dad?"

"God knows, but I intend to ask him. There are a lot of things I want to know . . . why I was brought here, who fixed it? It must have been someone connected with the casino, someone big enough to call the shots, perhaps one of the owners. And who told Richard's lawyers where to reach Vusi? That stinks of paid informers. Richard's landed us right in it, this time."

"I'm sure he meant well."

Ross said harshly, "Black politics isn't for well-meaning amateurs, Julie. It's like that sea out there, full of man-eaters. Because of Richard's action, we're tied to Vusi Matlala. We're down in the records as having tried to proposition him. If he gets killed, we're involved; Richard, you, me."

"But if Matlala refused the cheque . . . he did, didn't he?"

"Oh yes, he tore it up."

"Then that lets us out."

"No, it doesn't. The records exist in the Stormont Merchant Bank, in the register of this hotel, on the books of a prominent legal firm. I wish I could get my hands on the sods who set this up!"

She was looking at him with concern. "Was Matlala very angry?"

"Contemptuous is a better word."

"I don't see that he has any right . . ."

"He has every right. He reminded me that I live in New York, and he lives here. That's all the difference in the world."

"You've done your share."

"I made one down payment, a long time ago, and then I reneged. Vusi won't let up, this side of death. But I admit, I didn't expect . . ." He stopped, unable to voice what he was feeling.

"He was your friend," Julie said.

"A long time ago. He's changed. It's not surprising."

Yet he found himself surprised, and hurt, that the coinage of childhood should be debased. Vusi Matlala and Ross McRae, racing together across the hills of Halladale, swimming together in the dam, as close as brothers . . . that should have survived.

"He said something about Salectron," Ross said.

"What?"

"I don't know . . . hinting that we break the arms laws." Turning his head, Ross saw his reflection in the looking-glass, a face of angry disbelief.

"I'm bloody well going to find out," he said.

Julie stood up and came towards him. "My dear, I am so sorry. I know you didn't want to be involved."

He put a hand on her shoulder. "That's past. I don't mind for myself, I mind for you." He realised he meant that, and smiled at her. "Don't worry, love, we'll work things out. I'm taking you back to Joburg tomorrow. We'll talk to Richard."

She took his wrist in both her hands. "Stay with me now."

He tried for a light answer. "Is this a formal application to the Lonely Hearts Club?"

"No club. Just you and me."

As his arms closed round her, and the softness of the satin wrap gave way to the satin of her skin, he knew that in staying, he committed himself not merely to loving Julie, but to resolving the dilemma of his own life.

From a small back room in the police department block in East London, Dion Volbrecht conducted a telephone conversation with the man responsible for law and order at Bowers Bay.

They spoke English, which was the first language of neither of them. Volbrecht was frustrated and irritable. His opposite number was worried and resentful.

"We have this Matlala under observation," he kept saying. "We are watching him, around the clock."

"The other guests in the hotel. . . ?"

"We are watching, also. You have no need to worry. This side, everything is A-OK."

Volbrecht pressed for information about the guests at the casino. How many new arrivals, how many foreign passports checked at the border posts? He knew he was wasting his time. Vigilance at the posts was patchy, records seldom complete.

He asked about the deployment of police in and around the hotel and was told, more or less politely, that it was none of his business.

He next put through a call to his immediate superior in Cape Town. Their discussion quickly became acrimonious. No clearance had yet been given for Volbrecht to go to Bowers Bay. Diplomatic relations were strained, these things took time. The speaker was unable, or, as Volbrecht thought, unwilling, to say who was blocking the permit. After arguing for ten minutes, Volbrecht rang off, fuming.

He had spoken earlier with Mr Charles Sickert and Mr Derek Marciano of the casino staff.

He played over the tapes of these conversations. They did nothing to calm his temper.

Sickert had been loquacious, but unable to supply the information Volbrecht asked for. He referred Volbrecht to

Marciano, who insisted that the casino was co-operating with the local police, which was all that could be expected.

Volbrecht was scared. He felt like he was driving a car down a steep hill, and when he stood on the brakes, there was nothing there.

That was the trouble, these days. You couldn't trust the machinery. It was one thing for the President to give orders, it was another for those orders to be carried out. Orders got screwed up along the way. Some official, white or black, decided to be obstructive, and that was it.

A man was on his own, he had to do what he could, and hope it would be enough.

He looked at his watch and realised it was time to leave. He drove across town, to the factory area, and parked his car on a vacant lot.

The man he'd arranged to meet was already there, and restive. Volbrecht didn't blame him. Black informers didn't last long, and this one was already into injury time.

The man had a story that one of the Cheetah teams was in the district. The leader, he said, was Sousa. He'd been seen in Mdantsane, the black town just across the Ciskeian border. The informer thought the team had left Mdantsane now, and moved into East London proper.

Volbrecht paid him, and drove back to headquarters. There he put out an all-stations alert for the Cheetah squad.

He spent the rest of the night studying reports of the movements of trades union leaders, to and from the Eastern Cape, over the past few days.

After he left Ross and Julie in the roulette room, Charlie Sickert headed for the basement surveillance centre.

He was badly in need of a drink, which he couldn't have . . . not till he'd finished with Pampallas and Company.

If McRae was right . . . if the Greek had spotted someone in the foyer . . . the chances were it was a rat of the same breed, a pro who could take the casino for as much as Pampallas could.

Riding down in the lift, Sickert mopped sweat from his face

and neck. Things had gone way beyond him. It wasn't just the business with the Greek. That was part of his job. What wasn't his job was to deal with terrorists like Vusi Matlala. He'd said from the beginning, it was madness to allow a man like that near the hotel, but they'd overruled him. They never explained anything, just gave orders, and he had to obey them. He had no choice. Jobs like this weren't easy to find. He was fifty-four years old, he couldn't start again.

Tomorrow, thank Christ, Zidon Matlala would take his brother away and let the hotel get back to normal. In the meantime, thanks to McRae's tip-off, there was work to do.

The two men on duty in the surveillance centre greeted him without surprise. It was customary for him to check the area a couple of times during the night.

He walked through to the copying and storage room, and selected the batch of tapes made at the time of Pampallas's arrival.

He ran Tape Three, and quickly found the section he wanted. McRae was right. Pampallas's face stared out, bug-eyed, as if he'd seen a spook.

Sickert exchanged the tape for the one for Screen Two. He ran it through, freezing the frames in which Per Frolich appeared. He examined each picture with care, calculating the angles of cameras Two and Three, the relation of Frolich's position to that of Pampallas.

He sat thinking for a while, and then made a copy of Tape Two, put it in his pocket, and returned all the original tapes to their shelf.

Back in the surveillance room, he spent a few minutes chatting to the guards, then took the elevator upstairs, to the office behind the reception desk. There was a safe room in the north wall, and Sickert unlocked the door and went in. From a filing cabinet he extracted several stacks of passports, checked and ready to be returned to their owners next morning.

Sickert worked steadily through the piles until he found the passport he needed. He studied its details before returning it to its place.

Back at reception, he ran through the guest register and identified a room number.

At twenty-past two, he returned to his own suite on the seventh floor of the hotel. He poured himself a double whisky on the rocks and stood sipping it. When he'd finished the drink, he ran the tape through once more, on his own video machine.

Leaving the tape in position, he went to his desk, took a Smith and Wesson automatic from a drawer, made sure that it was loaded. Gamblers didn't usually get rough, but it paid to take precautions.

He crossed to the telephone and made a call, then settled in a chair close to the door, holding the automatic flat on his knee.

The knock, when it came, was barely audible.

Sickert glanced up at the security scanner above the door. It allowed him to see the man standing outside. He was tall and gangling, his hands hung loosely at his sides. He wore no jacket, only a soft cashmere cardigan over his shirt and slacks. There were cream-coloured loafers on his feet.

Well-to-do, Sickert decided, and looked harmless; but as he unlocked the door and waved the man through, he let him see the automatic.

"I'm sorry to trouble you this late, Mr Latimer, but there's a matter that has to be settled at once."

The thin man's gaze drifted from the gun, to Sickert's face. He seemed puzzled rather than angered by the summons.

"Settled?" he said. "What are you talking about?"

Sickert waved him to a chair. He himself remained standing, the gun at the ready.

"I examined your passport tonight, Mr Latimer. It seems to me you have some explaining to do."

"In what way?"

"Well, for one thing, you give your nationality as Swedish, but it's obvious from your permanent address, the way you talk, your . . . general appearance . . . that you're American."

"My father was Swedish. I was born in Stockholm. I'm a Swedish national by right of birth, though I haven't lived there since I was a kid." Latimer spoke quietly, almost tiredly, as if he'd been through all this before. "My passport's in order. You can check it with my consul."

"There's no Swedish consulate in these parts," Sickert said drily.

Latimer shrugged, apparently not much interested. His manner annoyed Sickert.

"I'd like to know your reason for being at this casino."

"I'm just passing through. Going to the Transvaal."

"Do you gamble, Mr Latimer?"

"Sometimes. When I got the spare cash. Don't make a habit of it."

"You were recognised tonight, by a professional gambler named Stavros Pampallas."

"Never heard of him." Latimer spoke coldly. "And I don't like your tone, Mr Manager. I'm a guest in this dump. I'm paying enough so I should get some respect."

Sickert wiped his face. If he'd made a screw-up, here, he could be in a lot of trouble.

"We have it on tape," he said flatly. "Pampallas saw you, and it scared him. He knows you, Mr Latimer. Now I won't make a big production of this. I'd like to settle it quietly, and I'm sure you would, too. So if you'll just tell me where and when you met Pampallas . . ."

"I don't know any Pampallas, and I don't know about any tape."

"I'll show you." Sickert backed towards the video machine, beckoning Latimer after him. Latimer rose and ambled forward. Sickert picked up the remote-control and started the tape.

The scene in the lobby rolled across the screen, Per Frolich smiling at the TV interviewer, the crowd moving behind them. At a certain point, Sickert froze the frame.

"There," he said.

"Latimer leaned forward, peering. "What's to see in that?"

Sickert edged forward to point. "There, on the right."

For an instant his attention was on the picture, and in that instant, Latimer swung backhanded, chopping the edge of his palm into the side of Sickert's neck.

As Sickert dragged in an agonised breath, knees sagging, he saw Latimer moving round, the goatface no longer puzzled but set in bleak concentration. The hand sliced in again, catching Sickert under the ear, knocking him cold.

Latimer caught Sickert as he fell and eased him to the carpet. He walked quietly across the living-room to the open door of the bedroom. From there he could see the windows, closed because of the air-conditioning.

Latimer approached the windows. Wrapping a handkerchief round his hand, he gently eased open the one nearest him. He leaned out a little and looked up and down the face of the building. He could see no lights. Directly below was a small courtyard, dark, a service area for the kitchens. Further to the left, a large rubbish truck was parked, and two workmen were lifting sacks of trash into it. There was no sign of movement on the roadway or in the grounds to the rear.

Latimer returned to where Sickert was lying. He felt the pulse in the fat throat. It was shallow and flickering. Latimer bent down, and bracing himself, raised the body in a fireman's lift. Grunting, he carried it through the bedroom to the window.

He took Sickert's limp right hand and pressed the fingers round the handle of the window. He pressed the left hand on to the dusty window ledge, sliding it out and over the rim. He stood still, supporting the body, watching the garbage truck and the silent grounds. The workmen threw in the last sacks, and closed the truck's doors. They climbed into the cab. As the engine started, Latimer heaved his burden through the window.

The impact as the body hit the ground, seven floors below, seemed very loud. Latimer waited in the dark bedroom, watching and listening, but nothing stirred.

Latimer went back to the living-room. He examined the carpet carefully. There was no sign of struggle. The automatic pistol lay where it had fallen, and Latimer slid a pencil under the trigger-guard, lifted the gun and laid it in the top right-hand drawer of the desk. He bent to sniff at the empty whisky-tumbler, left the glass where it was on the bar table.

The video machine was still running. Latimer switched it off, took out the cassette and tucked it under his arm, inside the cardigan.

He wasted no time on searching the room. By what the fat boy had said, nobody else knew about the tape.

It was now just after three a.m. He returned to his room, collected his luggage, and went downstairs to the foyer. There was a bus scheduled to leave for the north coast run at three-thirty a.m. and a bunch of sleepy tourists was gathered round the reception desk. Latimer joined them. He paid his bill and carried his bags outside.

The bus was on the tarmac. Latimer walked straight past it, entered the parking-garage, collected his car, and drove to the exit gates of the hotel. The guard there took no notice of him. Casino players kept odd hours.

In the wooded area twenty miles north of Bowers Bay, Latimer stopped the car. He strolled some distance into the forest. Presently he found a face of rock, seamed with clefts. He thrust the cassette deep into a crevice screened by bushes. Satisfied that it could not be seen, even at close quarters, he returned to his car. By four a.m., he was well on his way to East London.

Julie woke before daybreak.

She rose on her elbow to look at Ross. The light was on in the bathroom, and its beam fell across him. He'd thrown up an arm to shield his eyes.

He lay on his back, one knee raised, the blanket and sheet thrown back. Her eyes traced the heavy line of his thigh, the muscle curving down to the groin, the sex organs soft and relaxed. She reached out to caress them, but drew her hand back. There would be time for that, later.

The idea that one could take time, make time, for love, was new to her. With Dave, sex had been like one of his pit-stops, in and out as fast as possible, no speech to delay things.

There had never been any doubt in Dave's mind that he was good in bed. Plenty of girls had told him so. He preferred them young and silly, picking them carelessly from the groupies who

136

hung about the race-tracks. He made no attempt to conceal these infidelities. They weren't important to him, he said, and Julie believed him. Nothing was important to Dave but racing cars. To make love, one had to take time off from racing, so keep lovemaking as short as possible.

Ross had shown, that first time in Washington, and again tonight, that he wanted to please her. He'd given her time to reach her climax, he'd stayed with her as long as she needed. She had been allowed to feel that nothing mattered to him but her happiness.

He was her first lover. She'd been faithful to Dave, wanting so much to make her marriage work, to prove to all the critics, her father included, that they were wrong.

She saw now that her seven years with Dave had been a total waste, for them both. The man she'd believed him to be . . . no, that was unfair, the man she'd wanted him to be . . . was a figment of her imagination. No wonder he'd put himself beyond her reach.

Dave was over and done with, and she felt nothing but relief.

Which didn't mean she could latch on to Ross. He had his own problems, a sick wife, his work. She mustn't try to take him from them. She would not make the mistake of thinking she owned him. She would stay with him as long as he allowed her to. If he wanted to be free of her, she would let him go.

She could do that. She could let him go if he wanted to. She wondered if that was what love meant, and decided that love was a word to be used with caution, its value being much debased.

She leaned over and kissed Ross. He mumbled something, rolled his head, opened his eyes and stared up at her. His face relaxed in pleasure, and he reached for her with a sigh of contentment.

"What time is it?"

She glanced at the clock on the bedside table. "Half-past four. Maybe you should go back."

"Back where?" He began kissing her lightly, watching her at

137

the same time so that his eyes squinted a little. "Back why?" he said. His kisses became more demanding. He rolled over her, and she stopped trying to think of reasons why he should leave.

17

The Matlalas left Zidon's cottage at a quarter-past seven.

Their car drove up to the main entrance to the hotel, and Zidon Matlala alighted. He carried a small parcel wrapped in brown paper. As he was about to pass through the doors into the lobby, the doorman reached out and caught his arm.

"Hey, man, you heard the news? Charlie Sickert died."

Zidon stared at him dumbly.

"Fell out of the window," the doorman insisted. "Yes, I'm telling you, it's true!" He glanced at the waiting car, and lowered his voice. "You going on leave?"

"Yes."

"Then you better go now," the doorman said. "You put your nose through that door, you'll never get away."

Zidon looked at the packet of tapes he held. He could hand them to the doorman, but some instinct warned him not to. He nodded and smiled.

"You're right. Thanks, my friend."

He climbed back into the car. Themba Matlala, at the wheel, looked his surprise.

"Move," Zidon told him. "Fast."

Themba asked no questions. The car started quietly, rolled forward, gathered speed towards the main road north.

As Mathias was drinking his early morning tea, the bedside telephone rang. The caller was Derek Marciano, from Bowers Bay. He sounded close to panic.

"Sickert's dead," he said. "Fell out of his bedroom window, broke every bone in his body."

"Fell?"

"Yes. We found marks on the window-ledge. He . . ."

"Where was the body?"

"In the kitchen well, under his back windows. The kitchen staff found him half an hour ago. I had the house doctor look at him right away, but he was all smashed up, it's seven floors . . ."

"How did he come to fall?" Mathias cut through Marciano's near-hysteria.

"He'd taken a whisky, a stiff one. Charlie had a poor head for liquor. He must have gone to open the window, and slipped."

"When did it happen?"

"The doctor can't be sure. Maybe about three this morning. Charlie was down in the surveillance centre at twelve-fifteen, stayed there for a while, talked to the security guards. Then he went to the reception office and checked the contents of the saferoom."

"Was that usual?"

"Yes, he did it every night. He went up to his suite about twenty minutes past two. The maid went to wake him at six-thirty, couldn't get an answer, used her key, found no one in the suite and told the floor-porter. It took us some time to find Charlie. The well's only for ventilation, no one ever goes out there." As Marciano regained his nerve, his temper erupted. "I should have been told what was going on. Sickert brought people in, I wasn't told, I can't be held responsible."

"You won't be. Where was Ross McRae last night?"

"Look, I'm not the bloody house detective . . ."

"Pull yourself together, and try to think. McRae."

Marciano swallowed. "He was in the gambling rooms until midnight, with his girlfriend. A Mrs Aikman."

"And after midnight?"

"He went over to Zidon Matlala's quarters."

"To meet Vusi Matlala?"

"How should I know? I was tied up in the casino, all night. Why don't you ask the security men? The grounds were full of them, ask them."

"Where are the Matlalas now?"

"I think they left for East London."

"You think?"

"They left."

"Have the police been told about Sickert?"

"It was an accident . . ."

"And in the case of accidental death, there has to be an inquest. I want the police called in at once. What about the tapes?"

"They've been cleaned." Marciano felt on safer ground now. "All the tapes from yesterday, last night and this morning. There's no record, there."

"Good."

"You think McRae had something to do with it?"

"I think," Mathias said firmly, "that Sickert suffered an accident. Your job now is to hand over to the police, and see that the hotel runs as smoothly as possible. Play everything by the book, and you'll be all right. I'll keep in touch."

Marciano began to frame a question, but found that Mathias had already hung up on him.

Ross heard the news of Sickert's death at eight o'clock, from an elevator attendant. The man knew few details, merely that the security chief had fallen seven floors and was dead.

Instead of going down to breakfast, Ross went straight to Julie's room.

She had dressed, and was fastening the locks of her suitcase. Seeing Ross, she straightened up with a look of concern.

"What's wrong?"

"Charlie Sickert's dead. The story is he fell out of his bedroom window."

"Story? Don't you believe it?"

"It could be true. Either way, it's going to cause a rumpus. The police will be called in. We must leave at once."

"Won't that look bad?"

"Julie, I have to talk to your father. If the police find out he was trying to do a deal with Matlala, they're going to ask a helluva lot of questions."

"The cheque has nothing to do with Sickert's death."

141

"We can't be sure of that. I think Sickert brought the cheque here at your father's request. Even if that's all he did, it's going to make the police suspicious. Any death close to Vusi is going to get priority attention. I have to talk to Richard, get the facts from him, and if necessary we must work up some kind of a story."

Julie stared at him. "There's something you're not telling me?"

"There's a lot I don't know. I do know that Sickert's death will open a can of worms, and I want you out of here." He put his arm round her shoulders and gave her a kiss. "Get a porter for your luggage. I'll meet you downstairs."

The clerks at the reception desk were putting on a good act for the guests. Ross paid his bill and Julie's, then asked if a parcel had been left at the desk for him. The clerk searched the storage racks, and said there was nothing there for McRae.

So Zidon had changed his mind about the tapes. Ross didn't waste time wondering why.

He and Julie caught the hotel minibus to the airstrip, where the Beechcraft was already taking on passengers.

As they lifted off, they could see that the golf tournament was well under way, crowds lining the fairways and bunched behind the early players.

They flew low along the coast, and reached East London in time to catch the morning flight to Johannesburg.

The man called Latimer did not attempt to communicate with Mathias until he reached the small coastal resort of Port Edmond. There he sought out a public call box in a quiet area, and dialled the number Mathias had given him. Mathias himself answered.

"Moondog."

"Latimer. I had to abort."

"I know that. Where are you speaking from?"

"Call box in Port Edmond." Latimer gave the number and hung up. Mathias called him back at once.

"What happened?"

"I was recognised, is what. Stavros Pampallas, guy I used to know when I worked for Uncle Sam. I told you how it would be, using a place like that."

"Where's Pampallas now?"

"He quit. Sickert sent him packing. He lit out, last night."

"Will he talk?"

"No way. I told you, he knows me. He was glad to get away in one piece."

"Tell me about Sickert."

"He found out Pampallas spotted me. It was on the scanner tape. I warned you . . ."

"Did you appear on the tape?"

"Yeah. If you'd done like I said . . ."

"Never mind that." Mathias was savage. "What about Sickert?"

"He thought I was on a gambling scam, same as Pampallas. He called me to his pad, showed me the tape, started to pressure me. He was ready to call in the fuzz. I couldn't leave it that way, so I wasted him. It's OK, I made it look good, cleaned up the room after, no sweat."

"Was he dead when he fell?"

"No, but he sure was, after."

"And the tape?"

"I took it, dumped it on the way here."

"Your room at the hotel?"

"Clean. I said, you don't have to worry! For Christ's sake, I know how to handle things!"

"Did anyone but Sickert know about you and Pampallas?"

"There was McRae," Latimer said. "I saw him with Sickert. With the nigger from the surveillance centre, too."

"You think McRae knows about the tape?"

"How should I know? After Pampallas spotted me, I knew I'd have to abort. I stayed in my room." There was silence at the other end of the line. It annoyed Latimer and he said loudly, "Are you listening to me?"

"Yes." Mathias was calm. "Don't worry about McRae, we'll take care of him. All you have to do is fulfil your contract. I want

143

you to drop the Latimer identity, destroy those papers. From now on, use the papers for Randal Cooke. Go to East London, to the safe house. Sousa will be waiting for you, with the back-up team."

"What about Matlala? He hears Sickert died, maybe he'll change his schedule."

"Vusi Matlala left Bowers Bay for East London this morning. He travelled with Zidon Matlala and a black driver. He'll meet with Eastern Cape trades unionists this afternoon. This evening he'll address the rally in the Moroka Hall."

"He could make changes."

"He won't."

"You can read minds, that it?"

"I can read Vusi Matlala's mind," Mathias said.

Mathias informed Senekal of the events at the casino. The old man was deeply perturbed.

"Can we continue? There will be a great deal of adverse publicity. A murder at the casino will make the front pages."

"Not murder, General, it will be taken as accidental death, I assure you."

"What if it comes out that Cradock is one of the casino owners?"

"What if it does? The matter is entirely legal and above-board. No one will think anything of it."

"The young man, McRae?"

"He has a police record. If he becomes a nuisance, we'll knock him back into line."

"The tapes?"

"Marciano had them cleaned. There is nothing to link us with the events."

Senekal sighed. "I must respect your judgement. I leave it to you to instruct the rest of the group."

Mathias went to stand on the verandah of the cottage. The sea was grey, a wicked cross-current driving the water this way and that, so that the surf boiled with churned-up sand. Anyone who tried to swim there today would drown.

Mathias leaned forward, his thick hands gripping the wooden verandah rail.

The Matlala assignment had become as difficult and dangerous as that sea, but it wouldn't drown him.

The death of Sickert was troublesome, but it could be neutralised by quick action and enough money.

The question of the tape was more serious. Latimer said he'd scrapped it, but there could be other copies. Checks would have to be made at the casino, and with the Bowers Bay police.

McRae was a real headache. He'd been hobnobbing with Sickert on the night of the killing, he'd been with Zidon Matlala in the surveillance centre. He might have seen the tape. He might be able to identify Latimer.

It was time to talk to Cradock.

Cradock was, as always, slippery.

"Sickert? I hardly know the fellow."

"I think you know him very well."

"Thought is free, my dear Mathias."

"According to Breyten, the Stormont Merchant Bank is backing your attempt to bribe Vusi Matlala. In the circumstances, I demand to know if you've already made the approach, and if any other member of our group is implicated."

"Demand all you please."

"Put it this way; at our last meeting, the group voted against your proposal. You have deliberately gone against a group decision."

"What I do in my personal capacity is my own business."

"Have you, or have you not, approached Matlala?"

"Really, I don't propose to discuss it with you. I will tell you this much. I won't sit around, losing millions, while you indulge in Grand Guignol that has no hope of success."

"If you indulge in unilateral action, you will find yourself the star of a drama bloodier than any I can contrive."

"Don't presume to threaten me!"

"No threat is meant. I merely offer a friendly warning. Your operations have already attracted the attention of the UN Arms

Monitoring Committee. Matlala has friends in those circles. Any approach to him will tip your hand, which will make your customers abroad very unhappy. Of course, as you point out, that is not my business. What is my business, and what I shall not permit, is action that puts our entire network at risk. Why did you involve McRae?"

"Who?"

"Ross McRae, of Salectron."

"Never heard of him."

"You, or Rosendal, or Kestell, involved McRae, a man who's on close terms with the Matlalas. Thanks to that lunacy, McRae was able to spend time in the security centre at the casino. There's an excellent chance he saw our agent, on tape. If he puts two and two together, McRae could destroy us."

"Destroy him first."

"How? By more of my mindless violence? But that would be foolish, wouldn't it, if he doesn't know anything? It would focus attention precisely where we don't want it, don't you agree?"

Cradock said nothing, and Mathias gave the knife a twist. "My advice to you, my dear Professor, is that you stay home, see no visitors, avoid using the telephone. In short, do what you do best. Do nothing at all."

Rosendal calmly denied any knowledge of an approach to Matlala.

Mathias felt certain he was lying, but decided not to press the charge. Instead, he said, "We'll have to watch McRae."

"How?" Rosendal spoke with mild interest, as if the question was academic.

"I must first determine how much he does or doesn't know. I understand your company owns the block where he lives?"

"Yes. Why?"

"I want his apartment bugged. Nothing amateurish, and it must be done immediately. He's already on his way back to the Rand."

"What do you wish me to do?"

"Breyten will set up a phone tap in the building, and see that it's manned. You must ensure that he has free access to the premises."

"Very well. How about the East London deal, is that going to plan?"

Mathias found Rosendal's affability more infuriating than Cradock's rudeness.

"I'll keep you informed," he said, and slammed down the receiver.

18

When the three Matlala brothers arrived in East London, they drove straight to the house of Father Francis Césaire, whose church was on the southern fringe of the city, not far from the township of Mdantsane.

Father Francis shared a meal with them and gave them news of the situation in the Eastern Cape. When at last he departed about his parish business, Zidon and Themba went to their room to sleep. Vusi remained in his chair on the porch at the rear of the house.

It was pleasant to sit in the warm sunlight, and look out at the garden with its scrubby lawn and single tree . . . a white stinkwood, leafless at this time of the year.

Away to the left, in the church, the choir was at practice. Bursts of song alternated with the raised voice of the choir-master.

Vusi sat quietly. He had told the local organisers that he wanted time to himself, to plan what he would say to them two hours from now. That wasn't true. He knew what to say. There'd been plenty of time, in gaol, to rehearse speeches.

What was foremost in his thoughts, at this moment, was the President of the Republic of South Africa.

The man in Cape Town had done certain things, made an offer that Vusi Matlala couldn't refuse.

Vusi closed his eyes.

Years ago, when he was about fourteen, he'd hung a poster of Steve Biko over his bed. That was the time of Biko and black consciousness.

The trouble was, knowing you were black told you only the one thing about yourself.

The Black Man, people said. The Black Man this, The Black Man that.

Who was The Black Man?

Biko was black. So was the Ciskeian security officer who helped to secure Steve's arrest, and condoned his death.

Black freedom fighter, black police stooge.

Black banker, black pimp.

Black bishop, black pawn.

Black wasn't enough.

His father Simeon Matlala was black, born on the farm, a Master of Arts, teacher, poet, elder of the Christian church, friend of Albert Lutuli, believer in passive resistance.

The strategy of reason without muscle had failed.

The freedom fighters of the '80s were black, city-born for the most part, blue-collar, defiant through the days of emergency rule and detention without trial, the tear-gas and quirts, the bullets and torture. Committed to a matching violence, the bomb in the supermarket, the necklace, the AK47 hidden under the floor.

The strategy of muscle without reason had failed, too.

Stalemate, while the flesh of the nation rotted.

The man in Cape Town had moved to end the stalemate. Vusi Matlala must come up with a move to match.

He knew what he would do, knew it in his head and in his gut. Through the power of the workers, he would create a lawful political force that combined muscle and reason.

To create that force, he had to stay alive.

He half-smiled, thinking of the song they had danced to, when they were kids. Staying Alive, Staying Alive!

He'd been told, at the time of his release, that every effort would be made to protect him; and he'd said, stuff protection, I don't need that kind of help.

They'd got the message. The security boys had tried to be discreet, but they'd been there all the time, stationed in the plantations around Stannard's Post, trailing the bus that took him and Themba to Bowers Bay, hiding in the bushes at the casino.

There'd be a detachment on the street outside, watching this house.

No need to worry about them. Forget the President's men. Think about the President's enemies.

Those were the ones who wanted Vusi Matlala dead.

A man could be killed in a hundred ways; shot while resisting arrest, mugged in a back street, blown up by a car-bomb. No knowing how or when it would happen.

One clue he had. Ross McRae's warning.

That said the attack would come soon.

Maybe Richard Wragge's cheque was part of it, maybe not. Maybe Ross was involved, maybe not. No knowing.

The problem was, how to survive over the next few weeks. In that time he could complete his tour of the major cities. He could lay the foundations. Other people could build on them.

The next few weeks . . . days . . . were crucial. He had to use all the time he had, and use it well.

Inside the house the telephone began to ring. Vusi heard Zidon answer it. The conversation lasted only a few minutes, then Zidon appeared on the porch, looking anxious.

"That was Shozi, at the casino. The police are questioning people about Sickert."

"Are they still calling it an accident?"

"Yes, but they could change their minds. They could come after you."

"For what reason?"

"Man, they don't need a reason, you know that."

"If they come, I'll be here, doing what I came to do."

"Perhaps we should alter our plans, move to Durban? Harder to trace us, there."

"No. I have to stay visible. I can't run."

"What about Ross McRae? He spent a lot of time with Sickert, and he was with us. What's he going to say?"

"He won't say anything to harm us. He'll give us a better deal than we gave him."

"You don't know what pressure they can put on him."

"I do know. I can't waste time sweating about it. What Ross says and does is his problem."

"It's a good thing I didn't leave those tapes."

Vusi sat up straight. "Forget about all that. Tell me about the TU meeting. How many will be there?"

"Everyone except Zwelitsha. He's still inside."

Vusi nodded. He was mentally reviewing the men he would have to convince. Motsisi, restless and dynamic, Gcwabe who looked like a baboon and spoke like an angel, S. J. Lalla, Dirkie Hobbs, Zeke Dumisani . . . in each of the centres, he'd have to sell his vision to men who were not visionaries but practical people, with set ideas about how liberation could be achieved.

It was a big work, so big that there was no point in worrying about whether it was possible. He must go, one foot in front of the other, stride after stride, Vusi Matlala believing in Vusi Matlala.

Zidon bent forward, peering at Vusi. "Will you do as Themba suggested? Will you at least do that?"

Vusi looked up at his brother's face, a good face that belonged in a safe, clever job, not here.

"Tonight, yes, I'll do as he asks."

Zidon said with relief. "Good. I'll tell him. He better stay out of sight this afternoon. I'll drive you to the Union office."

19

Volbrecht felt like a shadow-boxer.

He had spent the entire morning trying to learn the facts of Charles Sickert's death.

The police at Bowers Bay were bloody useless, short on experience and long on bulldust.

The generalissimo who ran things down there was clinging to the theory that Sickert drank too much Scotch and fell out the window. He was also throwing a lot of twak about terrorists and revolutionaries, said his government didn't appreciate having people like the Matlalas in their territory, especially at the new casino, which was intended to be a showplace and a major source of income to the nation.

Volbrecht had asked the casino manager, Marciano, who actually owned the hotel. Marciano named the holding company, hedged about detail. He had his knife into McRae, hinted he knew something about Sickert's death.

What interested Volbrecht far more than McRae's link with Sickert, was his link with the Matlalas. McRae had visited them late on Sunday night, spent over an hour with them.

McRae had to be investigated. Volbrecht had the computer-check running, even before he hung up on Bowers-Bay-Fatso.

McRae's record was on his desk within minutes.

Detained during the student unrest of '86, resisted arrest and sustained injuries to the face and ribs. Became the focus, while in hospital, of a media row about police brutality. Released from detention two months later. Completed his university degree that year, and refused army call-up. Was charged (by the police, not the army), and stated in court that his refusal was on moral, not religious or political grounds. Went to gaol for eighteen months, morality not being grounds for civil disobedience. On release, was employed by an old pal of his Pa's, a Mr Richard Wragge, of Salectron Industries. Now represented that firm in the United States of America. Resident New York.

McRae would have to be looked at, Volbrecht decided; but care must be taken, no rhino charges.

After some thought, he deputed the job to Colonel Martin de la Rey, of the Johannesburg Special Branch.

That done, he returned to his main concern, the safety of Vusi Matlala.

The Matlala brothers were with Father Césaire. The church precincts were easy enough to secure, so were the Union offices in the centre of the town. The danger was the mass rally, this evening.

The Chief Magistrate wanted to ban it. Volbrecht sympathised with him. If anything happened to Matlala, there'd be mayhem, and the authorities would be blamed for letting it happen.

But the President had ruled that the rally must be allowed to go ahead. So it was a question of what to do about that.

Matlala's aides, the ones organising the rally, had been co-operative, up to a point, about their arrangements.

The crowd . . . a very big one . . . would be assembled by five in the afternoon. Factory-workers, most of them, from the nearby industrial area.

Vusi Matlala would arrive at the main entrance to the Moroka Civic Complex at five-thirty. You could expect them to frig around with the timing, a bit, if they were running late.

Volbrecht had talked to the organisers about security. He'd wanted a big police presence in Moroka township. The organisers had turned that down flat. They claimed their own vigilantes could guard the Complex, its entrances, parking-lot, and playing fields.

The best Volbrecht could achieve was consent to a limited police presence, a few patrol cars manned by blacks, and some plain-clothes men with the media teams.

There was huge media interest in the rally. Press and TV, local and foreign, were swarming to the city. Volbrecht had arranged to have some of his best men in there with them.

The township would be ringed by uniformed men, with Casspirs, choppers, the lot. If anyone at the rally moved one inch out of line, the Force would move in fast, and the hell with what anyone said.

It would be more comfortable sitting on a leaky petrol-drum, smoking a ciggie.

He'd studied the route the Matlalas would use to reach the complex. They'd be using two cars, Zidon and his brother Themba in the first, Vusi and the big Union cheese in the second. Neither car was bullet-proof, although both had dark glass fitted in the windows, which was better than nothing. Behind the Matlala cars, there'd be a parade of at least twenty vehicles, full of black heavies.

Volbrecht looked at the reports piled in his in-tray. He had a team sifting info. It was pouring in all the time. The trouble was, the informers sold to everyone. What the police knew at noon, the whole bloody world knew at five-past.

An informer he trusted swore there was a Cheetah team in the city. Volbrecht had promised big money for that address, but so far, no joy.

He felt sorry for Vusi Matlala.

Meneer die President had granted Vusi the freedom to die where and when he chose.

Volbrecht thought it was likely to be at the Moroka Civic Complex, around five-thirty this evening.

The Cheetah gang sought by Volbrecht . . . the same gang that had butchered Stendal on the Cape Flats . . . was at the safe house at Number 3139, Wallach Road, East London.

The word "house" was a misnomer. Number 3139 was a trucking-yard. Vehicles of every sort crowded its parking-lot, which was bounded by two large garages, a storage shed, and a repair-shop. All of these were maintained in peak order, to serve Mathias's operations.

Over the repair-shop was an apartment, ostensibly for a watchman/caretaker. In fact, it was used by Sousa and his men, whenever they had to spend a night in the city.

Access to the apartment was through the shop, but there was a fire-escape that led from the kitchen to the feeder-lane at the rear of the property. The kitchen windows overlooked the lane, the front windows were above the main gate.

The man whom Sousa was expecting arrived by this gate. He drove his car into the yard and stopped. Two members of the team went up to the car, one of them opening the driver's door and waving the occupant out. He took his time about it. The guard climbed into the car and drove it into the workshop, where a mechanic at once began to prepare it for a spray-job.

The new arrival was tall and thin, dressed in jeans and a black wind-cheater. He carried a golf-bag, and a sportsman's hold-all. Sousa thought he looked ordinary.

However, when they were face to face in the kitchen, Sousa changed his mind.

This one was dangerous.

He sat as quiet as a cat, relaxed, hands palm down on the pine table. He answered questions smooth and easy.

It was his eyes. They reminded Sousa of the demons carved on the church door, back home in Braga. You looked into them, and all you saw was holes. Space.

Eyes like that you didn't trust, and you didn't forget, ever.

"You should wear shades," Sousa said, not joking, and the thin man smiled.

"When the time comes, buddy."

"What do we call you?"

"Cooke, is OK. You got the maps? I'd like to look it over."

Sousa spread a large map on the table. Certain points had been circled in red. He'd had to do all that this morning, when he finally got word the rally was going ahead.

He ran through the programme.

"The Matlalas are staying at a church house, here. It's about eight Ks from the Moroka Civic Complex, here. We'll know when they start out. We'll have a radio car covering them all the way. You'll know which car the mark's in.

"They'll use the main road into the township. It goes right to the complex, which is on flat ground, see? With hills all round.

155

The slope's gradual. At the top of the hill on the south side is the reservoir, and the electricity supply system. That's all state land."

Sousa produced a second map, which enlarged the section showing the Moroka Civic Complex and the reservoir.

"You'll take this back road to the reservoir. We've fixed for a bit of electrical trouble to show up, tomorrow afternoon. You'll go in with the repair team . . . our boys. You'll fit in fine."

"How do we make it on to state property?"

"You'll have permits." Sousa's brutish mouth curved in a grin. "Plus a police escort."

"Your boys, too?"

"Sure."

"You coming along?"

"No. They know me. I'll be with the getaway team."

Sousa touched a small red circle on the map.

"That's the electricity tower at the north boundary of the reservoir. You go inside the tower and climb up to the upper floor. There's a room, with windows. You get a straight view down the hill, to the main entrance to the complex. The Matlala cars will stop at that entrance."

"Why not the parking-lot?"

"Because that's for the buses. Matlala will stop at the front entrance, to meet a reception committee . . . union bucks, township bucks, church bucks, all wanting to shake his hand. It'll take about ten minutes for him to do the whole line. You'll have plenty of time to hit him."

"Is there a back road to the complex?"

"Yes. It'll be used by the buses, coming and going all the bloody time."

"What sort of crowd do they expect?"

"Hundred thousand."

The thin man's head jerked up. "Shit! A mob like that can block the roads, cut us off."

"They won't come near us. I told you, the reservoir is government property. We'll have passes, they won't."

"Guards at the reservoir?"

156

"That's for me to worry about."

"Afterwards? How do we leave?"

"There's open ground at the reservoir. We'll bring in a chopper, fly the team out."

"Where to?"

Sousa shrugged.

The man called Cooke stared at him for a moment, then returned to studying the map, measuring distances and calculating angles.

20

Julie was silent through most of the flight to Johannesburg; staring out of the window, her hands idle in her lap. Ross knew she was thinking of her father.

The cheque had been a stupid, fatal mistake. People close to Richard might recognise it as the sort of grandiose gesture he enjoyed. Others would see it as hush-money, designed to cover up treasonable action.

Ross tried to recall details of the company's operations over the past few years. Any illegal deals would have been skilfully masked . . . dummy accounts, double lading, laundered money, all the tricks the sanctions-busters used.

To divert manufactured goods from any of Salectron's legitimate factories would be enormously complicated, calling for complicity by makers, shippers, and auditors.

Two possibilities remained.

There could be a secret factory, somewhere, set up for the sole purpose of making undeclared goods. The factory need not be on South African soil, indeed it would almost certainly be elsewhere; in one of the neighbouring states, or perhaps on another continent.

The second, and more likely possibility, was that someone in Salectron was selling formulae and blueprints, rather than finished goods; trading off the firm's programmes and techniques, and enabling pirate companies to copy its products.

Exposing that kind of racket wasn't a one-man job. It would take a team of experts, around the world.

According to Senator Cromlech, that kind of investigation was imminent. Salectron, and Richard Wragge, were synonymous. Destroy one, you destroyed the other.

So what was to be done?

The fact was that someone at Salectron must have been involved in double-dealing.

Richard Wragge's signature was on the cheque.

It always came back to Richard. The first step must be, could only be, to ask him for an explanation.

When the plane landed at Jan Smuts airport, Ross left Julie to collect their baggage, and went to put through a call to Salectron's Head Office.

"What will you say to him?" Julie asked.

They were at Wragge's home, Malbrook, having come straight from the airport.

"I'll ask him why he wrote the cheque."

"Can I be there?"

"I don't think he'd like that."

"You invited Hal."

"Hal's a friend, and . . . I need a witness." Julie had to face reality, whatever that turned out to be.

She blinked and seemed about to argue, then nodded. "All right, but tell me, after? You won't leave without telling me?"

He agreed, and she went upstairs. A short while later Richard and Hal arrived, and the three men moved to the study.

Richard flopped down in the chair behind the desk. He looked tired, annoyed, guilty all at once.

"Well," he said, "get on with it."

For answer, Ross produced the torn cheque and handed it to Hal.

"Do you know anything about this?"

Hal placed the fragments on the edge of the desk, slowly piecing them together. He lifted his head to peer at Richard in disbelief.

"You bloody fool! I told you not to!"

"You told? I'm not in the habit of taking orders from my employees."

Ross spoke before Hal could answer. "You owe us an

159

explanation, Richard. Hal warned you, I warned you, you went right ahead and did it."

"It was an act of goodwill."

"It was an act of bloody stupidity! You used Charlie Sickert as your courier, and now Sickert's dead, probably murdered!"

"Rubbish. It was an accident. It said so, in the papers."

"I hope they're right, but the fact remains, you've involved all of us, including Julie, in a police investigation. There's a good chance they'll find out about the cheque."

"Who's going to tell them? You?"

"I'll try not to," Ross said levelly, "but I'm not the only witness to its existence. The Stormont Bank may be forced to give information. The Matlalas may do so voluntarily."

"A fine return, for a generous offer!"

"Vusi doesn't see it your way. He sent you a message. Thanks, but he doesn't want to kiss any capitalist bums, right now. He doesn't believe in your goodwill. He believes you were trying to buy his silence."

"Silence? About what?"

"Vusi believes Salectron has been selling military secrets to illegal regimes."

Richard's face flamed. "Are you out of your mind?"

"No, and nor is Vusi. The rumours exist, Richard, there'll be an investigation, soon."

"There is no foundation for such a pack of lies. Salectron has a clean record. Ask our auditors, ask the national arms inspectorate, we're absolutely clean . . ."

"A million rand is a lot of money."

"I offered it to a cause!" Richard spread his hands in passionate emphasis. "Isn't there any decency left in the world? Any trust? A man tries to do something for humanity, and he gets a kick in the teeth." Richard was lashing himself into a fury. "As for you, what right have you to accept these slanders, what right have you to insinuate . . ."

"I'm on the Salectron board, for one thing. For another, my neck's on the block. You made damn sure I was dragged into your little scheme!"

"I? I did nothing of the sort."

"Oh, come on, Richard, you fixed it with Sickert."

"I did not! Sickert and I were talking, he told me he had security problems, I suggested he talk to you. I left the decision to you. You went to Bowers Bay of your own free will, don't try to blame me for it."

"How about Julie? Why did you send her to the casino, at this particular time?"

"I booked tickets for the golf, weeks ago. I was damn glad of an excuse to get Julie away from Theo's clinic, and all the troubles." Richard suddenly looked scared. "Where is Julie, is she all right?"

"She's upstairs, she's fine. We left before the cops started asking questions. But they will. We have to agree on what to say."

"If I'm questioned," said Richard stiffly, "I shall tell the truth."

"It's not that simple. For instance, are there other donors to the fund, or did you act alone?"

"There are others."

"Who are they?"

"That is a confidential matter."

"You'll be asked for names."

"I shan't give them. Not without the consent of the people concerned. For God's sake, Ross, the arrangements were handled by the Stormont Merchant Bank, which has a reputation beyond reproach. The lawyers we used are Ferrier-Gooch. Do you imagine they'd allow themselves to be party to a criminal conspiracy?"

Searching Richard's face, Ross could find there only a need to convince. He tried another approach.

"How did you trace Vusi Matlala? No one knew where he went, after he left prison."

"Ferrier-Gooch found out, for me. Old Gerard Ferrier's in touch with some top trades union men. He learned where Matlala's father lives. Where his brother Zidon works."

"And then, you just acted off the top of your head."

Richard half-smiled. "You know I have that failing."

"No one else prompted you to approach Vusi Matlala?"

For a moment, Richard's gaze wavered. Then he said firmly, "No. It was my own idea."

161

During this conversation, Hal Ensor had remained silent. Now he leaned forward. "What are you going to do?"

"About what?"

"The accusation that Salectron's breaking the arms code."

"There's only one thing I can do," Richard answered. "I shall start our own investigation, immediately. The computer must be secured, and the auditors must make an in-depth check of our dealings over the past few years. We'll have to run factory checks, as well. If there's the smallest indication that the rumours are true, then that will be reported to the proper authorities."

Hal stared at him, biting his lip and frowning. He poked a finger at the torn cheque. "You should get rid of this, shouldn't you?"

"On the contrary," Wragge said coolly, "I shall lock it away in my safe." He collected the pieces and dropped them into an envelope, which he put in his pocket.

"I suppose you're right." Hal shook his head. "What a lousy mess! If you don't need me, I'll be getting back to the office."

"I'll come with you," Wragge said. "Wait for me in the car."

As Hal walked away, Richard turned to Ross.

"You did the right thing in coming to me. I'm sorry I lost my temper with you. What you said . . . it was a very great shock, you understand? I knew nothing." He raised his head to meet Ross's gaze. "I built Salectron from scratch. I'm proud of it. I want it cleared, beyond shadow of doubt."

Ross nodded. He said, "How much do we sell to Lesurier?"

"A certain amount . . . components for jet fighters, for instance. It's all under SADF control. There is absolutely no chance that any of our material reaches unlawful buyers."

"You trust Lesurier?"

"Don't you?"

"There was a story, a few years ago, that he sold to the IRA, and Qaddafi."

"Not Salectron products."

"Can you be sure of that?"

Richard hesitated, then said quietly, "From now on, I can."

His manner had changed at the mention of Lesurier's name, as if it touched some uncertainty in his own mind. "You're thinking of a pirate factory?"

"Or pirated programmes."

"Also possible."

"Yes. Do you know if Lesurier is a shareholder in the Bowers Bay casino?"

Richard looked blank. "No idea. Why?"

"Can you get me a list of his holdings?"

"I think so." Richard stood up. "I must get back to the office, there's a lot to do."

"Shall I go with you?"

"No. I've stolen enough of your time. I'll see you tomorrow, perhaps?"

"Sure, I'll be in."

Richard nodded and followed Hal out to the car. Ross watched them drive away, towards the gate of the estate.

Julie came downstairs.

"What happened, what did Dad say?"

Ross reported the whole conversation, putting no interpretation on it. She listened attentively, and at the end said, "It is totally crazy to suspect my father of arms-running. He's arrogant, he's a political moron, but he has never in his life condoned violence, or terrorism. It's not in his nature, any more than it's in yours."

As Ross made no answer, she said sharply, "You, of all people, should trust him. He was there when you needed help."

"I haven't forgotten." Ross was thinking that whether Richard was guilty or innocent, he was finished in the big league. There was no place there for a man who didn't know what went on in his own back yard.

"He would never involve me in anything criminal," Julie said.

That Ross did believe, and he put his arms round her. She pushed him away.

"I have to know where you stand, Ross. Are you going to tell the police about the cheque?"

163

"Not if he keeps his promise about starting an investigation. If he reneges on that, I'll have to do something."

"Like what?"

"I don't know. I haven't had time to think. Julie, I don't want this to come between us. When will I see you again?"

She shrugged. "I'll be here. He needs me."

He leaned forward to kiss her but she turned from him, and walked quickly away, towards the back of the house.

21

At the time Ross was leaving Malbrook, a closed van arrived at the entrance to the Moroka Township in East London.

The van was painted dark green, and bore the city arms on its front door, with the words EAST LONDON ELECTRICITY SUPPLY along its side. It was accompanied by two uniformed policemen in a patrol car.

The two vehicles drew up on a strip of beaten earth outside the red-brick buildings that housed the township's administrative offices, and its police station.

The driver of the police car stayed at the wheel. His companion, a sergeant, climbed out and went into the station.

The air inside was cold and stale. Several uniformed men crowded the narrow space between the public counter, and the inner offices. In one corner of the room a black youth sat on the floor, crying, his head cradled in his arms.

The telephone on the counter rang and a black clerk picked up the receiver and began to talk rapidly in Xhosa.

The sergeant glanced about him, saw a warrant-officer emerge from the charge-office, and called out to him:

"Sir? I need clearance to go in."

The WO, a young man with buck teeth and a small fair moustache, shook his head.

"Nobody goes in today, sergeant."

"I'm escorting a detail from the Electricity Department. They have to fix a fault at the reservoir supply station."

"I said, nobody can go in. Haven't you heard about the rally, man? Nobody goes in, that's orders."

The sergeant shrugged. He was bull-necked, with a bright blue, up-yours stare. "The rally," he agreed. "You got a hunnerd thousand hysterical kaffirs, in there. What happens if the blerry lights go off?"

The WO sucked his moustache. The big man's stare became derisive. He leaned an elbow on the counter, seeming to enjoy the younger man's dilemma.

"Papers," the WO commanded, holding out his hand.

The sergeant produced his own ID, and a sheaf of forms tied together with a bootlace tag. They included a requisition from the reservoir supply station; an acknowledgement from the City Engineer's Department; an order form covering the work to be done, and giving permission for the van to proceed to the Supply Station, Moroka Village, on Monday afternoon.

All the forms carried the correct stamps and signatures.

Still the WO shook his head.

"So phone," the sergeant prompted.

"Phone who?" The WO was sweating. "The whole damn Force is out playing soldiers."

"I know. We passed them."

"They let you through?" The WO saw a gleam of light.

"Sure." The sergeant leaned forward and flicked over the top form. On the back was a police stamp, and a scrawled signature.

"Volbrecht," the sergeant said. "You know him? I din't recognise the name."

The WO sweated harder. He knew the name, all right, Volbrecht was God out there, but he was from the Cape. His signature was not familiar.

The WO called the Electricity Department. A clerk there confirmed that there had been a requisition, and that a van had been sent out.

"I'll take a look," the WO told the sergeant. He strode out to the parking-lot. The sergeant winked at the men behind the counter, and followed.

The white driver of the van had climbed down from the cab, and was perched on an oil-drum, staring into space. He wore a blue track suit, a blue peaked cap, and dark glasses. The rear doors of the van stood open, and a black labourer in white overalls perched on the back step, smoking a cigarette. A second

166

black man lolled on the bench in the back of the van. He was reading a copy of *Ilanga Lhase Natal*. He glanced briefly at the WO, then went back to his newspaper.

The WO scanned the interior of the van. He knew enough about electrical work to realise that the equipment it contained was genuine. Climbing in, he ordered one of the black men to open a wooden box. It proved to contain fuses. He climbed out again and checked the van's number plates. They seemed to be legitimate.

At his request the driver and the two labourers produced personal ID. All three wore security tags attached to their belts.

The WO added his stamp and signature to the sergeant's papers, and gave permission to proceed.

The reservoir was three and a half kilometres from the entrance to the township, in a shallow valley ringed by hills. The van made the journey at a slow pace, edging through the crowds already pouring towards the Moroka Civic Complex.

Presently the road forked. The left-hand fork led up the hill to the reservoir area, which was protected by high security fences. Guards could be seen patrolling inside the wire. There was a blockhouse at the gate.

The sergeant repeated his spiel to the chief security guard, who seemed relieved to see the repair team, and waved them on to the electricity sub-station at the north-east corner of the preserve.

The two vehicles travelled slowly along the grass track at the side of the reservoir. In the van, one of the labourers was lifting a section of the floorboards. He removed two long canvas bags of the type employed for carrying heavy tools. They now contained AK47s, ammunition, and grenades. He placed the bags alongside the genuine toolbags at the side of the van, and swiftly replaced the floorboards.

At the entrance to the control tower, an armed guard was waiting. The police constable leaned out of the patrol car and spoke to the guard, who presently signalled the driver of the van to approach.

A minute or two later, the driver and the two labourers, carrying the bags, followed the guard into the tower. As the driver passed the door, he hung an enamel disc on the handle; it read, DANGER KEEP OUT.

The hit-man glanced at his watch. Five to four.

The upper floor of the tower, in which he now stood, contained no electrical equipment. It was merely for cooling and storage purposes. Coils of spare cable were stacked along two of its walls.

The north window commanded an excellent view of the valley; the main road snaking from east to west, the Moroka Complex with its supermarket, soccer stadium, hall and parking area.

Keeping well to the side of the window, he watched the crowds massing for the rally. He had to admit that Sousa was right, this was the best point to work from.

The back roads to the stadium were clogged with buses, bikes, and cars, parked and moving. The public turnstiles were thronged. The stands and the playing-field were already two-thirds full.

As the thin man watched, the huge arclights at the corners of the soccer-field flickered, shone for a short space, then went out again.

Nicely timed, the thin man thought.

Below him, the van-driver and his assistant were working on the faulty unit. The armed guard, satisfied that they were what they claimed to be, had gone back to his post at the main door, and was chatting to the police sergeant.

The thin man turned to the rear window. It overlooked a stretch of rough turf to the east of the reservoir. Sousa and his team would land the chopper there, at the last possible moment.

He had assembled his rifle and hidden it under a length of hessian, below the north window.

He returned to his study of the target area. There was a broad plaza between the tarred main road, and the doorway to the shopping-centre. The big cheeses would gather on the plaza to greet Matlala. There were a lot of blacks there, right now; dressed

168

in khaki uniforms, with armbands and caps, carrying sticks, no firearms. A pushover.

He could see two police cars, one at each end of the complex. Over to the left of the entrance there was an area roped off for the TV teams and Press. The thin man grinned. He'd give them something to show for their trouble.

He arranged the support for his rifle, and sat down beside it, goat-eyes narrowed. He felt tense but not nervous, pleased that the moment of truth was near, sure of his skills.

22

The police were waiting for Ross at his apartment; two men in plain clothes. They identified themselves as Colonel Martin de la Rey, and Sergeant Gerhardus Ortlepp of the Security Branch. Ross invited them in.

"We're investigating the death of Mr Charles Sickert of the Bowers Bay casino," Rey said. "We'd like to clear a few points with you."

He was a strange-looking man, Ross thought; tall and lumpy in build, with a long narrow head, the eyes blue, protruberant and unblinking. His voice was precise and cold. He looked more like a Jesuit scholar than a policeman.

His sidekick Ortlepp was regulation tough, with the tucked-in stance and thickened knuckles of the street-fighter. Of the two, Rey was infinitely the more frightening.

"You know that Mr Sickert died last night?" Rey said.

"Yes. A liftman at the hotel told me."

"What time would that have been, sir?"

"About eight a.m. I left on the eight-thirty bus for East London."

Rey nodded. "How well did you know Mr Sickert?"

"Not well." Ross entered into a full account of his dealings with Sickert; the meeting at the trade fair, Sickert's appeal for help with regard to Pampallas, their tour of the gambling areas during Sunday morning, their conversation in the roulette room on Sunday night.

Rey listened quietly. It seemed to Ross that he already knew the answers to many of his questions, that he was talking to cover his real purpose. He returned constantly to Ross's last conversation with Sickert.

"Do I have this right, meneer? You asked Sickert if he had spoken to Pampallas about gambling at the casino?"

"Right. He told me he'd warned Pampallas to leave, and that Pampallas left without unpacking his bags. I said I found that surprising. I didn't expect Pampallas to fold so fast. I suggested that Pampallas might have seen someone in the foyer . . . someone who scared him."

"How did Mr Sickert react to that?"

"He said, perhaps Pampallas saw someone he'd cheated, in the past."

"Anything more?"

"I told him that as Pampallas had quit, there was no reason for me to stay on."

"Did you get the impression that Mr Sickert was going to look into the matter of the tape?"

"He didn't say so, to me. I felt he considered the incident closed."

The questions continued. Ross described the afternoon spent with Zidon Matlala, inspecting the repair shop. He said nothing about their private conversations. He mentioned having dinner with Julie, and their time in the gambling halls. Again Rey returned to the subject of the tape.

"To recap, Mr McRae . . . when Pampallas arrived at the hotel, you and Zidon Matlala were watching the TV scanners in the surveillance centre?"

"Yes. I asked Zidon to enlarge the picture on Tape Three, which covered the area Pampallas was facing. I saw . . ."

"One moment, sir. Why did you ask him to do that?"

"I felt . . . uneasy."

"Why?"

"I felt anxious about the set-up. Something seemed . . . out of kilter."

"I see. You asked for the enlarged picture, and you saw. . . ?"

"Per Frolich, the golfer, talking to the TV man. There were people behind them, a couple of caddies, some hotel guests. They were moving away, leaving the foyer." Ross paused. "You can check what I say by running the tapes."

"Unfortunately, they're not available, they've been reused. According to the casino manager, Mr Marciano, that's standard practice." Seeing Ross stare, Rey went on blandly, "The television set in Sickert's suite was set to 'video', but there was no cassette in the machine. So the position is, there's no record of the events in the foyer . . . unless, of course, there's another tape in existence. Do you think that's possible, sir?"

Ross thought quickly. The truth couldn't prejudice Richard Wragge, or the Matlalas. He said, "Yes, it's possible. I asked Zidon Matlala to make copies of tapes Two and Three. He may have done so."

"You're not sure?"

"No. He said he'd leave them at the desk for me. He didn't." Ross saw Ortlepp's gaze wander round the apartment. "You can search, if you want to."

Rey waved a hand. "Later, maybe. I'd like to inform East London of what you've told me. Could Sergeant Ortlepp perhaps use your telephone?"

"Certainly. It's in the bedroom."

Ortlepp rose and went into the next room. Rey said quietly, "Why didn't Zidon Matlala do as you asked, I wonder?"

"I've no idea. There was a television team in the foyer, maybe they have footage of Pampallas."

"No. We checked."

In the bedroom, Ortlepp's voice conversed in rapid Afrikaans. The words were indistinguishable.

"I was given to understand," Ross said, "that Sickert's death was an accident."

"Looks that way, at the moment." Rey pulled a notebook from his pocket and sat turning the pages. After some minutes, Ortlepp returned to the living-room and resumed his seat. Rey put the notebook away.

"According to the hotel receptionist on duty last night, you received a telephone call, soon after midnight, Mr McRae. Who was it from?"

"From Zidon Matlala."

"What was the purpose of his call?"

172

"He wanted me to meet Vusi Matlala, his brother. Vusi was staying in Zidon's quarters, as I'm sure you know, Colonel."

"You know Vusi Matlala?"

"I've known him all my life."

Ortlepp spoke suddenly. "Down on the farm? One of your Dad's cowboys?"

Ross looked at Ortlepp, who was sitting with legs sprawled, one arm hooked over the back of his chair. His voice and smile were intended to insult. His manner took Ross back ten years, he remembered with a drying of the mouth the batons swinging, the explosion of pain in his head and ribs.

He said levelly, "None of the Matlalas ever worked on our farm. Simeon Matlala helped my grandfather to build the school, and taught in it. His sons were my friends. We grew up together."

"So what do you think of your friends, now?"

"I think that Vusi Matlala is one of the most important men in the country."

"That so? What did you talk about, last night? Politics?"

"We talked about old times. Drank a few beers."

"Old times?" Ortlepp laughed. "Like, in gaol?"

Rey said with sudden sharpness, "Leave that!" Ortlepp straightened in his chair as if he'd been kicked.

"Since you gave us permission, Mr McRae," Rey said, "we'll give the apartment a quick lookover."

"Go ahead. Nothing's locked."

Ross watched the two men search the flat. They were quick, neat and thorough, but their faces showed no enthusiasm for the job. When they were done, Ross accompanied them to the front door.

"You've been helpful, Mr McRae," Rey said. "How long will you be staying in Johannesburg?"

"About three weeks. I came here to settle my father's estate . . . he died recently. I'm due back in the USA at the end of the month."

"We can reach you at this address, if need be?"

"Here, or at Salectron House."

173

Rey handed Ross a card. "If you think of anything else you'd like to tell us, will you please call me, at this number?"

"Sure." Ross put the card in his pocket.

When Rey and Ortlepp left, Ross locked the door.

He found he was sweating. He was not deceived by Rey's bland manner. Rey represented the power that could detain without recourse to the courts, without notification to family, priest, or lawyer. His was not a mind to leave stones unturned. He would go on probing until he had the full story of the events at Bowers Bay.

All that Ross could do was keep his mouth shut about the cheque, and hope that something would come up to clear Salectron, Richard, and himself.

23

In the patrol car outside the electricity-tower, the sergeant sat listening to a radio message.

It emanated from a plain van parked opposite St Ninian's church in East London. The voice was even, tense.

"There's about twenty cars lined up along the road. The priest's on the pavement outside the house, he's talking to the UDF top brass. Two of the Matlalas are with them. Not Vusi, the other two. Tall one, Zidon . . . he's in a dark grey suit, white shirt, wears specs, no hat. Shorter one, Themba, is in a red track suit, black running-shoes.

"There's two lead cars. First one's a 1984 Valiant, white body, dark blue glass, looks in good shape. Second one's a 1980 Merc sedan, cream, also got dark glass." The voice recited the cars' registration numbers, then broke off to announce, "The fuzz has arrived. I'll get back to you."

There was a pause of more then ten minutes before the voice resumed. "Two pigs on bikes, they checked all the cars. It's OK, no grief. We're still waiting to roll. The brother in the track suit went inside, the parade's hung up. The pigs are talking to a bunch of coons round the lead cars."

Another pause, then: "Action, we have action. Vusi and his brother came out of the house, Vusi is wearing a leather jacket, black, three-quarter length, a khaki cap with a peak, dark glasses. He's climbing into the second car with the UDF bugger. The track suit, and the other brother's in the number one car.

"OK, now, we're rolling, the whole thing's rolling. We're going to fall in at the back of the parade, we'll stay with it as long as we can, we can't get too near Moroka Township, too much fuzz around there.

"You got the picture, Vusi Matlala is in the second car. The time I have here is exactly four-forty-two. Over."

The sergeant checked his wristwatch. "Four-forty-two" he confirmed. "We'll be in touch. Over and out."

He picked up the walkie-talkie on the seat beside him, and checked that the men in the tower had picked up the message from the van. Satisfied, he climbed out of the patrol car and strolled over to where the guard and the police driver stood.

In the tower, the thin man waited for the cortège of cars to make its appearance.

Daylight was fading, but the lights of the stadium were full on, illuminating the whole of the Moroka Complex. He could see the dignitaries lined up on the plaza, the media with cameras at the ready, the police cars, five of them now, waiting at the roadside.

On the floodlit field, the crowd was singing. The thin man did not understand the words, but he recognised the fervour of the freedom songs.

He knew this was a political job. People killed a politico, they wanted good publicity. That was part of the deal, it was what made his money good.

The radio on the floor beside him told him that the cortège had passed through the circle of troops outside the townships, and reached the administration offices. If there was no hitch, it should be at the complex in around seven minutes' time.

He had already adjusted the telescopic sights of his rifle. He knew the exact angle and range of his target. He waited.

At the rim of the valley, to his right, he heard hooters blowing in unison. A line of cars appeared on the road, moving at a steady pace. The singing in the stadium surged higher.

There was a droning in the sky. An army helicopter swung into sight, hovered, banked, veered away in a wide circle.

The thin man kept his eyes on the line of cars.

It reached the complex. The white Valiant moved a short way past the entrance. The second car stopped exactly opposite the row of greeters.

176

The door of the car opened and Matlala stepped out, followed by a big, heavily-built man in the UDF colours. For a moment, this man's bulk obscured Matlala. Then he hurried forward, hand outstretched, preparing to introduce his companion to the waiting dignitaries.

Matlala stood alone, an uninterrupted target.

The thin man tensed. He did not see anyone of importance down there. Quality and destiny did not matter to him. He did not even see a man. He saw, on the cross-threads of the sight, a human head which he wished to destroy.

He squeezed the trigger.

Far below him, the head of his victim blew apart, the arms swung upward in a grotesque parody of prayer, the body lifted and crashed to the ground.

The sound of the shot was drowned by the roaring of the chopper as it came in to land on the stretch of turf. Two guards on the far side of the reservoir started towards it, moving uncertainly, rifles at the ready.

The thin man was already dropping down the ladder, joining the rush towards the main door. He did not see the turmoil on the plaza, the people scattering, the UDF man stooping over the bloodied pavement, frantically waving to the remaining cars to go, go, get clear.

The tower-guard, who had been staring at the chopper, turned in surprise and died as he stood, shot at point blank range by the police driver. Someone in the chopper opened fire on the approaching sentries, killing both. At the gatehouse, two men scrambled into a truck and began to race along the road towards the tower.

The sergeant placed oblong plastic boxes on the seat of the patrol car and in the cab of the van. He joined the other four men, who were running across the turf to the chopper. They were aboard, and the chopper was lifting off the ground before the guards' truck had covered half the distance from the blockhouse.

The chopper gained height, and swung east. On the ground, the patrol car and van exploded, spreading burning fuel across the grass, sending up columns of oily black smoke.

177

At the Moroka Complex, a group of men were carrying Matlala's body into the building, while a line of officials and policemen linked arms to prevent the media men from following.

A loudspeaker started to blare. Within the stadium, the singing faltered and died. For a short while the crowd was still. Then it began to boil like an ants' nest, sending its thousands out through the turnstiles and gates, into the streets of the township.

24

Ross learned of the assassination from Theo Kaplan. The telephone was ringing as he came out of the bathroom, and when he picked up the receiver, Theo said in the bald tones of shock that Vusi Matlala was dead.

"There was a news flash on the radio . . . he was shot about half an hour ago. Shot through the head, they think it was an explosive bullet . . . my God, Ross . . ."

Ross said urgently, "What about the others, what about Zidon and Themba, are they OK?"

"I don't know. The report just said, Vusi was shot as he arrived at the stadium in East London."

"Can you check with the Press, get more details?"

"I'll try."

"Pull every string you can, Theo. I'll come over to your place, but I must call at Wragge's home, first. See you in about an hour."

He hung up, his mind churning with questions . . . Vusi, his brothers, Simeon. The tape, the cheque, Richard's part in all this, and above all, his own failure to foresee disaster.

He dressed and headed for Malbrook, breaking the speed limits all the way. As the Lamborghini turned into the garage-yard, Julie ran out of the house to meet him.

"You've heard?" Her white face stooped to the window. "Oh Ross, I'm so sorry."

He shook his head, rejecting sympathy. "Where's Richard, do you know?"

"He was at the office a few minutes ago. I phoned to tell him about Vusi. He was terribly upset, he sounded distraught. We couldn't talk for long . . . he has the auditors with him, something about securing the computer against interference? He said he had a lot of people to see."

"Did he say who?"

"No. He said he'd be late home . . . that he might even stay in town, at the club. He said he was booked to fly to Harare tomorrow, but he wasn't sure he'd be able to make it."

Julie's voice shook. "Ross, I have to know . . . does Vusi's death have anything to do with . . . with what you told me about Selectron?"

"It could have."

"Then I want to hear about it."

"Darling, I can't talk now, I'm on my way to see Theo."

"I'll go with you, we can talk on the way."

"No!" He sounded sharper than he meant to, and said more gently, "You're safer here, believe me."

Julie reached down and jerked the key from the ignition. "Get out of the car."

He hesitated, then complied. She took a step back from him, staring at him with angry eyes.

"Do you think that's all I'm worried about? Being safe? I want to know what's going on!"

"I don't know, myself. I can only guess." Ross spoke slowly, trying to marshall his thoughts. "Back in the States, Senator Cromlech warned me that Vusi would be released, and that an attempt would be made on his life. Cromlech and your father have been good friends for years. He knew I'd pass the news on to Richard. Perhaps it was a tip off."

Julie frowned. "I don't see the connection between Vusi Matlala and Salectron."

"There's an overlap of interests," Ross said. "Cromlech heads a group that supports liberation movements around the globe. The same group acts as watchdog over the supply of arms to racist regimes. Over the past few weeks there've been rumours that our products are reaching such regimes. I think that when Vusi received your father's offer, he checked with Cromlech, and was advised not to touch the money."

180

"But Dad's started an investigation. Surely that proves he had nothing to do with illegal trading?"

"It may help, but the fact remains, Richard's signature is on that cheque, and Richard persuaded me to go down to Bowers Bay. The world is going to believe he tried to bribe Vusi, and that I was the bag-man. From there, it's a short step to believing that when bribery failed, a decision was taken to kill Vusi."

It was nearly dark in the courtyard, and someone inside the house switched on the security lamps at the corners of the building. The sudden blaze of blue-white light shone on Julie's frightened face.

"What are we going to do?"

"Find out who set us up." Ross tried to sound confident. "I have a couple of ideas . . . some people I'll see tomorrow. In the meantime, I have to find Zidon and Themba Matlala. That's why I must talk to Theo. If anyone can get a message to them, he can."

"Let me come with you."

"No, love." Ross put his hands on her shoulders. "I need you to stay here. I asked Richard to get some information for me. If he's not coming home, he may phone it through to you. If he does, write it down. I'll call you later, from Theo's. Don't try to reach me at the apartment. The line there is probably bugged."

As she opened her mouth to question him, he silenced her with a kiss. "I have to go. Stay in the house, Julie, and keep the staff with you. Do you have a gun?"

"Yes, but . . ."

"If any stranger approaches the house, use it. I'll see you as soon as I can."

He watched her walk into the house and close the door. At the gate of the estate, he stopped to warn the guard on duty to be especially vigilant, and to allow no strangers on to the property for any reason whatever.

Theo owned a bungalow in a run-down suburb close to the township where he had his clinic.

As Ross drove south from Malbrook, he overtook several police vehicles, and a line of Rakels packed with soldiers.

The conditioned reflex to any emergency, he thought; a flexing of the security muscle. The promise and hope of Vusi Matlala seemed over before it had begun.

Theo had news to give.

"I spoke to Matt Mulvaney of the *Star*. The murder was a gang job. Five men, armed with sophisticated weapons. Three of them, a white and two blacks, passed themselves off as employees of the East London Electricity Commission. The other two posed as security policemen.

"They used two vehicles; an ELEC repair van, and a police patrol car. They carried all the right identity documents and permits, including a pass signed . . . supposedly . . . by the man in charge of police operations in the area . . . a Brigadier Dion Volbrecht.

"After the killing, they left the scene in a helicopter that carried the indentification symbols of the SA Defence Force." Theo sounded despairing. "The effect is that the government had Vusi assassinated."

"Which shows that the government had nothing to do with it."

"Try convincing the people in the townships."

"Theo, do you remember, the night we dined at Richard's place, you told me about a gang that killed a journalist?"

"Stendal? You think this was the same lot?"

"I think there's a conspiracy. Right-wingers, probably. I think they hired a contract killer, to shoot Vusi. I think I saw the man."

"You what?"

"I saw him on tape, at the casino. Pampallas recognised him as a pro killer, and got the hell out. Sickert wasn't so lucky."

"What in hell are you talking about?"

"Sit down," Ross said, "and I'll explain."

In Cape Town an emergency meeting of the Security Council, in session since six p.m., was drawing to a close. The mood around the table was tense to the point of acrimony.

"Clearly," the President said, "we are faced with a conspiracy designed to destroy our credibility among blacks. The shot that killed Matlala was fired from State property, the hit-team masqueraded as State employees, they used weapons and vehicles of the type employed by our security forces." He tapped the pile of reports before him. "Whether the conspiracy is external, or internal, of the left or the right, we don't yet know."

"Internal, of the right," said the Minister of Defence bluntly. "The radical left would have killed you, not Matlala."

"In a sense," said the Minister of the Interior, "it's the same thing. With one shot, you eliminate two enemies."

The President glanced at the Chief of Police. "The townships," he said. "What is happening there?"

The Chief of Police, who had arrived late, lifted his shoulders. "There's been sporadic rioting. The crowd at Moroka broke loose when they heard Matlala was dead. Burned down the admin offices. There was some looting at the supermarket. Volbrecht moved his men in quickly and the situation is under control."

"For how long?" muttered the Minister of Defence.

"It requires firm action, of course." The Chief of Police was of the old school, unsurprised that Matlala had been murdered, sure of what remedies must be applied. "If we bring in the known activists, right or left . . ."

"I won't have a witch-hunt," the President said.

The Police Chief looked at him. "Sir, the unrest will spread like wildfire, when the news is out. There's already been stone-throwing on the roads round East London. A mob has fired a train in Port Elizabeth, by tomorrow morning there'll be unrest all over the place, and once the unions get organised . . . you can't dodge the issue, Mr President. A firm hand is needed."

"The people I want to see in gaol," said the President quietly, "are the people who murdered Matlala. Not a hotch-potch of political dissidents."

"As Carl has said," interpolated a senior Intelligence Officer, "the killing was probably arranged by right-wing extremists. Your own life is on the line, sir. For that reason alone, we have to take every precaution."

"No blanket detentions," insisted the President, "though I thank you for your concern." He glanced at the faces round the table. "Last week, I took a certain course, and I intend to stick to it. I'll be speaking on television tonight, directly after the news. I shall put my case . . . our case . . . honestly, to the people of this country. I shall appeal for their trust and their co-operation. I believe it will be forthcoming provided we all, each and every one of us, keep to our side of the bargain." He leaned forward, as if he might physically dispel the weight of scepticism about him. "Which means, gentlemen, that there will be no mass arrests, no show of force. Do I make myself clear?"

Before anyone could answer, the red telephone on the table pealed. The President lifted the receiver, snapped "Ja?", then said more quietly, "Dion. Yes, what is it?"

The telephone crackled. The President listened, and the men watching him saw his expression change from weariness, to incredulity, to a wild sort of hope. After some minutes, he said simply, "Thank you, Dion. Keep me informed, please." He replaced the receiver and glanced round the circle.

"Vusi Matlala is alive," he said simply. "The man who died was his brother Themba."

A burst of questions erupted. The Minister of the Interior raised his voice above them. "How could they make such a mistake? The report said categorically, Vusi Matlala was shot."

184

The President held up both hands. "Please, gentlemen." As silence returned, he said, "The victim's head was blown apart. There was no face to identify. The confusion at the scene was very great. The police on the spot checked the body and found Vusi Matlalas's identity book in the pocket of the jacket. The media got to hear of that, and spread the news that Vusi had been killed.

"When Volbrecht reached the complex, he was able to talk to the people who organised the rally. They told him that before setting out to the rally, Vusi and Themba exchanged clothes. It was a trick, designed to protect Vusi, and it did save his life. Volbrecht checked the dead man's fingerprints. They do not match those of Vusi Matlala, which we have on file."

The Chief of Police said urgently, "Where is Vusi Matlala?"

"Volbrecht doesn't know, yet. After the shooting, the other cars scattered, nobody knows where to."

"The killers are still loose, Mr President. They'll try again. We have to find Matlala before they do."

"Agreed, and that is your priority, Stefan, to find Vusi Matlala. Also his brother Zidon and his father Simeon. They have to be seen to be alive. I have to meet with them, talk to them, their presence at this time is crucial."

The President turned to his Press Secretary. "Walter, my statement. It must be amended. First check with East London, be sure we have the facts correct; then amend the speech and be ready to circulate copies to the media immediately after I've spoken. Oh, and warn the head of television. The news that Matlala is alive should be made public, but I shall be grateful if it is left to me to present the details. Paul," he turned to a man further down the table, "I want an urgent debate in the House, tomorrow, will you please arrange that?"

He was revitalised, his mind racing to meet the consequences of Matlala's survival. He had instructions for everyone, and quit the conference room only minutes before he was due to make his appearance on television.

His colleagues remained to tie up loose ends. An hour later, the Minister of Defence and the Chief of Police left the building together. A crowd had gathered in Parliament Street, and to avoid it, they left by a rear door, and strolled through the gardens to the head of Adderley Street.

The Minister said, "Will he survive?"

He was talking about the President. The Police Chief shrugged.

"Miracles happen."

"And will you find the Matlalas?"

"Finding a fox-hole is one thing. Persuading the fox to leave it, is another."

"You mean, because the killers are still loose?"

"I mean, because the Matlalas think we are the killers."

"How will you go about it? They could be anywhere . . ."

"There are people we can ask." The Chief of Police did not embroider on this statement. The Minister of Defence had many excellent qualities, but discretion was not one of them.

"Appeals!" snorted Theo Kaplan. He obliterated the image of the President with an angry stab of the finger. "Vusi Matlala won't respond to any appeals! Ducky, ducky, ducky, come and be killed!"

"At least he's alive." Ross stood up and moved to the telephone in the corner of Theo's living-room. He took out his pocket-book and found the number Simeon Matlala had given him, the number of the store at Stannard's Post.

A soft voice answered almost at once. "Vijay Ramdas."

"Mr Ramdas, this is Ross McRae. I'm phoning about the attack on Vusi Matlala. You know he survived?"

"Oh yes, Mr McRae, I was watching television. I thank God Vusi is alive, but the brother is dead and that is a terrible thing. A sad day, Mr McRae, a terrible day."

"Does Simeon know?"

"Alas, I can't tell. He heard the first news at six. He came straight to the village."

"Is he still there? I must get in touch with him, it's very urgent."

"No, I am sorry to tell you he has left the district. He took his brother's car and left . . . oh, nearly one hour ago."

"Did he say where he was going?"

"No, not at all. I only saw him for a moment, you understand? He came to the store to say goodbye. He said, 'Ram, it's best you don't know anything.' I think he's very afraid, Mr McRae."

"Simeon doesn't scare easily."

"Not for himself, no indeed, but for his sons, for what may happen next, of that he is afraid."

"Mr Ramdas, if you hear anything, will you let me know? I must talk to the Matlalas."

"Tell me your number."

Ross gave Theo's number. The storekeeper promised to do what he could, and rang off.

"A waste of time," Theo said, when Ross repeated the conversation. "Simeon will go into hiding like his sons, and quite right too. Those bastards will try again."

"I have to reach Zidon."

"Don't try, Ross. Keep out of the crossfire."

"I told you, Zidon has a copy of the tape, he has a picture of the killer. If we can lay hands on that, we may be able to identify the man. We may get a line on the people who hired him. We can at least publicise the picture, which should put an end to the contract, and buy us a little time."

"Ross, I'm telling you, leave this to the police. It's their job."

"The Matlalas won't deal with the police, they won't hand over the tape to any policeman, not after what happened today."

"What makes you think they'll hand it to you?"

Ross gave a lopsided smile. "We're all on the same hit-list. I saw the tape, remember?"

"All the more reason to keep your head down."

"I've kept it down too long. Everything's on the line, now; my career, my life, Julie's life, perhaps. The tape is the one chance we have."

"You realise you could lead the pack right to Vusi? You'll be watched by the police, by those other jackals . . ."

"The fact that I may lead them to Vusi is probably the only reason I'm still alive. Theo, I need your help. I want you to help me get a message to the Matlalas."

"Man, I don't have a hot line . . ."

"You know people who do. Talk to them, ask them to pass on the message. Say . . ." Ross thought a moment, "say it's from Polela. Say that Polela wishes to know the name of the dog that was given to him by his grandfather on his tenth birthday. Say that the parcel that was promised to Polela never arrived. Say that he needs it urgently, that he will use it for the sake of the people who stay here."

"'Stay here'? What's that mean?"

"They'll understand. See if you can fix a meeting, anything. If you have any success, call me at Salectron, not at my apartment, that line's probably tapped. Call me at Salectron. If I'm not in the building leave a message. Say, 'Anthony Rowley called.' I'll get back to you when I can. We can meet somewhere. At Malbrook, perhaps."

When Theo had committed the message to memory, Ross nodded. "Fine. I'll be moving about a bit, tomorrow. I'll be with my lawyer at nine-fifteen, my stockbroker after that, then at Salectron. If there's any change of plan, I'll call you here, OK?"

"OK."

"May I phone Julie before I leave?"

"Go ahead."

Julie said there had been no word from Richard. "I ran the message tape in his bedroom. There's nothing on it since Monday a week ago. The hall porter at his club says he hasn't booked in there."

"You could try Hal Ensor. He may know where Richard is."

"No. If Dad left no message, that's the way he wants it."

It was in both their minds that if Richard had decided to cut and run, raising a hue and cry wouldn't help him.

When Ross turned from the telephone, he found Theo standing in the middle of the living-room, holding out a stump-nosed automatic and a clip of ammunition.

"Take it. Don't shoot anyone I wouldn't."

As Ross hesitated, Theo said quietly, "You have to survive."

Ross dropped the cold metal into his coat pocket.

"Thanks, Theo. Thanks for everything."

The traffic on the road north was heavy. Ross kept an eye on the rear-view mirrors. He was fairly certain he was being trailed, by at least one car. It was a Mazda saloon, dark grey, fairly new, the kind of car he would not normally have noticed. What made it noticeable, now, was its persistence. It picked up speed when he did, slowed when he slowed.

Ross made no attempt to throw it off. For one thing, he didn't know if it contained friends or enemies. For another, he believed what he'd said to Theo, that his link with Vusi Matlala gave both factions a reason to keep him alive, at least for the time being.

He was certain that his apartment had been bugged. An organisation that could set up an operation like the one at East London, would have no problem bugging a flat or setting up a phone-tap. It could even have been done by Rey or Ortlepp, during their search that afternoon.

He tried to remember what he'd said to the police. He'd mentioned the tape, Pampallas, his talks with Sickert. Not the cheque. That gave Julie some protection, at least.

There was an underground garage at the apartment block, with an attendant permanently on duty. The car would be as safe there as anywhere.

Reaching the apartment, Ross made a thorough examination of the telephone, light-fittings, radiators and pipes. He found no listening devices.

From the flat he went to the caretaker's office on the ground floor. Sampie Cronje was an ex-prizefighter who had shared training-runs in the days when Ross was an athletics contender. He was watching a fight on television, but switched off when Ross appeared.

"Trouble with my telephone, Sampie," Ross said. "A voice cutting in, all the time. I asked my secretary to report it to the telephone company, last week. Did they send anyone to fix it?"

Sampie smiled. "Ja, they did, . . . this morning. Lessee, must've been ten o'clock."

"Did they go to my flat?"

"Ja, I took 'em up, and stayed there with 'em. They said the fault wasn't in the instrument, it was in the internal cables. They went down to the basement to have a look, nothing wrong there, so then they took a look at the service rooms, next to you, and that's where the fault was. They said they fixed it. Why, Ross? You still getting grief?"

"'Fraid so. Did the mechanic give you an order form to sign?"

"Sure. I wouldn't a let 'im in, else." Sampie leafed through a bunch of forms tacked to the soft-board near his door. He showed one of them to Ross. "Can't read the blerry signature, but it's the phone company's form, and the order's from Salectron, see?"

"How long did it take them to fix the fault?"

Sampie considered. "They were here about a hour this morning. Said they didn't have all the right stuff, they'd have to come back this afternoon. Four o'clock, they came, left again about six. So it should be fixed, after all that. If I was you, Ross, I'd fetch 'em back, make 'em do a proper job."

"Did you get the mechanic's name?"

"Nah, but I'd know him. About five-nine, good build, hunnerd-sixty pound, reddish hair goin' back on the forehead, blue eyes. I din't like 'im. Seen his kind too often. Put the knee in when the ref's not looking, that kind. The other one was just a donkey, carried the tools." Sampie frowned, then said surprisingly, "The first one reminded me of a cop."

Startled, Ross said, "One particular cop?"

"Nah. Any cop. Tried to boss me around. Stared at me when I told him he couldn't just march into your apartment. I din't let 'im touch any of your things. I kep' my beady on 'im, I tell you."

"Thanks, Sampie."

"You get the bees back here," Sampie repeated, "make 'em do a proper job."

Sleep did not come easily, that night.

Ross thought about Themba Matlala. In the old days at Halladale, Themba had been something of a clown, a blurred copy of Vusi, aping his god, never quite making it.

Once, when they were swimming in the dam, Vusi had fooled about, pretending to be drowning. Themba, no swimmer, had plunged in to save him, and had to be saved himself.

It would have been Themba's idea, that he stand in for Vusi for the drive to the stadium. Because of that devotion, Themba was dead and Vusi alive. Ross did not believe that Vusi would squander the gift.

He would do whatever it took to survive.

What would he do, where would he go? He wouldn't stay in East London. He'd make for one of the major cities. Natal wasn't his natural stamping-ground. It would be Johannesburg, or one of the satellite towns along the Rand, where the unions were strongest, and the name Matlala counted for something.

Everyone would be hunting Vusi. Sooner or later he'd have to come out of hiding. To lead, he must be visible.

Could Theo get a message to him? Could anyone, at this time? And if the message reached him, would he respond?

It was a question of trust. Trust was the vanished gold, no longer current in South Africa.

Ross thought of Julie, envying the emotional certainty that allowed her to make her decisions quickly, and stay with them.

Somewhere along the line, he had to trust his own judgement.

Accepting Richard's innocence, against the evidence, had been an act of faith.

Julie was trustworthy. Old Uncle James McRae. Simeon Matlala. Theo Kaplan.

Trusting them was easy. It was more difficult to accept that de la Rey was reliable, that he was concerned with keeping Vusi Matlala alive and therefore an ally.

Ross dozed for a while, and awoke to hear storm winds rattling the windows of the flat. He got out of bed to close them, and remained to look out at the downpour.

He could see the cars along the kerb, directly below. His adversaries were down there, waiting and watching. Fifty yards to left and right the lashing rain obscured all vision. What lay beyond, was dream. Reality was encapsulated in this narrow world of his own vision.

It came to him that what mattered was not whom he trusted, but who trusted him.

If Zidon Matlala trusted him, he would hand over the tape. If Zidon mistrusted him, that was an end of it.

The importance of Ross McRae, if he had any importance at all, was that he might be the focus of one man's trust.

Understanding that, he understood what he had to do, and the doubts of the lonely past, and the embittered present, fell away from him.

It was his moment of personal liberation.

26

In an office not far from Ross's apartment, Breyten confronted Mathias.

"We have to get rid of McRae at once," he said. "He knows about the tape. He told the police about it, we heard him. He knows about the arms deals. Rosendal confirms that."

Mathias made no answer. He poured coffee into a mug and sipped it, eyelids lowered. His lack of response infuriated Breyten.

"Did you hear what I said? McRae's dangerous. he won't let up. He's as stubborn as a rooting pig."

Mathias said softly, "I agree, he's troublesome, but we can't dispose of him yet."

"Why not? The longer he's left, the more damage he'll do."

Mathias sighed. "Use your head a little. McRae will try to get a copy of the tape from Zidon Matlala. If we can keep track of McRae, he will lead us to Zidon, who in turn will lead us to brother Vusi. Vusi is our prime concern. He's a far greater threat than McRae can ever be. Once we've traced Vusi Matlala, and dealt with him, we can worry about lesser matters."

"The trouble with you," said Breyten viciously, "is that you can never admit you're wrong. You've made one mistake after another. The casino, that big laugh in East London. If we'd used Sousa, Matlala would be dead, by now, the right Matlala, not some half-cock brother. Now I say we have to finish off McRae, and quickly. If you don't want to listen to me, I'll go direct to Senekal."

Mathias lifted his head, and his expression caused Breyten, no stranger to ferocity, to pause.

"Senekal knows the situation," Mathias said. "You won't make him change his mind."

Breyten sat back in his chair, breathing hard. If Mathias had got at the old General, there was no use trying that line. Better to talk to Kestell, who knew when it was time to cut the cackle, and act.

As if Mathias read the other man's thoughts, he said smoothly, "Kestell is out of the country. He left for Italy this morning."

Breyten's mouth jerked. "Why? Why the change of plan?"

"No change," Mathias answered. "There are some loose ends to be tied up, in Zurich."

"And your South American pal? Has he remembered some urgent business in Rio?"

"No. We have him safe. He won't leave until he's done what we paid him to do." Mathias set down his empty coffee mug. "Everything is under control, Breyten, so don't worry about what doesn't concern you. Your job is to make sure we don't lose McRae, a simple matter of intensive surveillance. I'm sure you'll perform it admirably."

Breyten left soon after. As the door closed on him, Mathias waved a dismissive hand. His eyes, coal black in his pale face, showed no displeasure at Breyten's intransigence.

There was nothing to worry about. Matlala, McRae, anyone else who stood in his way, would be removed. His own future was arranged, secure, certain.

He poured more coffee for himself, and drank it, smiling. The truth was that the psychopathic tendencies that Mathias had exhibited all his life, had now passed over into certifiable insanity.

27

Ross went out early to buy the morning newspapers.

The aftermath of the attempt on Vusi Matlala's life was already appalling. Across the country, workers were joining in a spontaneous stoppage of work, which, if it continued, would paralyse the harbours, railways, mines and factories. In the townships, the bus and railway stations were besieged by chanting demonstrators. The temper of these crowds was described as explosive.

The reaction of right-wing whites was as inflammatory. Groups of Vigilantes were mustering under arms, their spokesmen indulging in an orgy of racial vindictive, their Press condemning Matlala as a revolutionary, and demanding the President's immediate resignation.

In Cape Town, the President called for calm, and announced that the events in East London would be the subject of an urgent debate that afternoon.

The Cabinet was said to be firmly behind the President, the security forces keeping a low profile. How long would it be, Ross wondered, before loyalty and restraint gave way to disaffection and a call to the blood?

He left the apartment at eight-thirty. Down in the basement he checked the Lamborghini carefully before climbing in and starting the engine.

The traffic outside was heavy, and he edged his way slowly to the Killarney shopping centre. It was impossible to determine if he was being trailed, but he took it for granted. He found a pay phone and called Julie.

"Good morning. Did you sleep well?"

"In patches. Can I talk?"

"Yes, go ahead."

"Dad called, long distance, half an hour ago."

"Did he say where from?"

"No." Julie sounded anxious. "He gave me a list . . . names of companies and people. He said I must hand it to you personally, as soon as possible, and he wants to meet you, here at the house, at four this afternoon."

"Good. I'm due to meet Laurie Absolon at his office, at nine-fifteen, can you make that?"

"Yes. I'll see you there."

Ross's next call was to Colonel Rey at police headquarters. He told Rey about the listening device, pointing out that it had probably been in operation throughout the interview with Rey and Ortlepp. He passed on the description Sampie Cronje had given of the red-haired mechanic.

Rey was non-commital. He would, he said, "Look into the matter." Unnecessary, thought Ross, if the tap had been set up by the police, and if it had not, too bloody late to serve any purpose.

The legal firm of Ferrier, Gooch and Absolon was one of the most prestigious in the city. Dealing mainly in corporate law, it served many of the Rand's industrial giants, but it retained on its books a certain number of lesser clients, of whom Ross's father had been one.

Laurens Absolon was handling the McRae estate. He was also one of the team looking after Selectron's interests, so Ross knew him on both a personal and a business level.

The firm had large premises in a block near Eloff Street. Julie met him in the waiting-room a few minutes before nine-fifteen, and handed him Richard's list. He had time only to scan it before a secretary summoned them to Absolon's office.

The lawyer was a small man, plump, with a round red face, black hair smoothed back, and eyes the colour of dark olives. He greeted them fulsomely, and reached for the file on his desk, but Ross stopped him.

"Laurie, I'm not here to discuss the estate. Something else has

196

come up, which I think very urgent. It concerns a cheque for a million rand, signed by Julie's father Richard Wragge. The cheque was sent to Vusi Matlala at the Bowers Bay casino. It was accompanied by a letter from your firm."

Absolon glanced quickly from Ross to Julie. As she made no sign, he said, "Where did you get this information?"

"Julie and I were at the casino, last weekend. I spoke to Zidon and Vusi Matlala. They showed me the cheque and the correspondence."

"I see." Absolon's eyelids flickered, as if he was making a rapid calculation. "Did . . . er . . . Mr Matlala accept the cheque?"

"He tore it up, and asked me to return the pieces to Richard, with a message that he's not interested in taking money from white capitalists."

"Umh. Tell me . . . did Mr Wragge request you to meet with the Matlalas?"

"No, but he was instrumental in my meeting a man named Charles Sickert, the security chief at the casino."

Absolon looked up sharply. "The man who died in a fall?"

"Yes. Sickert invited me to Bowers Bay, ostensibly to help him deal with a gambler named Pampallas. I believe the invitation was a blind. The real intention was to get me to the casino and involve me in the transfer of the cheque."

"For what purpose?"

"So that if there is a police investigation into any criminal activity connected with the casino, Richard and I will be the scapegoats."

"Criminal?" Absolon's hands made a small movement of alarm. "What do you mean?"

"I think Sickert was murdered," Ross said.

"But the papers reported it as an accident!"

"The papers are wrong. Someone pushed him out of a seventh-floor window. I was questioned, yesterday afternoon, by a Colonel de la Rey of the Security Branch."

"Security, did you say?"

"Yes."

"Did you mention the cheque?"

197

"No, but I think I'm entitled to some explanations. Was Richard flying solo, or are there other donors to this fund?"

"That information is confidential . . ."

"Laurie, Vusi Matlala was offered a million bucks, he turned it down, and hours later, an attempt was made to kill him. There's going to be one hell of a witch-hunt, and if my neck's at stake, I'll have to come clean about the cheque."

"Well, of course." Absolon cleared his throat. "There is no need for shame, you understand, the offer was well-intentioned and entirely legal."

"Then you won't mind giving me the names of the people who put up the money."

"You know quite well I can't do that. My clients are entitled to protection."

"I'm your client too, aren't I? I may be facing a police charge. The man who invited me to the casino is dead, murdered. The man you sent that cheque to would also be dead, if his brother hadn't taken the bullet for him. There's a criminal conspiracy behind it, Laurie, and I want the names of the people who dragged me into it."

"I assure you, the principals are beyond reproach."

"In that case, they won't mind meeting me and answering a few straight questions." As Absolon still hesitated, Ross said bluntly, "If they're not on the level, your firm, and the Stormont Bank, are in for a lot of very damaging publicity."

Absolon touched a fingertip to an eyebrow. "Well, certainly, it can't hurt to ask them. Let me speak to my partners. Perhaps an approach can be made to the people concerned. If they agree to your request, where can I reach you?"

"At Salectron between twelve and one."

"Today? I'm not sure there's time . . ."

"Pull out all the stops. It's to your advantage. One more question . . ."

"What?" Absolon was clearly not eager to hear it.

"Who owns the Bowers Bay casino?"

"I've no idea, none at all. I always thought it was homeland-owned."

"I don't think so. I want to know the names of the holding company, the company that has the gambling rights, and any large shareholders."

Absolon nodded. "That shouldn't be too difficult." He drew out a handkerchief and pressed it to his neck. "I'll get back to you as soon as I can. That's a promise."

As they left the building, Julie said, "You might have got more out of him if I hadn't been there."

"I don't think so. You represent the Wragge interest. Laurie has a healthy respect for that."

"Where do we go now?"

"To see my stockbroker," Ross answered.

Lem Abramson was a large old man with a tired-lion face. Still a power on the stock market, he had an irreverent attitude to power itself. He greeted Julie with pleasure, and asked Ross what he could do for him.

Ross laid Richard's list on the desk. "These stocks," he said. "What would you advise?"

Lem glanced at the list and sniffed. "No," he said.

"Why not? They all produce for Armscor, and Armscor is the country's biggest exporter, right?"

"Right about Armscor, wrong about these companies. I'm told half their contracts have been cancelled over the past two-three months."

"Do you know why?"

Lem tilted his head, looking wary. "Times change. What was nice yesterday, isn't nice today."

"Nice as in wholesome, squeaky-clean, kosher?"

"Like that, yes."

"Have you heard anything definite, Lem?"

"Nah. Rumours only. But I tell you something, Ross. When I was your age, I wanted something definite. Now, I trust my gut. I don't like a man's face, I don't put money in his undertakings."

"Funny way to do business."

"I like it, my wife likes it, my bank manager likes it, who's to argue?" Lem flicked the list back to Ross.

Ross put it in his pocket. "Lem," he said, "have you heard any rumours about Salectron?"

The old man looked straight at him. "Maybe."

"Would you advise your clients to buy our stocks?"

Lem took his time over that one, and at length smiled. "I still like your face, Ross."

On the way back to the car, Julie asked who owned the companies on the list.

Ross told her, "Philip Lesurier."

Salectron House was in uproar. The upstairs foyer swarmed with sales reps clamouring for their schedules, the floor that housed the computer was sealed off and in the hands of the auditors. The executive suites above were under siege, every telephone ringing.

Ross took Julie to his own office. As he was technically on leave, his desk was bare. There was no message from Theo, yet, but several from Hal Ensor, angry in tone, demanding an immediate meeting of the full board.

Before Ross could call Hal's extension, Richard's personal secretary, Moira Finch, appeared in the doorway.

"Mr McRae, Mrs Aikman . . . I'm so glad to see you . . . do you have any idea where Mr Wragge is?"

"Not at the moment," Ross said, "but he spoke to Julie on the phone, this morning, and I'm meeting him at four."

She was not mollified. "He should have warned me. He said nothing, yesterday, about an audit. The computer's down, the place is a shambles."

Ross said evenly, "A snap decision, something that involves a big change in our programmes. No need to panic, tell everyone."

"I suppose we'll just have to muddle through." A smile touched her face. "It will be a chance for the younger staff to use their brains, instead of that damned machine."

She hurried away, to be replaced at once by Colonel Rey.

"Mr McRae. A word with you in private, please."

Julie stood up. "I'll go."

"No," Ross said. "You stay here. Colonel, if you'll come with me?"

He led the way to the board room, and set a chair for the policeman.

"You came alone, Colonel? Where's Sergeant Ortlepp?"

"Downstairs." Rey's protruberant eyes scanned the marble walls, the laminated steel ceiling, the thick grey carpets.

"Handsome," he remarked.

"Electronically secure," Ross answered. "No bugs. No one can eavesdrop on what's said here."

Rey smiled bleakly. "You don't trust your colleagues?"

"I don't trust my adversaries. We get a lot of industrial spying, these days." Ross sat down facing Rey. "Do you have any idea who planted the tap at my apartment?"

"It wasn't us, Mr McRae."

The directness of the answer startled Ross. He said, "Who, then?"

"Probably the same people who tried to kill Matlala. That's what I want to talk about. You're in a dangerous position, Mr McRae, because of your association with the Matlala family. Do you know where they are?"

"No."

"Can you find out?"

"Not if I'm hampered by a gaggle of police. My car's being trailed."

"It is. And there are people watching your apartment."

"Then why don't you arrest them, and find out who they're working for?"

"I doubt if they know." Rey's cold gaze was fixed on Ross. "We have to find Matlala. We have very little time to do it. You are withholding information that might assist us."

"I've told you all I know."

"That is a lie. Do you expect me to believe that you met with a man like Vusi Matlala, and spent the time chatting about old times? I want to know what was discussed." As Ross said nothing, Rey leaned forward. "You realise I can detain you, and keep you locked up until you answer my questions?"

"Oh yes. I also realise that that wouldn't help you to find Vusi. If I'm detained, he'll take it as a sign that you're tied to the old way of doing things. You have to leave me alone, Colonel. I'm the one person who has a chance of reaching Vusi, the one person with a hope of getting hold of the tape. Why don't we talk about that?"

Rey spread his hands. "Very well."

Ross said, "The man who scared Pampallas was not Per Frolich. According to the papers, Frolich went round in seven under par, yesterday. He didn't kill Themba Matlala."

Rey nodded. "And the TV interviewer was at work in Joburg."

"So . . . that leaves the people in the background of the picture. Three of those were black men, a caddy and two porters. Have you considered that the killer may be black?"

"We have, yes. But let me ask you . . . can you describe those three men?"

"No. I was concentrating on Frolich."

"You saw three black labourers. The people at East London saw two black labourers. We have no worthwhile description of any of them. If one of them was the killer, we don't know what he looks like."

Ross studied the man opposite him. Rey had come alone, without the witness that police procedure demanded. It could be a trick to entice Ross to talk more freely, but Ross did not believe that.

It seemed to him that Rey had been picked for this job not only because he was tough, and clever, but because he was capable of throwing away the rules when occasion demanded.

Ross said, "A few nights ago, at a party, we were discussing the Stendal murder, in the Cape. A friend of mine said that there are gangs . . . organised gangs . . . killing and looting, specifically to create racial unrest. Is that true?"

"Yes," Rey said, "it's true."

"Could such a gang have been involved at East London?"

"It's possible. Likely, perhaps."

"Two members of that team posed as policemen. Knew what to do, how to behave?"

"Yes." Rey's eyes were narrowed, now.

"An eyewitness at my apartment block told me that the mechanic who set up the tap, looked like a cop, acted like a cop."

"What are you suggesting?"

"I'm asking if there's any chance that members . . . or ex-members . . . of the police force could be implicated in a plot to kill Matlala."

Rey said stonily, "I don't like that kind of talk, Mr McRae."

"And I don't like feeling that someone may blow my head off, at any moment."

Rey made a sour mouth. "The aspect you mention is being investigated."

"An ex-policeman with a bad record, well built, five-nine, hundred and sixty pounds, red hair receding on the forehead, blue eyes and an aggressive manner."

"I'll bear it in mind."

"I need a favour from you, Colonel."

"A favour?"

"Protection for Mrs Julie Aikman and her father Richard Wragge. Mrs Aikman was seen in my company at the casino. It could put her at risk. She's at her father's house, Malbrook."

"I know it. I'll arrange something."

Rey got up to leave. At the door, he turned to face Ross. "Understand. If you learn anything about Vusi Matlala, it's your duty to inform me at once."

"There's only one way I'll ever reach Vusi."

"What's that?"

"I must have a free run. If I say the word, you must pull off your watchdogs."

Rey stared. "Man, you won't stand a chance, alone."

"It's the only way I'll stand a chance. My only chance, Colonel, and yours."

"I make you no promises," Rey said.

Back in his office, Julie said, "Absolon phoned. He's still trying to arrange a meeting with the donors. He says at this rate, it won't be till tomorrow. He got the other information you asked for."

She gave Ross a sheet from his message-pad.

The message read: "The hotel at Bowers Bay is owned by the homeland government, but all gambling rights are held by a Belgian firm, Charbonier, Ghent et Cie, which runs this kind of operation in various parts of the world. The major shareholders in Southern Africa are Messrs F. E. du Pont, C. L. Brive, and F. L. Sauzier, all resident in Antwerp; and Professor X. R. van der Sandt of Ster Hoogte, Cape Province."

Watching Ross's face, Julie said, "Dad stayed with Renier van der Sandt, the weekend you were at Halladale."

Ross nodded. He was comparing the note with the list of Lesurier's companies. There appeared to be no overlap. Frowning, he folded both pieces of paper together and slipped them into his inside pocket.

"Hal's been like a jack-in-the-box," Julie said. "He wants to take you to lunch."

"He can take us both," Ross said. "Will you go and break the news to him? I must phone Theo."

Theo had nothing to report, except that he'd "Passed on the message to friends." Ross told him that he'd be at the Portofino Grill Room for lunch, and at Malbrook after four o'clock.

28

"You're taking it all bloody calmly," Hal said.

"The calm of despair," Ross answered.

"Richard should have called a meeting of the board before he took such drastic steps. If it leaks out that we're in trouble, our shares will go through the floor."

"There's more at stake than a drop on the market. If the rumours are true, Salectron's finished."

"The rumours are crap. The audit will prove that." Hal's face was waxen, the birthmark on his cheek showing red as a burn. "I run the finances of this company. Are you saying I've missed fraud on a grand scale?"

"You know as well as I do that fraud by a smart computer operator can be damned hard to detect."

"The audit will clear me," Hal insisted.

"Hal, what shows on our records is only part of the problem. If the overseas investigators prove that our products are reaching terrorist regimes . . ."

"Not our products." Hal crammed a piece of steak into his mouth, chewed ferociously, and swallowed. "Copies, maybe. Somebody pirating our goods, maybe."

"Or somebody inside Salectron, selling our prototypes and programmes, under the counter."

"Rubbish," Hal said. He shifted his angry gaze to Julie. "Take my advice, tell your Dad to cool it! Playing politics, handing out cash to a lot of black monkeys, he could bury the lot of us."

"He did what he thought best."

"He acted like an idiot. He doesn't deserve to run things." Realising he'd gone too far, Hal said in a calmer voice, "If we're to get out of this mess, we have to keep our heads. Work together."

"All for one and one for all," Ross said.

Hal pushed his plate aside. "I'm sorry if I lost my temper, but I don't like being left out in the cold. Decisions taken without the board's knowledge, the computer beyond our control, Richard vanishing into the blue without a word to anyone. It's just not good enough."

"Richard created Salectron," Ross said. "He knows better than anyone where to look for cracks. As to acting alone, he's always done that. He'll include us when he's ready."

"It's all very well for you to talk!" Hal's rage surged up again. "Richard will see you right, knowing that you and Julie are such good friends! But what about the rest of us? Richard doesn't give a rap what happens to us."

Hal looked close to tears; and Ross thought, there's always been something childish in Hal, something unformed, an ambition so large that it leaves no room for any other emotion.

Aloud, he said, "We're all in it together. If Richard can save Salectron, he will, and we'll all be in the clear."

Hal hunched his shoulders, staring owlishly at Ross. He said abruptly, "Where's Matlala?"

"I have no idea."

"Are you trying to find him?"

"I hope he is found."

"Why?"

This was the crucial thing, Ross thought, to know how much to tell, to whom, and when. He said, "One of the Matlalas may have a tape that shows the man who killed Themba Matlala."

Hal sat quite still, his mouth a little open. Then he gave an incredulous shake of the head. "They'd never give it to you."

"They might. Hal, you do understand, this is confidential? You mustn't repeat it to anyone at all?"

"Of course I won't. I've no wish to pry, but I can't be expected to do my job if I'm kept in the dark. You do see that?" He raised a hand to beckon for the bill. "That policeman who was here this morning. Did he mention Salectron?"

"No. He came to discuss the people who bugged my apartment yesterday."

"Bugged?" Hal looked vague. "By whom?"

"No one knows."

"Crazy," Hal muttered, "the whole thing's crazy." The waiter approached with the bill. Hal paid it and stood up. "See you at the office?"

"No," Ross said. "I'm on leave, remember?"

They parted company at the door. As Hal ambled off towards the office, Julie said, "He knows about us."

"I think so."

"How?"

"Sniffing around," Ross said. "He's like an anteater." He was thinking that it was Hal who had told him about Julie's trip to Bowers Bay.

Leaving the restaurant, they walked through the rainy streets to the central library. There Ross spent an hour checking certain items in *Who's Who*, the *Chamber of Industries Year Book*, and the lists of foreign companies with holdings in South Africa.

At three-thirty they made their way back to Salectron House. Comparative order had been restored. There was no sign of Hal, who was reported to be visiting the Germiston factory. There was no message at all from Theo Kaplan.

They reached Malbrook at four. Richard was in his study, waiting. He looked exhausted, blue rings under his eyes. The first thing he said was, "The police are watching the house."

"I asked for protection for Julie," Ross said. "She shouldn't be here alone."

"They were at the office this morning, too?"

"Yes, but not about the company's affairs."

"What did they want?"

"Vusi Matlala's address. The tape."

"How much did you tell them?"

"That I couldn't help, on either point. Where have you been, Richard?"

"Digging." Richard ran a hand over his eyes. "I needed to make a lot of overseas calls. I spent the night at the Germiston works, used those phones. More private."

"Hal's there now."

Richard nodded, unsurprised. "He won't find anything incriminating."

"He doesn't expect to. He told me quite categorically that the audit will prove our innocence."

"No audit can do that. It may show that our records are in order . . . that there's been no misdirection of funds." Richard gave a weary shrug. "I spoke to Cromlech, last night . . . to the French police, and a man I know on COBRA, in London. It seems Wiesbaden has been asked to run computer checks. I'm afraid there's no doubt that a full-scale investigation will show that our products, or ersatz copies of them, are reaching terrorist groups. Which means that someone here has been selling our technology."

Ross said, "Lem Abramson says Lesurier is on the skids, that he lost his SADF contracts some months ago. If he had access to our programmes, his factories could churn out the goods."

"I know. I tried to reach Philip but he's out of the country. He left for Italy, before the shooting." Richard's fingers moved slowly along the edge of his desk. "My stupidity has tied us into that butchery . . . and God knows what else, around the globe."

"You were never a party to it," Julie said fiercely.

Richard hardly seemed to hear her. "My closest friends," he said, "people I've known for years. When I was at Ster Hoogte, with Renier van der Sandt, he told me Matlala was coming out of gaol, that a few people had launched a fund for him. Renier asked me to subscribe, and I felt honoured."

"Renier van der Sandt is water under the bridge," Ross said.

"Renier," Richard mumbled, "after all these years."

Ross moved round to stand in front of the desk. "Richard, you have to accept that van der Sandt is a liar and a cheat, that Lesurier is a butcher. You can do nothing to alter that. What matters now is who sold the company out."

Richard shook his head dumbly.

"The three main suspects," Ross said, "are you, me, and Hal Ensor. We all have access to the top-secret material, we all have the means to lift it, and to cover our tracks, after. You signed the cheque, which will count against you. I was involved in the hand-over, I travel in the States and Europe, I could have been the leg man for the illegal sales. Hal is our financial controller. He could have run the money side of the deals. He handled all the Lesurier accounts."

Richard raised his head. "I'm sorry, Ross. I can't apportion guilt and innocence. I'm to see the Minister tomorrow, in Pretoria, and I shall turn the whole matter over to him."

"Richard," Ross began, but Julie stepped forward.

"Not now. He's too tired." She put an arm round her father's shoulders. "Pa, come upstairs and rest."

He rose, and put her gently aside. "Let me be, Julie. I want to be by myself, for a while." He saw the alarm in her face and shook his head. "Don't worry. I won't do anything foolish."

At the door, he turned and looked back at Ross. "You do whatever you think best, for yourself and for Vusi Matlala."

They heard his steps go up the stairs, and the door of his bedroom close.

Ten minutes later, the guard at the gate called to ask if he should admit Dr Theo Kaplan.

"Send him through," Ross directed, and he and Julie went out on to the driveway to meet the car.

Theo was elated, already talking as he climbed out. "I got an answer," he announced. "I can't tell you how, everyone's very nervous at the moment."

"Did you speak to Zidon?"

"No, but the answer is from him." Theo closed his eyes, reciting. "The name of the dog given you by your grandfather was Mongane, and he had no bark. Right?"

"Right."

"Good, so the message is genuine. The parcel promised to you will be handed over, but only to you. The place will be the gymnasium where you trained when you were a student. The

209

time is tonight. You will have to prove your identity. You will have to answer questions, and ask none. You must go alone. If you are followed, there will be no hand-over. If you try to lead anyone else to the meeting-place, they, and you, will be killed." Theo paused. "What gym are they talking about?"

"It's in Braamfontein." Ross turned to Julie. "If I'm to shake off pursuit, I'll need a fast car. May I use the Lamb?"

"You may, provided I do the driving."

"No way!"

"On wet roads, at top speeds," Julie said, "the Lamb needs real handling. I'm a pro, better than you'll ever be. Either I drive, or it's no deal."

"I can't take you, woman. You heard the terms. I have to go alone."

"So we'll compromise. There's a service-station in Brixton, owned by a man called Mickey Uys. I've driven in rallies with him. If I ask him, he'll lend you a car that's fast and reliable. We leave here in the Lamb, lose the competition, and make for the garage. Park the Lamb there, you go on to your appointment in something less conspicuous, and I catch a lift home with Mickey."

"It's too risky."

"Take it or leave it."

Reluctantly, Ross agreed. They spent some time working out the details of the plan, marking certain roads on the map Theo produced from his car. When they were done, Julie said, "I must phone Mickey."

"Not from here," Ross said. "I don't trust the lines. We'll go across the road, to the club."

Theo went off to talk to Richard. Julie and Ross walked down to the roadway. There were several cars parked at intervals along it . . . It was impossible to see, through the drizzle, whether they were occupied, but Ross was sure some of them were.

It was a foible of the Salectron board that its executives should be members of the Melton Club, and for once Ross was glad of the ruling. On a wet Tuesday night, the place was ill-patronised, and the writing-room, with the members' phones, was deserted.

While Julie called Mickey Uys, Ross looked up the number of the Press attaché at the American Embassy, Jason Hopner. Jason, on the point of leaving to cover a function at the Embassy, was first impatient, then attentive, and finally excited.

"Sure, sure, Ross, you got it, what time will you reach us?"

"Late. Perhaps after midnight. Can you keep the shop open?"

"For this, yes. I'll square it with Himself."

"We'll need to lift still photos from the video, and fax them to Washington, or wherever. Do you have a high-grade fax? The pic must be clear."

"No problem. I'll alert Washington right away, so they can do some work on the Pampallas angle, fix the dates he was with them, and determine his known associates."

"Will they co-operate? It's sensitive information."

"Cromlech must pull strings for us. I think he'll fix it. By the time you get here, we'll be ready to roll."

Ross next dialled the number Colonel Rey had given him. Rey's soft voice answered.

"McRae," Ross said.

"Yes, Mr McRae, what can I do for you?"

"Something I can do for you. A name. Professor Renier van der Sandt, of Ster Hoogte, in the Cape. Do you know him?"

"We've met."

"Talk to him, Colonel. He has a financial interest in the Bowers Bay hotel, and I think he was friendly with Sickert."

"How did you. . . ?"

"I don't have time to talk. I'm going to a party. A very private party. I don't need company. In fact, company would be very uncomfortable for me. You understand?"

"Where are you now?"

"At the Melton Club, across the road from Richard Wragge's property. I'll be going back to Wragge's now, and I'll leave again in half an hour. I'd be grateful if you will keep in mind what I said to you this morning."

211

"McRae . . ."

"It won't help if I'm had up for speeding, either. Perhaps you can use your influence?"

"McRae, I must insist . . ."

"Sorry, Colonel, no time. Goodnight."

In his office at police headquarters, Rey switched off the machine that had recorded the conversation, and signed to the sergeant at his elbow.

"Tell Cape Town I want everything they've got on Professor Renier van der Sandt, of Ster Hoogte in the Du Toit's Kloof area. They'll have a dossier on him, he was Defence Adviser on communist strategy in Africa, about ten years ago."

As the sergeant departed, Rey turned to the man seated on the other side of his desk.

"You heard?"

Dion Volbrecht nodded, dropping the receiver of his phone back on to its cradle. He had had no sleep for forty-eight hours, and it felt like longer.

Rey hunched his shoulders. "The prick knows something important. Maybe he's found Matlala."

"You could bring him in."

"I could. He lied about what went on at Bowers Bay. He lied about the Matlalas, and about his boss. Salectron's in big trouble."

"He told us about the tape." Volbrecht straightened up in his chair. "McRae's an unusual man, the kind that goes on quietly for years, and then does something mad. And he's stubborn. He went to prison for his opinions. You can bring him in for interrogation, but I don't think he'll break fast . . . not fast enough for it to help us. Now he's asking for a free run. It must be he thinks he can get hold of the tape, doing it his way. If you interfere, you could get him killed, and lose the tape as well."

Rey ran his tongue over his lower lip. He was wondering which was worse, to take the wrong decision himself, or to let Volbrecht win the credit for taking the right one.

At length he said, "OK, then. We give him this one chance. Then finish."

Volbrecht smiled. "I agree. After all, Martin, it's a calculated risk. If it comes off, they'll give you a decoration. If it doesn't, there's always the Salvation Army."

29

The drive with Julie was not something Ross ever wanted to remember.

For some time after leaving Malbrook, she took the Lamborghini along at a steady pace. As they reached the N1, she said, "Three of them, I think. A Merc, a Riley, and a BMW. But are they cops or robbers? We don't know?"

"Doesn't matter," Ross said. The traffic was heavy, commuters heading for Pretoria and the northern suburbs, heavy vehicles lumbering towards the ring roads for Modderfontein and Randburg. The drizzle had lifted, but the roads were still slick with moisture, and dangerous.

The three cars stayed in pursuit. Julie, keeping an eye on the rear-view mirrors, pronounced the Riley a sea-cow. "Wallows on the bends," she said, "and the driver's chicken. We'll lose him before Buccleugh."

She was right. The Riley left the race minutes later, penned between a milk-tanker and a mine-company bus.

"The cars may be radio-equipped," Ross warned. "They could pull one out and replace it with another."

"They won't have time," Julie said. She eased the Lamb into the fast lane and put her foot down.

For a few miles, Ross tried to watch the traffic behind them. After that, he concentrated on what lay ahead. They fled north towards Pretoria, but before reaching the city, Julie switched to the new freeway that swung west and south, by-passing Krugersdorp and Randfontein.

They overtook everything ahead of them. Hazards appeared and disappeared, like the moon that came and went overhead. An error, at the speed they were travelling, would have meant death.

Nerves taut, Ross waited for the sound of pursuing sirens. They never came. Rey must have fixed it, which meant they were indeed without police protection. It did little to steady his thoughts.

As Randfontein fell away in their wake, Julie said, "Only the Merc left."

The road they were on had been open only a few months. It ran arrow-straight across flat country. To their right was the vast sprawl of Soweto. To their left, open ground, some housing developments.

"Now," Julie said.

The speedometer climbed yet higher. The Mercedes followed for a mile or two, began to rock, dropped back and back.

There was usually a speed-cop at each of the main exits from the freeway. If they were about tonight, Ross never saw them.

At Riverlea, Julie slowed to check the mirror.

"Lost him," she said triumphantly. She left the freeway and turned north once more, threading through the small streets, punctilious about stop streets, running no risks. They were not followed.

They reached a canyon of factories, turned left, and left again. A neon sign loomed up: "Mickey's Car Hire." The wide doors of the service station were open. Julie drove the Lamborghini through them, and slowed to a beautiful, silent halt.

The car Mickey Uys lent Ross was a Peugeot. The bodywork bore the scars of stock racing, but the engine was sweet enough.

Ross drove through avenues of dreary bungalows, small cafés, run-down cinemas. To his left was the snake-slough of the railway track. Beyond that, on higher ground, the snail-tracks of Hillbrow glittered.

A railway bridge appeared, and he pulled to the side of the road. He waited there for ten minutes, but the only vehicle to come by was a bus, half-empty, chugging towards Ellis Park. Satisfied that he had not been followed, he drove under the bridge, turned left along the embankment wall, and after five minutes reached Siddley Street.

This cul-de-sac lay squeezed between two rows of warehouses. The gymnasium, a made-over workshop with walls and roof of corrugated iron, blocked the northern end of the alley.

Ross remembered it as a noisy place, echoing with the sounds of physical exertion, music, the voices of the boxers, wrestlers and runners who looked on the place as a club, as much as a training centre.

Tonight, there was no noise at all. The door was shut, the steps leading up to it empty. To the left of the door, a row of soot-encrusted windows showed a faint bloom of light.

Ross turned the car and reversed down the alley, stopping at the foot of the flight of steps.

As he stepped out of the car, he saw the men at the mouth of the alley. There were some twenty of them, dressed alike in track suits, with balaclavas that half-hid their faces. They came towards him in a rush, surrounded him, feet still prancing and breath coming in a sort of unified, rhythmic hiss. Ross stood quite still, saying nothing.

A man in a red balaclava held out his palm. "Gimmie the keys."

Ross obeyed.

"Search him," the man said.

Hands ran over Ross's body, none too gently.

"Clean," a voice said.

The outstretched palm wagged impatiently. "Identity book."

Someone flicked the book from Ross's pocket. Red Cap examined it under the street lamp.

"OK. Take him inside."

The door was unlocked, and the crowd half-thrust, half-lifted Ross through it. They entered a narrow lobby. To their left, at the entrance to the gymnasium proper, stood a man with an AK47. He stared briefly at Ross, then gave a jerk of the head. The crowd of runners dispersed, fading back into the street. The street door slammed shut.

Ross walked past the guard into the gym.

The room was long, cavernous, reaching up to iron rafters. The near end of it was dimly lit. Ross could see the shapes of the

216

exercise machines on his right, and on his left, the door that led to the ablution section.

Ahead of him was a blaze of light. It came from the huge fixture above the boxing-ring, and from the row of spotlights on the rail of the spectators' gallery. That had always been the preserve of the sporting élite, promoters, owners and sponsors. There were people up there now, but to Ross, dazzled by the lights, they showed only as a dark blur.

He heard the click as someone switched on the public address system. A voice said, "Step into the ring, please."

Ross moved forward, the guard two paces behind him. He reached the ring, hoisted himself up and rolled through the ropes. He could feel the heat of the lights, he was isolated by them, pinned like a moth.

Up in the gallery, voices murmured. He couldn't pick up the words, or even be sure what language was used.

The voice came again.

"What is your name, and where are you from?"

"Ross McRae. My home is at Halladale Farm, Stannard's Post, in Natal."

Saying that, he found it to be true.

The questions proceded, general at first, then specific. He was asked for the names of old associates, events near-forgotten. The questioner switched to Zulu and Ross answered in the same tongue, giving details of his time as a student, in prison, in America.

There came another pause, more muttering in the gallery.

The heat in the ring was unbearable. The sweat ran down his body, soaking his clothes. He stripped off his jacket and dropped it at his feet, dragged his tie loose.

A different voice spoke, gravelly, deep, unmistakable.

"McRae? Do you remember me?"

Ross put up a hand to shade his eyes. "I ought to. You broke my nose."

"What is my name?"

"Masinda. Tok-tok Masinda. Light heavyweight, good hands, bloody slow feet. Thought he knew about horses. Had a wife who ran a fat-cake stall in Orlando West."

217

Someone laughed in the gallery. Ross turned his head sideways, speaking towards the microphone.

"I am who I say I am. You're wasting time. Give me the tapes."

"What will you do with them?" demanded the first voice.

"I will try to identify the man who killed Themba Matlala. If I succeed, I will give his picture to the police, and to the world Press."

"Give? Perhaps it has occurred to you that such a picture could bring you a lot of money?"

Ross shrugged. "How long would such a seller live?"

There was a chuckle. "For as long as it took us to find him."

"Give me the tapes. If you are Vusi Matlala's people . . ."

"We are The People," corrected the voice. "We brought you here to look at you. Now we know you, and we will not forget you, be sure of that. Go back to your car."

Ross stood for a moment without moving. Then he picked up his jacket and left the ring, walked to the door, the guard at his heels.

The outer door stood open. He stepped into the alley. It was cold, and smelled of fresh urine. The Peugeot was where he had left it. Leaning against the bonnet was Red Cap. He straightened as Ross approached, and held out a parcel wrapped in brown paper. The car keys lay on top of it.

Ross took the articles, walked round and climbed into the driver's seat. By the time he closed the car door, the street was empty, and the door to the gym shut.

He did not stop to unwrap the parcel. He knew it contained the tapes. He started the Peugeot and drove quietly across town to the Embassy of the United States of America.

"Stop there," Ross said.

He was in the Press Room at the Embassy. With him were Jason Hopner, and the Embassy's security officer, Rad Marcus. Tape Three was on the video machine before them. The frozen frame showed Per Frolich, in close-up, talking to the TV interviewer. In the background of the picture were three other men, two of them in profile to the camera, the third stooping in the act of lifting a bag of golf clubs.

"Move on in slo-mo."

The picture moved. Slowly, the stooping man straightened. He lifted his head, facing the camera. For a count of five they had a clear view of a thin face, coffee-brown, the mouth first slightly open, then snapping shut in an expression of annoyance. The eyes were hidden behind dark glasses, the forehead was shadowed by a peaked cap, drawn well down.

"That has to be him," Ross said. "The angle's right, and you can tell he saw Pampallas."

"We'll fax this whole section to Washington," Jason said. "Frolich, the interviewer, and the three other men. If we get nothing on any of them, we can do blow-ups of the folk further back."

He went off to the processing-room. Ross turned to Marcus. "How hard is it to identify a man wearing cheaters?"

"Doesn't help, but they can do surprising things, nowadays. They'll check the skull measurements, also. It's a clear pic." Marcus lit a cigarette and blew smoke, "You know, your own police will have checked out the staff and guests at that hotel pretty thoroughly. They may already have some kind of feed back from the FBI. Can't be many black contract killers on their books."

"We need positive identification, a picture we can publish."

"Yeah, well, let's hope you get it."

Marcus left to make his final round of the night. Ross phoned Malbrook and spoke to Julie. Safe home, she reported, and Richard was asleep, having been given a sedative by Theo.

Ross found a notepad and pencil and settled into the one easy chair in the room. He made some notes, added them to the list of Lesurier's companies, and Absolon's note about the casino shareholders.

Jason appeared. "They have the pictures, they'll work on them. It'll take an hour or two. Get some rest, you look bushed."

Ross closed his eyes. He must have slept for some hours, for

219

when Jason shook him awake, the sky outside the windows was red with dawn.

Jason was exultant. "We got it, Ross. A short-list of one. The man in the cheaters worked with Pampallas on a Federal scheme to break the gambling rackets. They both went bad at the same time. Pampallas turned pro gambler, and this guy started doing contract killing, for the Mob. Then he crossed them up, result is, he can't work anywhere in the States, or Europe. He operates out of Rio."

"What's his name?"

Jason held out a sheet of paper. "Take your pick. And here's the official mug-shot from the Fed files."

Ross took the faxed photograph. It showed a thin face, long-jawed. The eyes watched him, sly, the lids thick and creased like a goat's.

"What next?" Jason said.

"A big envelope," Ross answered.

Jason fetched one. Ross turned the photograph over, and while Jason watched, wrote across the back, "This is the man who shot Themba Matlala." He added his signature, and put the photograph, the list of aliases, and the papers from his own pocket, into the envelope, which he addressed to Colonel Martin de la Rey at Security Branch headquarters. He handed the envelope to Jason.

"Can you see that Rey gets this, without involving the Embassy?"

"Sure," Jason said, "but he's going to arrest you, Ross, you can count on it."

"I want him to put out a warrant," Ross said. "I want my name in the Press, as well as that photograph. If the picture doesn't appear in the early editions of the evening papers, I want you to see it's leaked in the USA, to the world Press. Can you do that?"

"I'll end up a bum in Central Park," Jason said. "Anything else?"

"I need a set of handcuffs."

"I don't want to know why," Jason said. He went away and came back a few minutes later with the cuffs, and a key. "They belong to Marcus. He'd like them back without any blood on them. Where do you plan to go from here?"

"I'll check into a motel for the day."

Jason reached into a pocket and produced a key. "Go to my pad," he said. "There's food in the fridge, and the bath water's hot. If you need a change of clothes, take what you want."

"Thanks Jason."

"Stay under cover," Jason said. "I get the early editions here. I'll let you know if you've become famous."

On the way to Jason's flat, Ross stopped at a hardware store and bought a pocket-sized tape recorder. He would have liked one of the sophisticated jobs available at Salectron House, but that was out of bounds. The recorder he chose was light enough for his purpose.

From the chemist next door he bought a roll of adhesive tape.

The apartment block where Jason lived was in a quiet street lined with plane trees. Ross parked the Peugeot and entered the building unnoticed.

In the flat, he drew all the curtains close. Then he dialled the Malbrook number. Julie answered, and as soon as she heard his voice, started to ask questions. He cut her short.

"I'm OK," he said, "I just called to tell you I love you."

"Ross . . ."

"I can't talk. Whatever you read in the Press, don't worry. I'm OK, and I love you."

He hung up, before she could answer. He bathed and shaved, made himself a breakfast of eggs and bacon and coffee. He washed the dishes and put them away. Then he went to the desk in the living-room, and sat down to put various ideas on paper. He addressed four envelopes, one to Julie, one to Rey, one to Jason, and one to his lawyers.

At noon, the telephone rang.

"You're on page one," Jason told him. "They printed the photograph, with the usual caption. 'The police wish to interview this man, who may be able to assist them with their inquiries into the death of Mr Themba Matlala, who was murdered at Moroka

Village yesterday afternoon.' You're a footnote to the main story. 'The police would also like to trace Mr Ross McRae, a friend of the murdered man,' etc. Anyone knowing your whereabouts is asked to get in touch with Colonel Rey."

"Is my picture in?"

"Not yet. It probably will be, in the later editions." Jason paused. "I'll be home around six. Until then, you'd better just sit tight, and keep your head down."

At two-thirty that afternoon, Ross phoned Hal Ensor. Hal came on the attack, at once.

"Where the devil have you been? I tried all last night to reach you. Where's Richard?"

"Gone to Pretoria, I expect, to see the Minister."

"Minister? What for?"

"He's going to hand over the whole investigation. He's going to throw us to the sharks. It's over, Hal."

"What the hell are you talking about? The auditors haven't found anything. We're in the clear . . ."

"It's not the audit, it's what happened at Bowers Bay. Richard has admitted that van der Sandt put him up to it. The police are questioning the old fool, now."

"What's van der Sandt got to do with us?"

"You know damn well."

"I do not."

"He owns a chunk of the casino. He ran Sickert. The money was laundered there. Sickert told me . . ." Ross bit off the words.

"What?"

"Nothing."

"What did Sickert say. Ross? Do you hear me?"

"I can't talk about it on the phone, but the police know about van der Sandt, and Lesurier. They're looking for me. It's in the papers. I'll be arrested . . ."

"If you just keep your head . . ."

"I can't take any more! They've been following me around, I've been questioned twice, already, Christ, Hal, I won't go inside again! You have to help me. I need cash, and my passport. My

222

passport's in the safe, at the office, I can't go there, they'll be watching for me, but you're right on the spot, Hal. You can get it and bring it to me, with the cash . . ."

"Like hell I can!"

"Hal, please . . ."

"No ways. All we have to do is keep our heads, and stay where we are. There is absolutely no evidence against us. For God's sake, pull yourself together."

"All right." Ross's voice was fast and mean. "All right, have it your way, but I warn you, if the police arrest me, I won't look after you. I'll tell them what Sickert said. He knew about the deals, about van der Sandt, and Lesurier, and you. I'll talk, Hal, and you'll go inside with me. That's a promise."

There was a short silence, then Hal sighed. "Well, Ross, for old times' sake . . . as your friend . . . I'll help you, but on one condition. You get out of the country."

"Why do you think I need the money? I want fifty thousand, that'll buy me out. Used notes, fifties and hundreds."

"I'll see what I can do."

"Where can we meet?"

Again there was a silence. Then Hal said, "You know the small-boat marina, at Lakeside?"

"Yes, sure."

"I'll meet you there at seven o'clock tonight. You come alone."

"You think I want witnesses?" Ross said.

He made one more call, a very short one, to Colonel Rey.

30

Lakeside was a resort serving the small-craft sailors of the southern suburbs. Once a rural dam, it had been overtaken by urban sprawl, and now lay among small-holdings and bungalows, enclosed by a loop of the southern bypass.

The expanse of water was large, and there was ample parkland surrounding it, much of it covered by bush and indigenous trees. At the western end of the lake a building had been erected to serve as clubhouse and restaurant for the water-set. From the clubhouse, a wooden jetty extended some fifty feet, to deep water.

The ground behind the building had been grassed to provide picnic space, and there was a stretch of tarmac where cars and boat-cradles could park. There were approach roads from the north, south, and east.

Ross reached the parking-lot well before seven, stopped the Peugeot and climbed out. There were half a dozen cars drawn up along the back wall of the clubhouse, and judging by the lights and the thump of beat music, someone was throwing a party inside it.

Far away, on the ring road, there was plenty of traffic, but the park itself was quiet. A near-full moon blazed across the water, and caused stark shadows to streak the surrounding land. A small breeze stirred the encircling trees.

Ross stood still, looking about him. He could see no movement in the woods. No car had followed him into the park, so far as he knew. He was apparently alone, and surprisingly, that didn't bother him. He felt light and free and sure of himself.

He raised his right hand to touch the tape recorder strapped to his chest, under his shirt. His left hand rested on the cold metal in his jacket pocket.

Hal arrived exactly at seven. Ross saw the headlamps of the car coming along the southern feed road. They were lost for a time among the trees, then reappeared. At the edge of the clearing the car stopped, and the lights were doused.

Ross waved his arm. Hal climbed out of the car and walked across the turf. He was wearing dark slacks and jersey, a rain coat with the collar turned up. The upper portion of his face showed as a chalky wedge, the light glinting on his thick spectacles. He carried a small briefcase.

He stopped a short way from where Ross stood, staring at the cars along the clubhouse wall.

"This is too bloody crowded."

"They're all inside," Ross said impatiently. "Come on, give me the stuff."

As Hal still hesitated, Ross moved forward. "You did bring it, didn't you?"

"Sure," Hal said. He reached into his raincoat pocket, brought out a passport and dropped it on to Ross's outstretched palm.

"The money," Ross said.

"How do you propose to repay it?"

"Through Lesurier. It's all arranged, don't worry."

Hal's eyes were restive, scanning the tree line. "Do you have a gun?"

"No. You know I hate the things, and I couldn't take it on the plane."

"Where will you go?"

"Botswana, then Europe."

Hal muttered something under his breath. He seemed unwilling to conclude the business, and again Ross said, "The money, Hal."

"What did Sickert tell you?"

Ross took a breath, blew it out. "I'm in a hurry, man."

"What did he say?"

"He said that van der Sandt worked with you, and others, to sell our technology to Philip Lesurier . . . that Lesurier's

225

factories manufactured stuff and sold it to the IRA and Qaddafi. He said that Richard and I were tied to the deals, because of the cheque."

"Lies," Hal said, "total crap."

"I'm not going to wait for the police to arrest me. I had enough, last time around."

"Where did Sickert get such crazy ideas?"

"I don't know."

"Why would he tell you about it?"

"He was scared. I suppose he thought it would protect him. I don't want to go the same way."

Hal laughed.

Behind him, Ross could see car lights approaching. Late-comers to the clubhouse party, police, whoever, it didn't matter any more. It was between him and Hal, now.

One for Themba Matlala.

"Give," he said.

Hal raised his arm straight out, offering the briefcase. "You want to count it?"

Ross shook his head. "Thanks Hal, I'm grateful."

Hal's smoky gaze lifted to Ross's face for a moment, then dropped. At that moment, Ross pulled his right hand from his pocket, leaned over and grabbed Hal's wrist. He snapped the free end of the handcuffs on to it. The other end was already attached to his own wrist. he stepped close to Hal, and spun him round so that they stood in tandem.

"My car or yours?" he said.

Hal stood stock still, staring at the cuffs. "What are you doing? Are you mad?"

"Choose," Ross said.

"I'm not going anywhere." Hal began to strain against the metal circle. His head twisted round to stare at Ross. "Let me go! I did what you asked . . ."

"Which way, Hal?"

Hal shook his head. His eyes went to the line of dark trees. "No! Let me go!"

Ross's left arm was across Hal's shoulder. "My car, then," he d, and started towards it, half-lifting, half-dragging Hal with him. Hal kicked out, planted his feet, thrusting back against Ross.

"No, don't! They'll kill us both!"

"Who will?" Ross tightened his grip. "Your useful friends? The ones who killed Themba Matlala?"

"Please," Hal said, "please, Ross, let's talk, we can work something out, we can . . ."

"I don't think we have time," Ross said.

He could see figures at the edge of the woods, men moving purposefully forward. Up on the ridge where Hal's car stood, car doors slammed and other figures ran.

Ross swung half-circle. "Run," he said. Hal stumbled beside him towards the jetty. Behind them, a gun stuttered, and a line of bullets spurted past them, kicking up dirt. Hal was sobbing.

They reached the water, its icy cold engulfed them. Ross struck out towards the shelter of the jetty, pulling Hal after him. Two men with machine pistols appeared on the bank, running. Up on the ridge, rifles barked, and one of the men fell. The other came on, half-crouched, peering across the water. The jetty was close. Ross gave one last, desperate heave. The water between him and the shore seethed, something hit him in the chest, Hal screamed and sank under the surface. In the spinning darkness, Ross saw the red-haired man caught in a beam of light, saw him take one stiff step forward, arms spread-eagled, and then topple face down into the water.

People were rushing down the slope. The moon became enormously big, then very small. Ross slipped into black oblivion.

At his cottage on the Cape coast, Mathias was preparing to emigrate.

He sat at his desk, a briefcase open before him. There was not much in it; certain necessary documents, a package of uncut diamonds, always useful, and the pills he used against travel-sickness.

He had a long journey ahead of him. In fifteen minutes, the helicopter would carry him to the rendezvous with the ship that waited outside territorial limits.

Mathias leaned back in his chair, running a mental check. The computer was clean, everything of value had been transferred to other countries, days ago. What could not be used had been erased. A search of the cottage, which was bound to come sooner or later, would reveal nothing more than a magnificent machine. The loss of that bothered Mathias not a whit.

The loss of his erstwhile colleagues bothered him even less. They had never, in his opinion, been better than mediocre, swayed by emotion to a dangerous degree, unable to sink their differences in a common cause.

Their stupidity had decided their various fates. The old gasbag Cradock was now talking to the police in Cape Town. Rosendal and Breyten, dead in that ridiculous shoot-out. Kestell on the run in Italy, facing the attentions of the international arms watchers, the legitimate munitions-makers who disliked being undercut, and very likely, the Mafia as well.

Senekal, alone on his farm, would no doubt take the way of his forebears, and blow out his brains.

Latimer, as befitted a man unable to fulfil his contract, was disposed of, and no trace of him would be found by the police, or any other predator.

The staffs at Bellville and Lusaka, the teams around the country, were of no interest to Mathias. As mercenaries, they could fend for themselves.

The boy Abram was somewhat different. He had pleaded to be allowed to accompany Mathias. Mathias, as fond of Abram as he could be of anyone, had given the request serious consideration, but dismissed it as impractical.

"Where I'm going, my dear, you'd be a fish out of water. Unable to speak the language, lacking the training to fill any worthwhile position. Believe me, you will be better off here, in your country, among your own sort. I've made provision for your needs, be sure of that."

Abram had taken the decision badly, but had had to accept it.

Now Mathias rang the bell to summon the boy from the kitchen. Abram appeared, carrying an empty tray, which he ıd pressed against his chest. There was a forlornness in the posture that touched Mathias, and he smiled kindly.

"So, Abram, we come to the parting of the ways! I have a present for you." He held out an envelope. "One hundred thousand rand. The money is clean, and I've written a little guide-line about how you must place it, so that it will cause no talk. Talk is something to avoid. Remember that, in the future."

Abram nodded, not raising his head. He did not want the man on the far side of the desk to see the mistrust in his eyes, and the fury.

All this time, he'd been true, keeping secrets, looking after Mathias in every possible way, and now he was to be left behind to face the dangers Mathias wouldn't face himself . . . the police, Sousa, the whole pack.

It wasn't good enough. It wasn't going to happen.

Abram, too, had done his thinking.

He knew his own worth . . . and that of Mathias.

"Time to move," the big man said. He shifted his wheeled chair back a little, started to rise to his feet. His head came forward.

Abram swung the tray. The heavy metal edge struck Mathias under the left ear. He gave a sound between a grunt and a cough, and crashed face down across his desk. Abram swung the tray a second time, on to the back of the thick neck. The body jerked but did not shift its position. Abram bent and felt for the jugular vein. There was no pulse.

He set the tray down, went round the desk and pushed the chair against the back of Mathias's knees. Grasping the body under the armpits, he eased it back on to the chair. He turned the chair, and moved it close to the door of the computer room.

Lifting Mathias's right hand, he pressed it flat against the electronically-controlled panel beside the door. The palm-print identified, the door slipped open. Abram bent his shoulder to the back of the chair and thrust it through the door. The impetus carried chair and cargo some feet into the computer room.

Returning to the desk, Abram pressed the button that closed the door again.

He thought about cleaning his prints off the tray, but decide
against it. Self-defence would be his story. It would be believed.
Disinformation was his speciality.

From his pocket he took a flat black video cassette. It was the
one Fouché had told him to burn, the one taken at Site Nine by
the photographer Stendal. Abram thought the police would find
it interesting.

He put the cassette into the briefcase. The envelope with the
money, he kept. The diamonds and the papers he left where they
were. He closed the briefcase and snapped the locks.

He went out to the station-wagon in the garage, ignoring
Mathias's car. He would first take his money to a safe place. Then
he would go to the police, tell them where to find Mathias, and
give them the briefcase.

They'd give him a hard time, but Mathias had taught him how
to handle that.

He started the engine, and drove away.

31

Ross was in hospital for two weeks.

The first face he saw was Julie's. It swam towards him out of a stink of ether. The mouth, curiously blurred, said, "Don't talk, darling. Just sleep."

After that, she was there most of the time, sitting in a chair, reading or knitting. Ross told her, "It will take time."

"What will?"

"Us. A lot to sort out."

"We have time," she said, smiling at him.

Theo came. "You were lucky," he said. "You caught it, here." He touched the left side of his chest. "Missed the heart by a hair."

"Hal?" Ross said.

"Hal's dead. Better, don't you think?"

Richard came, didn't say much, pressed Ross's hand and said things would work out all right, not to worry, they'd pull through.

Colonel Rey came, standing stiff at the end of the bed.

"You were bloody late," Ross said.

"You had to do it your way."

"The tape recorder?"

"It was OK."

"Vusi Matlala?"

"He hasn't showed up, yet. He will. We'll crack the case. I'll need to talk to you, when you're fit." And then, grudgingly, "You did well, Mr McRae."

Finally, when Ross was almost ready for discharge, Vusi Matlala came.

"Polela! How are you, man?"

"Fine. I'm going home soon."

"Home to the farm?"

"Not yet. To my boss's house."

Vusi nodded. "I owe you, Polela."

"No, you don't."

"We won't argue." Vusi grinned. He looked thin and tired, but the diamond-shaped eyes were bright, the stance full of energy and confidence.

"How's it going?" Ross said.

"Busy, man, busy. Talking, plenty of that. Might even talk to the Big White Chief, some time. Not yet. We're not ready, yet."

"Don't leave it too long."

Vusi tipped a hand back and forth. "We'll strike a nice balance." The grin faded. "Come back, Polela, we need you here."

"Soon. I have things to attend to, overseas. I won't leave it too long."

"Good."

"My Uncle James wrote to tell me about Themba's funeral. He said it was very big."

"Very big."

Ross was silent, imagining the people moving in groups along the paths, coming from the farms nearby and those further away, from the distant villages and cities, to pay tribute to Themba. He thought of Simeon and Zidon, and all the thousands coming together, there, in pride and love.

He looked at Vusi.

"The singing filled the valley," he said.

"Yes," Vusi answered, "it did."